Murder in Cloud City

Janet E. McClellan

Writers Club Press
San Jose New York Lincoln Shanghai

Murder in Cloud City

Published by Writers Club Press
an imprint of iUniverse.com, Inc.

For information address:
iUniverse.com, Inc.
620 North 48th Street
Suite 201
Lincoln, NE 68504-3467
www.iuniverse.com

ISBN: 0-595-09765-0

Printed in the United States of America

To the next adventure

1

As the morning sun washed through the kitchen, it came to him that he would leave her. The swelling light reflected pale pastels on the walls and urged him to be on his way. Snuffing out his cigarette in a breakfast plate, he rose reluctantly from the table, and slugged back the last drop of coffee in the cup.

"Places to go and things to do, Hon," he called through the kitchen door and down the brief hallway where she lay. He was pleased to think of her lying in the bed waiting his further attentions. He admired her obedience. He particularly liked the way she waited for him.

Moving across the room, he hesitated, trying to decide if he should freshen up his coffee again. He gave in to his need for caffeine and lifted the pot from the stove. Cup in hand, he walked through the tiny living room to the back of the cabin and the master bedroom. Her attentive devotion to his needs had earned her a final moment of his company. A moment, and then he would have to go. He wanted to say goodbye.

As he passed the bathroom door, his eyes caught his angled reflection in the long bathroom mirror. Momentarily distracted, he admired his distant face and form. Drawing up taller, he let the memories of last night play across his mind. His reflection hitched up its belt and extended its chest. He thought how intertwined his and Beverly's lives had become in the short time they had available. The hours had flown. He grinned broadly at the mirrored double, reliving the feel of their bodies. Her receptivity had been a marvelous thing to witness. It had made all the difference in the world. They had come together and moved easily toward the final destination. He had prepared himself for her. When he had finally held her, he knew she must have prepared herself for him. It came together like the magic he had hoped for and hoped to control.

Smoothing his hair back from his forehead, he conceded that a man could not afford to spread himself too thin or be too incautious. The world was too dangerous not to be a little leery of every woman who wanted him. Finding the right woman had been important. Last night Beverly had been the right woman. He had awakened the lust and passion essential in their relationship and felt pride in his ability to control himself, to anticipate and overcome her first anxious tremors. He had found himself enjoying her feigned reluctance. Those beguiling regrets had helped to fuel his desire and increase his longings. She played him just the way he wanted her to.

Winning lovely prizes took time and careful planning. He was not usually a patient man, but the rewards were always greater when he did not allow his zeal to carry him away. Earlier on the progress toward his desires had been frustratingly slow but the effort had paid off in spades. He had learned from his mistakes and success. Beverly had been proof of that last night.

She had not seemed too surprised to find him standing on her doorstep. He felt as though Fate had stood at his shoulder as the sudden glare of the porch light washed over him.

"Yes?" Beverly said, blinking at the man on the stoop. Peeking through the window blinds of the door, she frowned at the stranger.

"What do you want?" she called as irritation crept into her voice. The pounding on the door had shaken her out of her self-containment. Alarm and surprise intruded into her solitude. She had put down her novel to answer the door and loose her concentration on the steamy love scene between the hero and heroine. Rafe, the dashing pirate of the South Seas, and his captive Katrina, daughter of the Vice Counselor had finally given in to their long denied attraction for each other.

The man on the other side of the door responded to her question but Beverly did not hear him. Her reverie had been replaced with frustration. She would have to reread the section again to recapture the effect of emotion as Rafe finally took his lover into his arms.

"What do you want?" Beverly repeated.

"I...I've had a little mishap back up the road. I need to use your phone." His voice bit through bone chilled teeth as the cold night air cut through his clothes and scored his flesh with pins of ice. A dusting of snow swirled in the dark behind him. Annoyed, he stood under the glare of the light, hugging his arms to his chest and stomping his feet in cold protest.

Silently he cursed her and himself. He had been a fool and coward to stand so long staring at her door before knocking. He should have already been inside the cabin. He had hesitated and waited under the shadows of the trees, staring at her cabin like a lovesick schoolboy freezing his ass off. He gathered his courage to plead again. He did not want to lose the moment.

"I'd like to use your phone," he said as he pushed his face closer to the tiny window.

Latching the chain, Beverly opened the door a few inches. She stood in the crack of the door letting the frigid night air rush past her as she looked closely at the man. There was something about him she could not place. She wondered where she might have seen him before, or was the memory a trick of the night? She had taken the mountain cabin a week ago and imposed a discrete distance between the people of the small town. Had he been in town, at the grocery, at the liquor store?

"Hey, Lady! Can I use your phone?"

"I, I don't know…?" Beverly said hesitantly. She held onto the doorknob and backed away from his sudden bellowing. Caution moved her hand. She began to close the door. Her urban survival skills called to her as she felt a sudden panic that the solitude of the mountains had lulled her urban wariness. Lowering her eyes, she tried to block out his glares as she steadily pushed the door toward its latch. She wanted him away from her space and sanctuary. Beverly wanted to return to the glass of wine and the book on the couch.

"Lady!" he shouted at the narrowing crack of light.

Startled, Beverly looked up at him and her hand froze on the doorjamb.

"Lady," his tone softened as he watched her hesitate. Seeing his opportunity, he let the words rush. "I'm freezing out here. I just need a tow. For heaven's sake, you can call someone to get me. But tell them to hurry. A man could die in this weather!" He did not want her to panic or ruin his chance and have to bully his way into the cabin. He wanted her to let him in. Taking a small step back and away from the door, he tried to give her room to relax. He waited for a sign. He did not want this one to get away. He had been waiting too long. A few seconds more would not matter to him either way. Not now.

She faltered. The warm interior of the cabin beckoned him. He longed for her, and her shelter from the night. He worked to keep his confusion and impatience from overriding his judgment.

"I'm sorry…certainly you can use the phone." What could it hurt? She gestured him inside and slid the chain from the lock. She knew she should not be rude to someone in need. Beverly heard her mother's voice whispering, "just be nice." Shrugging inwardly, she wondered how long it would take a tow truck to arrive. After he left, she would return to her solitude and book.

He smiled as he closed the door behind him. He was amused and proud to have turned the trick. His mother had always told him his good looks and winning ways would make him a lady-killer.

"The phone is in there," Beverly said as she pointed toward the kitchen doorway. She turned away from him and walked to the fireplace to stir it alive again. As he disappeared into the kitchen, Beverly settled onto the couch. Finding her voice, she called after his retreating back to make up for her initial hesitancy.

"Did you have to walk far to get here?" she asked and looked up to see him standing in the doorway watching her as she raised her glass of wine to her lips. He did not respond. She eyed him curiously as the lip of the wineglass rested on her own and smiled at him uncertainly.

A sudden crash of logs in the fireplace brought a startled leap to her hand. The glass fell to the floor. Beverly saw his eyes narrow on her as a new hardness settled over his face. "Just be nice," her mother's voice whispered to her as a confused gasp broke from her throat.

Moving toward her, he noticed how clean and shower fresh her scent was. He wondered how she had gotten the logs to leap from their resting-place. It did not matter. She had revealed herself. He knew what she was. A rush of blood weakened his knees, and fear gripped him as he moved to capture her. Cringing, the skin on his face taut in anxiety, he had to stop her before she became wickedness.

The hair on the back of Beverly's neck and arms stood at attention and, called to her in ancient warning. She moved swiftly off the couch and grabbed at the tongs resting near the fireplace.

He lurched unsteadily toward her.

"No!" she screamed, and swung the tongs at his head. The blow landed and bounced hard off his left shoulder driving him to the carpet.

He fell heavily, rolled on his uninjured arm, and cowered as she ran past him to the kitchen. . Sudden panic shook him as he realized she might have gone to the kitchen to get a weapon. He felt like giving up, and lowered his head to the carpet to hide. It took ever nerve he had left to pull himself up and off the floor.

He crossed the floor and walked toward the kitchen door, he found her standing uncertainly at the narrow windows looking for escape. Cornered. She raised her hand and screamed a curse at him. The knife blade shone like a wicked promise. His heart exploded with longing and he rushed toward his fate. He hoped she would be quick and a little kind.

The pink sky of morning continued to advance and insist that it was time to go. Looking down at her from the foot of the bed they had shared, a wide grin spread across his face. She had only been testing him, making sure that he was the right one, and the one she had waited for. He misunderstood her at first but now he knew her and knew her completely. He had proven himself and she rewarded giving herself to him and sweet memory. She had surrendered the life force and courage. Beverly would be with him now and always.

In quick salute, he held his coffee cup aloft and inclined his head gallantly at her. Beverly had been a marvel. No matter how many others ever wanted him, she would always be first in his heart. She had given him new life and he had been born again through her flesh.

The tilting lip of the coffee cup splashed coffee onto Beverly's foot.

"Stupid!" He screamed angrily at her. Just as quickly, the old fear came straining to the surface of his nerve. He did not want her to take his tone as a challenge. He did not want to be pulled back into his weakness. Control was essential.

Motionless, she kept her most tempting poses toward him. Wanton and unashamed she silently called to him.

"You want some more, don't you? Don't you, bitch?" He said as he pinched her hard on her naked buttocks and ran his fingers gently across the punished flesh.

"Trouble with you," he offered, testing his new boundaries," You're frail. You can tempt but you cannot endure. You rob us and want us to be grateful for you're little favors. That's trickery, cunning and deceit." He waited for her response but her silence and posture betrayed her.

"Damn it!" Emboldened, he screamed down at her. Grabbing her leg, he rolled her over on her back and pulled the stained bottom sheet from beneath her. Stripping all the sheets and pillowcases from the bed, he jostled her side-to-side, doing it for fun. He enjoyed the sight of the bounding sway of her flesh as it responded to his rough motion. The sight of her sweet skin hardened him. He wanted to take her, hesitated, and then unzipped his pants.

A few minutes later after he finished, he walked back to the kitchen and returned with the tablecloth. Positioning himself behind her, he splayed her legs apart. Pursing his lips in determined artistry, he raised her buttocks off the cloth and shoved her knees under her stomach to make the picture perfect.

As he achieved the result, he wanted he ran his fingers over her ass and patted her upturned cheeks for good luck.

"There. That is better. Now, don't you go waiting up for me tonight. I might be late." He thinks he might come back, if he has time. There is a lot more exploring he would like to do.

Stepping out into the cool morning air, he softly closed the door behind him. With the sunrise shining in his face, he waited as he looked at the surroundings to the roadway and beyond. Straightening his shoulders, he shifted his load, and moved to the side of the cabin. He quickly crossed the hundred yards of hard snow covering the field behind. He stopped at the weather-shattered barn to look back one last time. Satisfied that he was unobserved, he headed toward the tree line and the truck he had hidden there the night before.

"Brunch," he muttered to himself as he looked at his watch. "Denver in three or four hours, and then lunch, or maybe I'll just crunch a brunch." He settled comfortably into the truck and hummed to himself.

2

The campfire was finally beginning to create warmth beyond its tight centered flame. Lynne Fhaolain brought the blue speckled coffeepot closer to the fire and settled it firmly on the grate. A tremor of chills raced across her chest and down her arms. It was an uncomfortable recognition of the cold and damp air in the abbreviated valley of Tennessee Pass, Colorado. She knew that spring came late to the mountains, but the light dusting of snow that had fallen in the night suggested more than winter's struggle against spring. Her long-john's, layering of sweaters, and down-jacket was not enough to protect her from the frigid morning air.

She pulled down her favorite winter hat, snuggled it securely over her auburn hair, and tried to hide her frosting ears in the fleece lining. She squinted and glanced toward the peaks on the valley's eastern rim where the sun was still hiding. Sighing heavily to herself, she knew she was not ready for the demands required of the day. She was tired of facing the cold and tired of hiding in the deep granite range of the valley. Lynne did not have the energy to go on but she did not have the heart or will to stay longer. Resigning herself to the next leg of her journey, she danced against the cold creeping up her legs and tried to hurry the sluggish flow of blood through her veins. The valley had been her hideout from the world, but now she had to make her return.

The nights of sleep and days of restlessness in the valley had, at first, been their own form of peculiar comfort. In the weeks that had followed Shelby's death the pain and confusion had driven her from her home near the banks of the Missouri River haunted her here.

Despite the warmth and comforts she managed to pack into camping, her heart had become a frozen wasteland long before she had ever reached the chill of the Tennessee Pass. Once she reached the valley she spent days huddled in her bed, drifting and dozing through dreams. Consciousness had been too painful. Sleep had been her escape. Sleep brought memory without regret.

The dark depression firmly settled over her on the second day and she stayed in her cocoon willing the day to end. When she was finally able to rouse herself, three days passed.

She could almost imagine Shelby chastising her to pull herself out of her funk. It would have been the tone Shelby used when worrying that Lynne could not put on enough weight to provide protection from the damp winters.

Rope muscled and slender and the same five-foot four inches and one hundred thirty-five pounds she'd been when she and Shelby had first met she would not accept thickening or padding of arms and hips as a natural course of life for a woman of forty-five

She had tried to convince Shelby of the advantages of a life dedicated to fitness and her metabolism rates. But, Shelby remained unmoved and persisted in remaining primarily sedentary. They agreed to disagree. Lynn's chosen profession insisted on fitness while the life of a college professor made Shelby less interested in such exertions. Lynn had accepted that rationale as easily as she accepted the soft Southern drawl that marked Shelby Montgomery as a native of North Carolina.

The older she got and the more life threw cruel curves at her, the less she was inclined to easily accept circumstances as preordained. When she was younger, she had not accepted the fact that her father, Sergeant-Major Fhaolain, could not afford to send her to college. Instead, she had accepted the fact that ROTC and a stint in the Army were the only way she could afford it. She had even accepted the fact that she had grown to enjoy military life, and did not leave the Army until she had in her twenty years. She realized that promotions for women were slow in coming. She accepted the fact that she had retired early to live on the pension of a Major. Not the full pension that would have come if she had stayed thirty years but a handsome one anyway.

Of all the accepting of the facts of life, she still could not accept the fact that Shelby was gone. The loss had put her in greater pain than she had ever known. Lonely and lost, she was unwilling to easily accept events as natural, life course or happenstance. She was not in the mood to just let it ride.

Lynne had come to the Tennessee Valley for its peace and quiet. It nestled the remains of an abandoned training ground used only once during World War II. The grounds shattered streets, ruins of barracks, and concrete bunker foundations crumbling near the river were the only company she was keeping. After two weeks in the valley and no closer to knowing or trusting her desires than when she had arrived. Habit was all she had left.

"Lifestyle," Lynne said, glancing at the creeping rays of the sun as they broaden on the eastern peaks. She could tell the slow onslaught of light and warmth would melt the dense fog hovering over the creek. She sat down in the camp chair near the fire and she settled into her morning ritual. By centering herself and huddling close to the heat, she wanted a gentle introduction to the morning as she waited to decide what to do.

With her supplies running low, she willed herself to move and go on with her life. She discovered to her dismay that her dwindling self-willing resources had not been replenished by the solitude. Abandonment and loss ambushed her every idle thought.

Reluctantly, Lynne rose from the fire and stretched. She moved her hands to stretch down to the tops of her boot-covered toes. Leaning slowly and deliberately to the left and to the right, she began a slow rhythmic bending and stretching. A runner's light muscle-warming strains were a comfortable habit for her. It was a dependable way to relieve her mind when nothing else was dependable. Finding her own rhythm of motion and pull of muscle, she relaxed into the routine. Her breath came deeper as she finished her sit-ups. Pushing herself off the canvas space, she balanced and flexed into deep leg lunges. Each muscle and tendon stretched and warmed in its turn. Pulling herself up on her toes and extending her arms as far above her head as she could reach, she felt oxygen and blood answering her efforts. Twenty minutes of warm-up satisfied her as she jogged in place, looking across the valley floor. A little run was the right thing to do. In mock challenge, she nodded to the birch trees like fellow contestants at the blocks.

She took off in a slow run, carefully picked up speed across the snow, and watched for ice glazing the roadway. The awkwardness of running in hiking boots made her plant her feet in an uneasy, flatfooted lope. Once on surer ground, she let her feet pound and her mind took its liberty.

Shelby had hated running. The dislike had not been finicky. Shelby could not understand or abide the idea or running day or night. It was Lynne's military law enforcement occupation and her lack of size had required her to develop endurance and strength. Shelby's southern sensitivities allowed a gentle joking harassment to emerge between them about

Lynn's efforts to fit into the culture of the military. As part of the argument and on her cue, Lynne she would explain how ROTC and the Army had made it possible to go to college, and really be all she could be.

Truth was, Lynne had needed the body skills, the offensive and defensive abilities and confidence to do her job. Initially, she needed those hard won physical and mental skills to protect herself from the lame and intrusive mania of male officers. She found she needed the college classes to keep her mind from being swallowed up by the narrow vertigo of the "us versus them" mentality sometimes present in the provost offices. After the required training schools, Lynne found herself being one of the few women officers in the military police. Her endurance, physical agility, and agile mind had won her respect from even the most begrudging male detractors. A few hand-to-hand victories and investigative successes had assured her acceptance.

Finally, and most appreciatively, the Army had led her to Shelby, although the circumstances at first had not initially been particularly pleasing. Shelby had been a civilian professor of political science hired by the Army to teach political theory to select field staff officers working on their master's degree at the War College.

On the morning of their meeting, Shelby had been speeding toward the General Staff and Command College at Fort Leavenworth, Kansas, late again. Major Fhaolain did not usually deal with traffic offenders but when the little sporty red car missed the stop sign and roared its engines as it blasted through, the enforcement instincts of Major Fhaolain kicked in. Major Fhaolain issued a ticked and got a phone number.

The following week during their first dinner together, Shelby confided to Lynne, in hushed conspiratorial tones, that the idea of dating a law enforcement officer was novel and interesting. There had been something in the sweet undercurrents and tone of voice that told Lynne there were several other things Shelby had never done with an officer, but might be persuaded to try.

That dinner had been the start of their eight years together through a course of several difficult separations and ecstatic reunions. Lynne was reassigned to Germany for three years and another at Fort Williamson, Arkansas for another two. Those assignments had taken her away from Shelby until the Army had finally reunited when she had been allowed to return to Fort Leavenworth, Kansas for her pending retirement.

Over the years, Shelby had occasionally voiced deep concern regarding the dangers of Lynn's job and had seemed particularly uneasy when Lynne had been promoted to the Criminal Investigation Division (CID) and alarmed when she was assigned to homicide during her last three years of duty. Although, homicide investigations had been Lynne's particular ambition since she had joined the Army. It had been a long hard haul to achieve her goal. Lynne had found it necessary to complete her master's degree before she could coax and kick the powers-that-be to consider her worthy of a promotion to major and the command of a provost marshal's office. But, she had arrived at the pentacle of her dreams. She had enjoyed all the previous tours that had found her in charge of patrol, routine investigations, and the adjunct general's office and as investigative trainer.

Shelby had quieted her concerns and learned to keep whatever fears, however uneasily, hidden and mostly unmentioned. Shelby had been a loyal and loving partner who provided Lynne with the buoyancy of love. The gentle academician did not feign to understand violence and was at home with the comfortable intrigues of politicians and wicked ballot box manipulations. Shelby had been Lynn's center of sanity. With Shelby, life had felt focused, meaningful and connected. Those years turned out to be precious and few.

Lynne ran distractedly along the valley floor. She stumbled. Righting herself to keep from falling, she shook her head to shake the past away from her mind. Reaching the end of the weathered pavement, she jogged around a tumble of bushes marking the farthest point of the brief valley. As she turned, she saw the campsite smoke rising among patches of juvenile birch near the spring-fed stream. The valley had been as remote from her past life as anything she could find. It had been satisfying solitude. Even the cold mornings that had caused the exposed flesh on her face and hands to feel brittle and tight were a relief from the weight she carried in her heart.

As she ran back to the campsite, she realized how satisfied she had become in her discontent. In her irritation she began to pump her legs more vigorously to speed herself across the ground. She wanted distraction. Coming back to this valley, a place they had shared had been a mistake. She wanted to be able to forget the future and escape the past. Instead of freeing her, she had become more bitterly entrapped. Each plan, hope, and dream stood in sharp relief. Nothing was real. The only things left were the plans they had made together. None of those plans made sense anymore.

It had been inexplicable. In an instant, an aneurysm ended everything Shelby and in that instant everything Lynne had come to believe and rely upon ceased to exist.

The loss of Shelby torn Lynne's world asunder and sent her down a slow spiral of darkening misery. Lynne had continued to live but in the half-light of sorrow and gloom that nothing could penetrate. As her twentieth year in the Army approached, Lynne tendered her resignation for retirement. No one could change her mind and nothing could stop her from leaving. She would not remain where everything yielded only to memory and sorrow. She left the Army and headed away from the pain and towards the comfort of mountains, fly fishing streams and cool night air.

Suddenly, a shadow of a cloud in the valley seemed to pass directly over Lynne as she tried to concentrate on cooling down from her run. A heavier phantom flitted across her mind, and she felt a quickening of awareness. Glancing around, she could not locate the source of her discomfort. Someone or something of malice moved across her perceptions. She was transfixed with awareness as a shadow of death moved through the valley. The high clear notes of a hawk called out on the wind and made the hair rise up on the back of her neck. Lynne reached into her backpack near the campfire and pulled out the Smith and Wesson .357 from its resting-place. She held it against her leg and cocked the hammer back as her eyes searched the valley and the highway sloping toward up through the pass.

It had been there, near the highway. Nothing moved but the breeze and her own frosty breath on the air. It had passed on. She was alone again. Shaking her head, she slid the revolver into her pants next to the small of her back. A long time ago she had learned to pay attention to her intuition and that it was easier than paying the price of ignoring it.

The coffeepot began making bubbling noises as small puffs of steamy aroma rose through the air. The smell recalled her to the present and she relaxed her guard ever so slightly. Sighing, she took a cup from her gearbox and poured herself some coffee. She raised the cup to her lips and cautiously cooled the liquid as memories sank below the surface of her mind.

Smiling wryly down at the fire, she realized she had to rouse herself out of her mood. She ran a hand through her hair and lightly fingered the first hints of gray that lay at her temples. The streaks had begun after the funeral and were advancing with each day. Lynne wondered how much time it would take until the dark auburn would disappear forever. Forty-five was merely the zenith of the summer of her life. She tried to remain philosophical about the passing of that summer. It was all connected to the other losses in her life but she did not want to dwell on it too long.

The small chores of breaking camp would have to carry her body. Her heart was on its own to find a way to healing.

After breakfast, she packed up the truck and tried to mentally prepare herself for the next stage of her journey. When she glanced at the map, she knew she could be in Leadville in a little less than two hours. There were people waiting for her and the time to move on had come. Tennessee Valley had held her while she had tried to find the courage to begin again or denounce it all for the last time. She had found she could not just leave life behind. Not yet. She hoped she might be living long enough to know joy again. Habit would have to do for now.

Turning the truck up and onto the highway, she resigned herself to leaving heart and soul behind. She did not believe she would need either of them for a long time and was resigned to live with the little that remained. She had decided to call the agent back, agree to the assignment, and hope that the travel prospectus the publisher had in mind would be interesting. She hoped that the creation of the bookstore and the prospect of beginning a career as a travel writer would tether her more firmly to the world.

3

"No need to hurry," Lynne said to herself as she began the downward drive to her new home of Leadville, Colorado. The morning was gaining on her. She had wasted a few precious minutes phoning the realtor to let him know she was on her way. Mixed emotions raged through her. Lynne felt the tug of tomorrows as keenly as the pull of her yesterdays. She glanced at the western horizon and noticed the setting of a ghostly pale moon.

"No need to waste time either," she countered her argument.

Lynne and Shelby had visited the small community five years ago. Both agreed that it was a wonderful place to visit. Frowning to herself, she now wondered seriously if "a fine place to visit" was any recommendation for a place to live. All she could remember was a high country retreat, and how much they had enjoyed the cool shore of Turquoise Lake during the summer that had blistered with humidity in Kansas. It had been their escape from work. Now it was her escape from the past.

They originally visited Leadville because Shelby enjoyed the tales of the town as much as she enjoyed the simple escapism from the grind of teaching. The stories of Leadville's heyday had been fascinating and would regale Lynne with the history of the place at every opportunity.

Leadville was situated at a breathtaking 10,152-foot altitude. Forgotten now by the high tech world, once it had been listed amongst the greatest names in the mining annals of the United States. Its remote past had seen the mountains and surrounding hills mined for all variety of precious minerals. First, it had been a gold mining camp, and then a rich silver vein gave its wealth, then lead, and finally manganese. The gold and silver had been mined from the late 1860's into the early 1930's. Leadville's denuded hills and short canyons crowded with tiny ramshackle cabins did not vanish or become hidden by nature's recovery until the late 1970's. But underneath the surface, old scars unexpectedly protruded through the tender earth. Mounds of slagheaps lined the southern route out of town. Everywhere there were reminders of greed and destructive tendencies.

Lynne turned her truck on the curve of the highway and caught a glimpse of Leadville dozing in the early morning light. Unburdened by the six thousand souls it now held, it was hard for her to imagine that Leadville had ever had a reason or the audacity to call itself Magic City. It had been the second largest city in Colorado, and boasted a migratory population of over 42,000. Impressed with itself during the fever of gold and silver, the town fathers had even considered changing its name to Cloud City. Its precarious perch two miles above sea level made the idea realistic.

Lynne had tried to gather as much information about the town as she could before deciding to live there. The Chamber of Commerce had sent Shelby fliers describing the advantages of the community. Neither of them had been prepared for the frankness of the advertising. A brochure mentioned in a very matter-of-factly how the weather and climate of Leadville were "ten months of winter and two months mighty late in the fall." It would suit her and her loneliness. The land would be as chilly as her heart and as resistant to spring as she was toward life.

She steered the truck to the side of the road. She was alone in an unfamiliar country. Her heart raced. She looked across the great expanse toward the mountains and down into the valley, and felt her nerve slipping. To the east and below was the aging pine flat of the Arkansas River as it secretly threaded its way toward the Kansas plains. Somewhere, twenty miles or so on the western horizon, Mount Massive and Mount Elbert hid in the haze. The crests of the Sawatch Range spread south below her like the prone vertebrae of some fallen giant. The high Mesquites, with their tumbling and rolling slopes of Carbonate, Iron and Fryer Hills, had recovered from the disembowelments of an earlier time. Patient nature, and the efforts of generations gone, had covered the hills with a gaining forest of trees and shrubs. Lynne steeled her courage and turned the truck down into Leadville.

The town was a fascinating contrast of past fact and current reality for Lynne. She had a lot of difficulty trying to imagine the effect of 40,000 people mining and camping in and around Leadville. In the 1880's, the town had stretched away from Main Street in a dance of decent hotels to prostitute hovels for blocks in either direction. The flare of red kerosene lamps at the pleasure houses and green lamps for the dining halls had lined all but the streets occupied by the churches. Nowhere could Lynne see or imagine the antebellum prostitute cribs framed by wide windows and well-hinged swings playing across the sidewalks, holding their temptress wares. They would swing there and beckon to passers by with what must have passed for suggestive solicitations. The last brothel had closed in 1967. The town's notorious past seemed buried and politely silent.

She wondered if the publisher would be interested in that sort of information about other small tourist attracting towns in Colorado. Lynne knew for certain that writing a travel book would certainly be a lot different than the small contributions of witticisms she use to create for the various base newspapers. She and Shelby had had a deal after Lynne had received positive inquiries from the publisher, Shelby would run the bookstore and Lynne would write the travel guides. Fate had seemed to dictate other. The bookstore had been Shelby's dream and Lynne was determined to make that dream come true if it was the last thing she ever did in the world.

Driving down Harrison Street to the real-estate office, Lynne resigned herself to her present state of affairs. She figured that Leadville must have managed to forget its past, or at the very least had recovered from it. She could do the same. It would take time. And time was all she had.

4

Trying to escape the icy fingers of the wind as they reached down into his upturned collar, Doctor Will Kennedy pitched open the door to the Watson and Son Realty and Insurance Office.

"Charlie! Charlie Watson, you in here?" Doc Kennedy yelled as he stamped his feet on the doormat. Clinging clumps of snow skittered across the polished wood floor. He was irritated and annoyed with the cold. He did not wait for an answer as his stomping brutalized the welcome mat inside the door.

"Charlie! Where the hell are you?" Doc Kennedy bristled. Taking off his hat, he looked around the office. The two-story, wood and native stone building smelled of varnished oak, leather chairs, window cleaner, and the faint perfume of wilting roses. The vast open space was partially broken by the neat alignment of desks hugging the wall. Each workspace had been politely shielded from the other by smoke-frosted glass panels. The computer screens on the desks sat in mute testimony of the orderly and efficient habits required by the sales staff. Tasteful green-glass desk lamps, wooden letter baskets, and leather chairs contrasted sharply with the buff tones of fax machines, computer terminals, and telephones. It was a study in contrasts and therefore not incongruous with the nature of the owner, Charlie Watson. He had always had a fondness for the past and a penchant for gadgetry.

Its visual clash of time and culture seemed to further irritate Doc Kennedy. But it was an old habit of irritation about the rightness of tradition that Charlie Watson did not share. Doc had been putting up with Charlie for more than fifty years and managed to gain some comfort with the constant inconsistencies of Charlie's personality. Doc knew that Charlie had been reluctant to lose all the polite comfort of the past to modern business necessities. Long after old man Watson, Charlie's father, died, Charlie had done little more than allow practical business considerations to intrude into the family-owned business.

The ancient vault of the converted bank loomed across the back wall providing a natural break between front offices and the rear section of the building. The layout made the secretary, accountant, and the filing cabinets invisible to potential clients. Only the sales staff and Charlie were to be seen by Charlie's customers. Charlie's sense of order and decorum dominated the business in structure and form.

Doc Kennedy walked toward the pewter-colored vault that towered near Charlie's walnut desk. Next to the desk, an old fashioned roll-top desk bordered the window. The memento from the past was Charlie's refuge from the complexities of the world.

The bank had belonged to his grandfather. It had gone under in the Wall Street silver panic of 1890. Charlie's grandfather had been part speculator and part squirrel. The old man had bought the bank outright at the county tax auction. Over the years, the family had secured prosperity while the county's quicker fortunes slipped away. Charlie was a big fish in a small pond. It suited his political conservatism. And being a friendly big fish suited his nature.

As Doc Kennedy moved toward his favorite chair near Charlie's desk, a slamming of doors and heavy steps echoed from the interior. The soft thud of a body making contact with a doorway caused Doc Kennedy chuckled. He knew Charlie was anything but graceful, and could prove it several times a day. Over the years, as they had begun to grow old together, Doc Kennedy had felt a professional inclination to warn Charlie about the need to take better care of him. Absent-mindedness was not a terminal condition, but Doc Kennedy worried about the cumulative strain Charlie's blunders caused his body.

"Cripes, Doc, can't a man take a leak without being disturbed?" Charlie Watson's face was flushed. He half-lumbered toward his desk chair as he pulled and pushed his suspenders into place. Doc Kennedy tilted his head and studied Charlie's face. He saw the red blotches across Charlie's cheeks and the pulse beating in the wide temple vein. His physician's mind conjured up elements of cause and effect. Doc did not like the way Charlie looked, but he could not bring himself to chastise his friend about his continued weight gain. Not yet, anyway. He would consider it again after the effects of a good breakfast had an opportunity to work on Charlie's morning attitude.

Doc Kennedy and Charlie were in the same leaky boat of aging. Charlie had turned sixty-two in January and Doc sixty-three in February. Neither were old men, at least they would not concede to the idea. But Charlie's sedentary life was a great leap from the robust course Doc had chosen. Doc Kennedy liked hunting and fishing.

Doc and his wife had not had children. He was alone now. Widowed for five years, Doc had rejoined and rejoiced in his hobbies. It had been easier and safer than allowing being too quickly captured by eligible widow women in the area. His friend Charlie could still count the blessings of a wife, children, and grandchildren.

Charlie looked at Doc Kennedy. Doc studiously ignored his friend's fixed glare.

"Well?" Charlie demanded.

"Well?" Doc intoned slowly. "Aren't you the one who scheduled this sunrise breakfast?"

"So?"

"So, your lights were on. I figured you were ready to buy me that cup of coffee. And here I am." Docs Kennedy studied a small fissure in his thumbnail and waited for Charlie's response. It was a ritual, an ancient game of harassment, and a bait-and-wait they had invented forty years ago. They secretly kept a score. Doc had gotten two points ahead of him as of last Friday.

"Unlike some people I know, I still have to make house calls to make my living, and I do it at all hours, too." Charlie sat behind his desk and eased forward to see if the barb stuck.

"Unlike some people we both know, I retired, satisfied with my savings, investments and county pension, and a part-time job, rather than allow avarice to control my life." Doc Kennedy squared the score. A sneaking smile crossed Doc's lips. Over the years they had become the types of men who believed that too much courtesy to one's real friends might lead to outbursts of messy emotionalism. They preferred the discrete embrace of antagonism and feigned disdain.

"You buying coffee or not?" Charlie asked as he rose from his chair. He reached into his hip pocket to check for his wallet. He had lost the last round of verbal barrages and knew he would be pressed to buy breakfast. Suddenly, some physical discomfort gnawed at him and his reach faltered. He glanced at Doc, but Doc had not noticed the twitch. Charlie moved his hand toward his shirt pocket and rubbed his heart. He masked the message by pretending to search for a lost packet of matches.

"Hell, no. You invited me and in polite society, the person who invites pays for the invited. I am the invited. Or don't you feel very polite today?" Doc insisted.

"Who said anything about me taking you on to raise?" Charlie asked as he felt the tightness loosening its vise grip from around his heart. "Besides, I'm expecting some business sometime morning. A lady called from up the road the other day and said she'd be here to check into the campground next to Turquoise Lake this morning."

"Look. You can kill two birds with one stone. Put a sign on your door. She'll find you. If she can't find you, then you won't be wasting her time or yours." Doc stood up, ready to leave.

"All right...all right. You go ahead and get us a table. I'll be along shortly. But hold off ordering until I get there." Charlie waved Doc toward the door.

Doc walked out onto the sidewalk and glanced back to see Charlie busily writing the sign. He thought Charlie was too driven. Seven in the morning was a fine time for breakfast, but too damn early for business. Shaking his head, he turned to walk down the street. His feet guided him to the distant glow of the neon lights above the Double Eagle Bar and Grill.

"Cripes," Charlie silently cursed as he pulled on his coat and headed toward the door. Satisfied with the lock and the legibility of his sign, he followed stiffly in Charlie's direction.

Hunching against the cold wind, Charlie understood and supported the love-hate relationship that existed between tourists and locals. Tourists were pesky immigrants to the quiet mountain town. They always brought money, but sometimes they also brought trouble. Tourists rarely became residents, and the residents believed that to be best. As a Realtor and life-long resident, Charlie often found himself in both of the warring camps. He rented and sold property to the interlopers. That made him money.

But he was part of the old crowd, so his profession set him at odds with his soul. He could not win. He could only make money.

Smiling to himself as he approached the Double Eagle, Charlie speculated what it would be like if the town could devise a test for potential newcomers. A test should be developed which could check the mettle of the personality. What they needed was some means of detecting grit and style. He wanted something certifying, separating the wheat from chaff, and the welcome from the other ones, who should move-along. Winners would be allowed to stay. Losers would have to go back where they came from and not bother folks. Charlie liked the idea.

Opening the door of the Double Eagle, he felt a rush of warm air on his face. Charlie would offer his idea as grist for the conversational mill at the breakfast table. He hoped for a good size group and conversation. The Double Eagle had been built in 1878 and had quickly become a notorious bar and brothel. The long bar, cozy curtained seating for ladies and gents of the day, pool tables, dining rooms, and delights of the second floor had made it the most popular and profitable location in town. The ancient oak, walnut and polished cherry woods still gleamed in the chandelier lights. But time and circumstance had changed some of its demeanor and civilized most of its customers. The antiquated mounted heads of dead hunting trophies stared and lights winked through the stained glass entrance at every newcomer approach. Opening every day at six a.m. it fed and watered locals until abbreviated closures at two a.m. Tourists rarely visited the Double Eagle. If they did manage to visit, they were generally ignored by the locals and not invited to stay.

"You're getting as fat and slow as a sway-back mule, Charlie," a grating voice bellowed across the room the moment Charlie stepped through the door.

Charlie could not see the man's face. He did not have to. He knew who it was. The gravel voice told him, and his hope of good breakfast companions had been shot to hell. He wished his property prospect would show up early and save him. He walked toward the table, glanced at the three men waiting for him, and decided to ignore the vicious taunt. Temporarily. He took off his overcoat and added it to the pile of parkas on an adjoining chair.

"Yes, sir," Greg Hanson persisted. "Every year old Charlie here gets a little older and a whole lot slower. Looks like you're puttin' on a bit of extra weight, too." Greg nudged Doc Kennedy to get him to join in the conspiracy against Charlie. Doc moved away from Greg's touch in mild revulsion. He objected to being touched by anyone who could manage to look so dirty and unkempt that early in the morning. And he objected to being included in anything Greg might ever be involved in.

Charlie was disappointed. The climate and altitude might sort out interlopers into the community, but it seemed that even the natives had their own perversities.

What Doc and Charlie called poor hygiene, Greg claimed as a befitting and naturally musk masculine aroma. Greg had spent his life if what nature had given by accident was his own manifest destiny. Right, bright penny, proper to be a man and happily middle aged. Greg figured he was all he needed to be. Nothing else mattered. An obnoxious and frequently dangerous drunk, he spent his time as an unemployed fixture in town.

Charlie looked to Doc and then to Ray Billings sitting at the table. Both men shrugged and silently confessed what Charlie suspected. Greg had made himself at home among them without their direct permission. It was a small town and its least tolerable member had an acknowledged right to exist. They would allow Greg his small intrusion.

"You boys settle down and play nicely," Bevs McLeary asserted as she suddenly appeared at their table. Bevs was part owner and part-time waitress at the Double Eagle. She demanded respect, and would not take less. She was a commanding woman of uncertain age and black dyed hair. Her feigned schoolmarm propriety was a hallmark of authority and mixed easily with the clear voice.

"Well?" Bevs threatened.

"Yes ma'am?" the men at the table agreed in mock contriteness.

"Order up or get up," she said as she readied her pen above her pad.

Orders for breakfast came quickly, and the table settled back into a general discussion of politics and the impersonal.

Ray Billing's long lanky legs tipped his chair back against the wall while he waited for the food. His long fingers were clasped together behind his head making his elbows stand out akimbo. He had not entered the earlier fray between his table companions. In the years since he had arrived in Leadville, he would become conditioned to the sparring of the town's habitual friends and foes. He had learned to ride it out and let the dust of familiarity settle the arguments.

When Ray had first arrived in Leadville, it had taken him quite sometime to get over the culture shock of living in a small community. He had been used to the shifting fortunes of a large university set in a metropolitan area. The move had been a blessing. Escaping the pressures of academia, and found a sanctuary for his research and curiosity at the local junior college. It had been a good decision then. It still was. He counted amongst his friends Doc Kennedy and Charlie Watson. And in that he knew he was fortunate. Greg and others like him were merely part of the compromise to be made in life when all else was going well.

From where he sat with his back to the wall, Ray had the best view of the entrance to the Double Eagle. He liked it that way. He was a people watcher and by that stroke of luck, he was the first to see the woman dressed in a blue parka walk through the door as she swung her backpack off her shoulder. His natural curiosity and training as a sociologist was brought to full alert, as he realized, she was not a regular or local.

The woman's steady gaze across the tables in the room caught his interest. Ray thought he detected an interesting air of confidence and hint of studied purpose in her demeanor. He watched her take off her hat and release a bounty of short auburn hair. She was poised ramrod straight and within that posture seemed to convey coiled vitality. Her eyes struck him as those that had been closed by the sun. There was a hint of lines that might have been shaped by weariness from having gazed too long at things, which were best-left unseen. They were her most striking features. A hint of green seemed to flash to him even at that distance. He recalled that other; older cultures might have marked her as a warrior, with weapons or without. He wondered if she knew she carried it so visibly. Ray thought of mentioning her to his tablemates, but declined. He could not have explained it to them, and they would have chided him for being too easily overheated by women or too philosophical for the time of day. Ray's eyes followed the woman as she found a booth. He made a mental note to introduce himself to her if she remained in town for any reasonable length of time.

5

"Sheriffs Department," Deputy Lon Gradey huffed into the phone as he shifted his thick leg and swollen knee to a more comfortable position on the side chair. He placed his index finger on the page of the book he had been reading.

"Lake County Sheriff's Department?" a hesitant male voice asked at the other end of the line.

"That's right,...what can I do for you?" Gradey let weariness seep into his voice. He was not in a good mood. His knee was still swollen from the fall he took Wednesday at the racquetball court. He had had a miserable night of it. He was disgusted with himself for having missed the shot, and disgusted at his continued lack of skill in the game.

"Officer?..." The man's voice continued reluctantly. Gradey unconsciously moved the phone a few fractions of an inch away from his ear. He disliked whining men. The caller gave Gradey all the wrong signals, and he wanted to reduce his contact with behaviors that might be contagious.

"Officer?" the man insisted.

"Deputies…sheriff department officers are called deputies, mister. Now, what can I do for you?" Gradey's voice had dropped to the tone he reserved for the criminal element and other worthless civilians.

"Deputy, my name is Terry Bodeen. I'm calling from Denver about my wife."

"Yes?…And?…" Gradey was already tired of the conversation. He hated his injury-imposed desk duty and was anxious to be on the road enforcing some law, any law. He swiveled in his chair, and jumped from the pain the move provoked.

"Look,…I'm concerned about my wife. "A measure of steel crept into the caller's voice as he registered Gradey's impatience.

"She's been on vacation…in your area for a week, and was due home yesterday. It's just not like…."

"She may have got a late start or the road conditions could have held her up," Gradey interrupted with the patent answers.

"Yes, well, I thought of that. I tried to reach her at the number she left but there's no answer. I called the Highway Patrol. There's been no report of unusual road conditions or accidents involving our car." The voice gave a clipped recitation of facts.

"Well, then, I'm sure she's on her way home. 'Course, she could have decided to take a longer holiday without letting you know." Gradey chuckled derisively. His meaty hand propped open the pages of his book, and he eyed it searching for the paragraph he had been reading when the phone interrupted him.

"Look,…Deputy, I'm not crying wolf here. I know my wife. She is very responsible and reliable. If she had been delayed, or had decided to stay longer, she'd have let me know."

Gradey could begin to see where the conversation was heading. The man's imagination was beginning to conjure up all sorts of nightmarish visions involving his wife. Gradey took a deep breath to try to prepare for the onslaught of spouse anxiety and searched for a means of avoiding the confrontation.

"Have the two of you had any difficulties lately?" Gradey offered as a solution. "You know, something that would cause her to take her irritation out on you,...like, not showing up when you expected her?" He said as he warmed to the subject. "She got a friend...or...you got a friend and she found out about it?" Gradey had learned how unforgiving a scorned woman could be. Two ex-wives and a ton of alimony were constant and aggravating reminders.

"No," the caller said. "No, nothing like that," his voice had taken a sharp turn toward anger. "Look, let's get this straight right now, deputy. I'm calling for help. I need to find my wife. I want to know she's O.K. You are a cop. Your job is to help me. So, you can either help me or continue to be an asshole. If you can't, or won't, help,...I'll speak to your supervisor." Frustration and fear moved Terry to the point of losing control of his anger.

"I am the supervisor, this week..." Gradey began defensively. Sheriff Bret Callison had gone on vacation at a convention retreat in Las Vegas earlier and was not expected to return until Saturday. Gradey was left in charge. Gradey liked being in charge. He liked having authority but not having it questioned.

"Look," Terry said, taking a slow deep breath, trying desperately to control his emotions. "All I want you to do is to help me. Beverly could be injured...or worse."

"I understand your concern, but you have to understand, too,...I have a lot of responsibilities here." Gradey warmed in the glow of being in control of the man's needs. He wanted to hear him grovel.

"And you could be unemployed next week!" Terry interrupted heatedly.

Gradey's mind flashed on the member of the county council and the Sheriff during his personnel action last month. Gradey had been warned and reprimanded for what had been termed "heavy-handed and officious behavior." He had to look up the word "officious" to understand what they had accused him of. He stung from the rebuke. The Sheriff had barely saved his butt. A three-day suspension without pay had dented his pride and his wallet. Gradey was too close to the fire to want to have anything fan the flames. He took a slow breath to cover his alarm. The hostile silence on the line grew louder.

"Deputy," Terry began with calm purpose. "My wife was staying in a cabin in your county. I have the address and directions. She is not answering my calls. She is not home. Nor has either of us been involved in any affairs. The Highway Patrol assures me that she has not been involved in an accident. Could I ask you to go to the cabin and check on her? It would give me one less thing to worry about." His composure wavered, but he maintained his strident tone.

"Where's the cabin?" Gradey asked, surrendering to his sense of enlightened self-interest. Frowning, he knew he would have to write a damn report to cover his ass from the irate taxpayer.

"Thank you," Terry exhaled in relief. "The cabin is at a place called the Half Moon Creek Ranch. Beverly said the ranch belongs to a Bob and Marian Peavey. Her cabin is about two miles west off Highway 24...."

"I know the Peavey's and their ranch, too," Gradey said without writing down the information.

"Oh,...good, all right. She's staying at cabin number four."

"Yeah, I know the outfit. I will give them a call and maybe run out there, if we don't get an answer. Give me your phone number, and I'll have a deputy go out there and give it a check. OK?"

"Great. I appreciate it. I need to know she's all right," Terry said, hoping he had finally heard concern or competence in the deputy's voice.

"Ok. We'll see what we can do," Gradey promised as he hung up the phone. He gingerly swung his damaged knee off the chair. "Creep," the hushed curse slid under his breath. "I'll get back to you." He figured his need to go out and do something interesting had been answered by an exercise in futility. Gradey limped to the dispatcher's office and pressed the communication center mike. There were three deputies on the road. He decided to take the closest available with him on his fool's errand.

"Which one of you is closest to town?" Gradey asked as he punched the mike. Faint static crackled through a relay booster station's whispered bounce. The radios were always jumpy during days when the clouds hung low. A signal could bounce and miss his deputies.

"I'm 'bout three miles north, just off twenty-four. Do you need something, Sergeant?"

"Whose that?" Gradey asked as he adjusted the static and volume controls to get a fix on the returning signal.

"Joe. What's up?" Joe Larks responded eagerly and slowed his patrol vehicle to a stop. He figured he would lose the signal if he dropped into the valley. His fair-haired youth and enthusiasm had yet to be replaced by cynicism or boredom.

"Get in here and pick me up," Gradey ordered.

"On my way. Whatcha' got going?" Joe liked working with Gradey and admired the big man's tendency to take control of situations. He wanted to be just like him someday.

"Just get in here. We got a little run to do," Gradey said, decided to make the best of a bad situation. He ran his hand through his thinning brown hair and sighed to himself. As unwanted as the errand was, it was the best excuse he had had all morning for getting out of the office. He reached for the phone to call in the part-time dispatcher, Susana Weller. But he stopped when his stomach reminded him of its earlier complaints.

Stabbing the microphone, he called Joe again. "Listen, Joe, get me a cola and a couple of burgers at Carroll Grill before you come in here."

"O.K.," Joe responded. Gradey had once told him the real learning of law enforcement had nothing to do with the weenie-book offered at the state's training academy. Joe had already memorized the Gradey approach to "scrotes and shit-bags" one would encounter in the real world. "Whatever you need, Sage."

"Right," Gradey looked around the office and, hopping on his good leg, reached the locked gun cabinet and saw his favorite toys. He retrieved his black leather gear and hefted the weight of the holstered .44 magnum across his waist. It was like an old lover resting against his hip. "Natural," he crooned, and felt complete again.

Twenty minutes later, he was lounging in the patrol car, eating his hamburgers, as Joe drove south out of town. He managed to finish the hamburgers and wash them down before the patrol car passed the city limit sign. He had forgotten to phone the Peavey's after his mind had settled on an early lunch.

Gradey decided he liked being "sheriff" even if it was only for a week. Gradey liked having someone at his beck and calls. It seemed to him to be a natural extension of his leadership capabilities. Gradey nodded imperiously at a truck driven by a local rancher and romanticized about what it would be like to be the sheriff for more than a week.

To Gradey's way of thinking, Sheriff Callison had all but retired after his reelection three years ago. The only problem was, the man's body kept showing up at the office. What the county needed a real man in the Sheriff's job, and Gradey happened to know the man who could fill that bill. He was not exactly sure how it might all come about. He did not have the training Callison could boast about. But Callison had been gone for fifteen years after joining the Colorado Bureau of Investigation. Gradey figured he was as much a tourist as any other he had ever seen.

"What cabin we looking for?" Joe asked, turning the patrol car onto the Elm Creek Gulch road.

"Number four. I think if you just keep to the road here, there will be a posted sign leading back off to a clearing. We'll have to check. I hope the Peavey's posted numbers on the mail boxes," Gradey said, as he shifted his weight and tried to get his legs in a more comfortable position. The patrol car's bench seats had been moved to fit Joe's shorter legs, which made Gradey's bad knee rest perilously close to the glove box. And the jostling it was taking from the ice-rutted road began to wear on his nerves.

"There…there, that's the cabin number." Gradey said pointing to the number nailed to a post next to a short driveway. The cabin sat back in a tree-sheltered circle.

"There's a car there," Joe noted as he slowed to turn into the drive.

"Yeah. I can see it," Gradey said, and wished the annoying caller could be with him to see for himself. Gradey was already sizing up how he'd play the old "I told you so" line for the idiot husband when he got back to the office.

"What do you want to do now?" Joe asked, as he brought the car to a stop next to the silver gray sedan.

"Hasn't been moved in sometime," Joe concluded as he noted the hoar-frost caking the trim.

"What I want you to do is to get your ass up to the door and tell that bitch to get on the horn to her hubby. That's what. 'Cause if I do it, I'm just as likely to tell her what I think of her and her whole Damning family," Gradey roared, and motioned angrily toward the cabin.

"Sure, Sarge," Joe nodded and quickly got out of the car. The weak spring sun filtering through the dissipating fog did not warm him as he trudged toward the cabin. As he put his boots on the frosted boards of the cabin porch, the boards snapped and groaned under his weight. Joe did not notice that his boot-prints were not the only one's on the porch. He stood quietly for a moment before the cabin door, listening for sounds inside the cabin. He raised his fist, pounded heavily on the door, and waited for a response. Nothing stirred but the wind past his ears. He tried the doorknob. It caught and confirmed itself as locked. Joe clinched his fist and hammered louder and longer on the door with a glass-rattling jar that could have raised the dead.

"Bet 'ole Gradey's right. She's snuggled up in there with some new squeeze," Joe chuckled under his breath. There was still no answer. Joe turned back toward the patrol car and heavily shrugged his shoulders at Gradey.

Gradey rolled down the passenger window and stuck his head out, all but knocking off his dark brown Mountie hat. "Christ, Joe. Do I have to come up there and hold your hand? ! Go 'round, check the windows. See if there is a back door. Watch the windows as you go," Gradey yelled. He figured that Joe might be a nice enough kid, but he had obviously not paid attention to anything in the police academy. He settled back into the car and leaned over to the driver's side to turn up the heat while he waited for Joe. He keyed the radio and called in the license plate so Norma would check for the identification of the owner. Norma had verified that the car did in fact belong to Beverly Bodeen. He waited. He realized Joe had been gone a long time, more than it should have taken to walk around a small cabin. He stretched and rubbed his aching neck.

"What's keeping him?" he wondered aloud. Mumbling to himself, he wondered if he was going to be doomed to spend his entire career working with idiots. Gradey called to Joe as he got out of the car and leaned against the doorframe. The engine's rumble made it impossible to hear anything. He limped around the side of the car, stretched over the steering wheel, and shut off the engine.

The faint sound of retching met his surprised ears as his head emerged from the quieted car. Dread spread up from the base of his crotch to his heart. Caution pulled his hand toward his revolver as he hobbled toward the cabin.

"Joe?". Gradey called his voice in uncertain croaking. He cleared his throat. "Joe?" he called again as he walked toward the side of the cabin Joe had disappeared around. Running footsteps came at him. Gradey raised his gun to gut level.

"Sarge!" Gradey heard Joe's voice just before the rookie stumbled and fell around the side of the cabin.

Hot adrenaline shot through Gradey's arm and down to his outstretched weapon. He was barely able to keep his trigger finger from lapsing into a pull. The shock forced him to jerk his revolver up and over Joe's pin-wheeling body. Joe collapsed on his hands and knees as a patch of half-frozen mud pitched him to the ground.

"Christ on a crutch! What the Damn is wrong with you?" Gradey stared stupidly at Joe, his gun still waving in the air. Fear and alarm mixed uncertainly in Gradey's mind. His heart hammered hard against his chest walls. He would come close to blowing off the other man's head.

"In the window," Joe said gasping as the dry heaves claimed him again. "I can't," he said as he looked up at Gradey through tear swimming eyes.

"What? What window? Where?" Gradey demanded. He knelt next to Joe and raised his revolver to the cabin.

"Back. There. This side," Joe said as he glanced at Gradey and then shook his head in resignation. "She's,......" he sputtered to a whispering halt.

"Come on. Get up," Gradey commanded as he pulled at Joe's arm. "You get up and help me, right now!"

"All right," Joe whispered angrily.

"Straighten up and pay attention! If something has happened here, I need you."

Joe nodded weakly and tried to stand.

Gradey pulled and pushed Joe to his feet. They moved cautiously around the side of the cabin. At the far west end, Gradey shoved Joe under and past the window, he had pointed to.

Carefully, Gradey peeked through the side of the window. A curtain edge partially obscured his view. He bobbed his head to the unobstructed opening, hoping to get a better look. He focused. At first, he could not decide what he was seeing, and blinked to fine-tune his vision. Then he saw the fixed grimace, her blind gaze reaching past the window to some far point beyond the meadow and above the mountains. As he felt the bile rise at the back of his teeth, Gradey's heart lurched at the astonished pain forever locked in Beverly's eyes.

6

By late morning, Charlie Watson had returned to his office to sort through the stack of envelopes that represented the end-of-the-month bills and receipts. Although he had an accountant, he found it comforting to have his hand in on all aspects of the business. He always wanted to know where the dollars were coming from and where they were going. He worked quietly through the morning.

When he had been a young man working for his father, he had told his mother the only thing he wanted from life was to be comfortable. He could still see her smiling in amusement at him.

"Charlie that may be true. But your definition of comfort would be most people's idea of rich." Her eyes had danced as her gentle laughter washed over her eldest son. He had been indignant and accused her of not knowing him very well. She had touched him lightly and assured him of both her love and understanding. As the years passed, he began to understand himself almost as well as she had. She had been more right than wrong. He remembered her smile every time he restrained himself from being grasping or greedy.

His mother's chiding had held him in check and he saw to it that good fortune and success did not become a failing. She had not wanted him to be a narrow or lonely miser in either money or life. And so, he had married his childhood sweetheart who could share his love of the small mountain town and his personal struggle to be a decent man. His wife of thirty years was the one who helped him define the difference between the cost of a thing and its real value. He was not the richest man in the community. But with the woman he loved, he had become both prosperous in his business and generous in his charity toward others.

A slight frown caught on his forehead, and pulled his thick wavy, gray hair toward his eyebrows. He was not unhappy with the quarterly totals but he would have preferred them to be as firm and fat as was typical for the summer and fall traditional showing. He leaned back in his chair, his concerns eased by remembering that spring would bring the buyers. As he reflected on his need for patience, the magnetic chimes on the office doors signaled that he was no longer alone. Rising from his chair, he realized just how much he truly disliked the mechanical tone of the chimes. He did not care for their pretensions of soft civility; the clanging of the chimes jarred his ears.

The sun was streaming brightly through the windows and reflected sharply on the polished hardwood floors. The glare masked the body and face. Charlie raised his hand to his forehead to reduce the glare and get a better look at the person who had walked past him to stand midpoint in the room.

"Are you Charles Watson?" a woman's cool resonate voice asked from out of the glare.

"Yes," he said, pushing his right hand out in front of him. He felt his hand clasped full and firm. No fingertip touching, shrinking violet here, he thought.

"Though most people around here call me Charlie," he offered casually.

"Yes,…well," she said, looking around the office at the fixtures. "I'm sure they do, but I imagine most folks know you better than I do, Mr. Watson."

"Would you have a seat?" Charlie asked, and motioned to his desk. He wondered if she had really meant to put a chill in the air that he suddenly felt. Over the years, he had developed the practiced air of country tried-and-true goodwill. Charlie had found it would work with most people, but he suspected it might not work with her. He decided he would have to get the full measure of her quickly to stay even. Being off balance was the last thing a Realtor wanted to have happen. He watched as she moved around the far side of his desk and looked at the waterfowl lithographs on his wall. She touched his desk with her hand, gazed at the papers and smiled lightly to him as she took her seat in the green leather chair.

"I don't mean to be rude, Mr. Watson. It's just that you and your office have the look of a man who knows how to make a goodly profit but are not too prone to flashing it," she said as she cleared her throat. "Because of that, and the information provided by my attorney, I'd rather call you Charles or Mr. Watson. That way we won't confuse casualness with business." She took off her parka and laid it across an empty chair next to her.

Her green eyes locked on him and he noticed the slight creasing of her smile line's highlight her words. He felt a mild discomfort. He wondered at the feeling, and then to his surprise he recognized it as intimidation. He did not know whether to be startled or amused. There were damn few men who could intimidate him, and there had not been a woman since his mother who could raise that specter in him.

"As you will. How might I help you?" Charlie wanted the weight of the conversation on her side of the desk while he sorted through his consternation. He glanced at her as he walked around to his chair. A practiced quick observation he used to take the measure of his clients told him to go formal. It was not just the formal tones or insistence. It was more. He squinted to get a better look but the casual parka and glare of the morning light hid her from his full view. But there were things he could see, like the sharp pressed button-fly jeans, crisp oxford shirt collar, V-necked dark blue sweater, and polished boots. It told him volumes. Here was a place and in one person where propriety and protocol blended in her nature. She was the kind of woman who would not be known for professional playfulness. She was business even in the early light of day. He could see where her mind and heart lived comfortably entwined.

"My name is Lynne Fhaolain. I believe you've been expecting me?" she asked, and began removing legal sized papers from her backpack.

Charlie nodded and glanced down at the light penciled notes he arranged on the top of his desk. He found what he was looking for and quickly ran the words through his mind. "Sharp as a tack, a bit caustic, shrewd, Major, retired Army...watch your step, there are some loss issues..." The attorney in Kansas City, Missouri had shared his analysis of the seemingly formidable Ms. Fhaolain. It sounded more like a warning. He glanced back up and found her watching him intently. He shuffled the papers to hide his notes but remembered her walk around the desk, and figured he was had. She would show no deference to him, that much was apparent. He decided he would have to watch his footing until he knew how the ground was laid out. Over the years he had taught himself to know the difference between solid ground and the shifting of sands. Here there are sands.

"The Gellmore property, right?" Charlie said, deciding that going straight to business was the best way to firmer footing.

"Yes. I'm hoping we might settle whatever financial matter remains unattended. I'm assuming, of course, that my attorney contacted you weeks ago?" Lynne moved the chair in front of his desk and spread her documents across her side of the desktop.

A quizzical smile fled across Charlie's lips. He was amused that she had moved herself into his space and domain like an unabashed cat burglar moving about a house. Since he had not immediately responded to her territory encroachment, he knew there was little he could do to protest her gains.

He rose and scanned the walnut cabinets behind him for the one holding the documents he needed. Pulling open the drawer of the cabinet containing currently available properties, he found and retrieved a manila folder of papers and turned back to his desk.

"Right. I have been working with your attorney. I hope what we have done is according to your wishes. I feel certain they are keen to have your interests at heart. I...." Charlie looked up to find Lynne moving the ashtray to her side of the desk. She smiled at him as she removed her cigarettes and lighter from a parka pocket. He wanted to make some remark about her space claiming tendencies, but thought better of it. Charlie searched helplessly for some light topic of conversation. Then time ran out.

"Well, I didn't hire them..." she placed the cigarette in her mouth and lit it, "...to have any heart. I've found that heart and conscience in attorneys is an oxymoron of purpose and intent." She sat back in her chair and flashed a smile at him through the rising smoke. "Wouldn't you agree?"

"True, too true," Charlie chuckled. She did have a sense of humor, but it came with the glint of a knife.

"I have gotten my money's worth from them. Anyway, about the Gellmore place, I am not terribly familiar with it. Frankly, I have no more notions about it than what my attorney advised me."

"You didn't drop by there then, before you came here? The Gellmore property is just a short walk from here. Not more than 200 yards, I'd say."

"No, I haven't taken the time. But, ahh…a friend of mine saw it less than a year ago. I take it that it is still in good condition." Lynne asked as she ground the cigarette out. Shelby had come to Leadville to make inquiries about the building. Lynne did not care for dealing with sales people and wished that Shelby was with her to help deal with the complications. Lynne felt that sales people had a habit of intruding into her otherwise controlled world. It always made her feel vulnerable and suspicious of their intentions. Drawing in more breath, she tried to relax. "…And I want to be able to see more than just the outside."

"I understand perfectly. Just to let you know we have maintained a modicum of heat in the winter and ventilation in the summer to prevent unnecessary deterioration of the building from extreme weather conditions. It's the tendency of buildings to deteriorate more quickly if left to the ravages of our seasons up here," Charlie explained as he scanned the building inspection form for any glaring notations or suspicions of structural weakness.

"However," he said as he leaned across the desk, "any deterioration or flaw that varies from the condition you expect could be remedied, or we could assume the variances as points of negotiation in your purchase of the building."

Charlie wanted to unload the Gellmore building. It had been vacant for three years, with only infrequent use as a warehouse during citywide garage sales. He enjoyed making the gesture to the community but he was in business. The building was becoming too expensive for him to continue to heat, even to delay structural weakening. He did not want his original investment to vanish at a county tax auction.

"Well, let's get to it then. First, I want to look over the..." Lynne began.

Screams of sirens and the dash of emergency vehicles interrupted the conversation. She turned in her chair in time to see the flashing strobe of lights from a speeding vehicle bounce off the office doors. The sirens warbled to a crescendo and faded into the distance.

"Lots of noise and commotion, isn't it?" Charlie said.

Lynne turned around in her chair and raised an eyebrow at Charlie, waiting for further comment. He hesitated and then offered no explanation.

"That happen often around here?" she asked, feeling the tug of questions raised by the emergency vehicles. In the line of duty, or official curiosity, she generally had all her questions answered. But, she reminded herself; her only official function now was as a young retiree. That and fifty cents would buy her a cup of coffee. She wondered how odd it would be to know no more than the average citizen about such emergency comings does and goings does.

"No, we're pretty quiet. You might have guessed. More than likely, there's been some accident on the highway. Get your blood up, did it?" Charlie asked deciding a personal approach.

"My blood?" Lynne responded, looking at him quizzically. "Oh,...I see. Yes, I suppose I'm as bad as any old war horse."

"Your attorney told me you'd been a Major in the Army. With investigation divisions, as I understand it. How long were you in service?" Charlie prodded.

"The bare maximum. Twenty years. Investigations were just part of the job." Lynne took another cigarette from a pocket, looked at it, and decided to put it on the desk instead. "I've since retired. Spent my time, all the time I intended to, I saved some money and to start over again. I'm looking for a new career."

"Well, so you're a lady of leisure?" Charlie asked, finally liking the general conversational tone in her voice. He did not like to rush to formalities. Business could be done in a kind and gentle fashion.

"I'm really not sure how leisurely I feel. For that matter, with what I have in mind as a business venture, the idea of leisure is at cross purposes," she said, shifting the papers in her hand.

Sirens wailed faintly in the distance and were joined by clarion blasts of ambulance and fire engines.

"Must have been a hell of a crash," Charlie interjected.

"Must. But nevertheless,...we should probably get on with our business. Can't do anything for anyone from here but speculate."

"Right you are. Let's see,...you wanted to look over the blueprints, appraisal, and proposed terms of the contract, no doubt," Charlie said as he handed the papers to Lynne.

"Yes. To begin with this would be fine," Lynne said as she reached for the papers Charlie offered. She put on a pair of gold-rimmed glasses and began to read through the documents. While she read, Charlie busied himself by pretending to read other documents. Periodically, Lynne referred to her notes and made notations in a book she had retrieved from the seemingly cavernous parka.

Charlie was a patient man. Half an hour later, he momentarily absented himself with the excuse of making coffee. He took the time to quickly call his wife and tell her that it looked like he might not be home until later. He was glad his wife conveyed neither great surprise nor impatience in her voice. She was used to him and his infrequent Saturday ventures.

When he returned with the coffee, Lynne reached up and smiled lightly at him. It was a vanishingly small smile. Business, money, and planning had seemingly taken over her concentration. Time marched on, and Charlie tried to keep himself busy halfheartedly reading the morning paper. He wondered what questions she might have for him once she finished her thorough study.

"All right," she said, looking up from the papers that now drifted over Charlie's desk. She was prepared with more questions.

"Everything looks good then?" Charlie stretched his neck and rolled his shoulders to get the kinks out that had settled in them.

"I don't want to assume too much of a fixer-upper, Mr. Watson. My intentions are always as good as gold in such instances. But, as I'm sure you know, good intentions and reality are often two very different things," she said, her voice whispering softly as though it was weighted under by the volumes of information she'd digested. She stretched in the chair and looked at the clock on the wall.

Charlie followed her eyes and felt his own search for the face of his wristwatch. It was 1:30 p.m. His stomach, cued by his realization of the lateness of the hour, began to growl and rumble. Breakfast had been a long time ago.

"Could we run over there now? I'd like to look at exactly what I'm talking about when and if I agree to move forward in this venture," Lynne said, as she reached for her coat and gathered up the papers. "I might have some questions and suggestions," she added, when she saw the blank look on Charlie's face. She had heard his internal growling and mentally acknowledged the need for food in herself.

"That is, I'm not unhappy with the way it looks on paper. I'm sure you understand that before I can commit myself, a thorough tour of the premises is important to me," she said as she walked toward the door.

"I'll get the keys," he called to her retreating. After some befuddlement, he managed to grab his coat, scoop up the file, and find the keys for the Gellmore place. But none of it was easily accomplished. He had made three aborted trips across the floor toward the door, trying to remember everything he might need. He tried to keep his face from reflecting the annoyance he felt.

He found Lynne standing on the sidewalk waiting for him. Charlie had just motioned in the direction they were to take when he saw Doc Kennedy's car come rolling slowly up the street. He waved at Doc, but Doc never looked in his direction. Doc's gaze stared fixedly forward. Then Charlie noticed the two sheriffs' cars moving at the same subdued speed behind Doc. Charlie stood transfixed and wondering as he watched the cars continued up to the Sheriff's office and park.

"Something's wrong?" Lynne asked.

"What?…. Oh? ," Charlie said, finally remembering Lynne. "I don't rightly know."

"A friend of yours in trouble?" Lynne asked, trying to sound solicitous and genuinely concerned.

"No, no. That would be Doc Kennedy, a friend of mine all right, and county coroner. There must have been to the accident. He looked like he's seen more than he wanted to today."

"It's hard sometimes, I know," Lynne said.

"Might as well get to it," Charlie nodded toward the Gellmore building.

7

They walked the three blocks in silence. Lynne's pace pulled her away from Charlie; her mind racing while her feet tried to keep up. It was a short three-block walk. Lynne observed that Leadville must have undergone some restoration during the 1970's and again in the late '80s when money and historic preservation interest had been available. Lynne noticed that the town seemed to have taken an interest in itself. Everywhere the signs of fresh paint, colorful hues and a return of the gingerbread trims on businesses and homes abounded. Specialty shops, hotels, eateries, and basic supply stores of clothes and goods had returned to the main street. Harrison Street had been paved and the streets leading off the main drag for a block in either direction seemed to sport new asphalt through the thin covering of snow. Harkening back to the proud spirit of its heyday, minus the bordellos, brightened the town and made it appealing to the eye.

When she refocused on her immediate surroundings, she heard Charlie's labored breathing. "Everything, O.K.?" Lynne asked self-consciously. She realized she had been making the poor man fairly run down the street after her. She slowed her pace and took in the sights of the town. She realized there was not need to continue her headlong flight down the street.

"Fine," Charlie coughed into his gloved hands.

Lynne paused and turned to Charlie. "Sorry. Lots of things on my mind. Things I need to be settled. I've been dragging my feet, but I don't want my general aggravation with the world to affect you." She touched his jacketed sleeve to convey her sincerity and lapsed back into silence.

As she walked to the front of the Gellmore building, Charlie felt the need to speak to her. "I'm aware of your loss, Major. You have my sincere condolences," he said in a low tone.

She halted. A slow exhalation of breath escaped her pursed lips and she turned to look back at him.

"My attorneys?" she asked soberly.

"Yes, it was. No invasion meant. It was just their way of letting me know that whatever plans you might have had could be subject to change," Charlie said, nervously scratching at the left side of his face. The social misstep made his face itch and he tried to catch up to the nervous tick with his woolen glove. "I'm sure they meant no harm."

"Fine. I guess. I always heard that small towns were sieves of information but I didn't expect to be on the pipeline so soon," she said noticing how the warm afternoon air felt on her face. "Let's just not share too often or too much more, shall we?"

"Agreed," Charlie said, moving toward the doors of the Gellmore building and searched his key ring for the right set of keys.

Lynne listened distractedly as Charlie recited the building's history and snatches of the lives of the people who had populated it. The native stone, bricks, boards and mortar wrapped in Charlie's stories colored the building with well-preserved freshness. It seemed to Lynne that buildings had lives and that this one might have been waiting for revival. She wondered if the ministrations and efforts she had in mind would make it possible for both of them to come back from the brink.

Charlie said the Gellmore building had originally been built in 1925. As a family-owned clothing store, the bottom two floors held clothes, offices, fitting rooms, tailors, sales clerks and skeins of fabric for the do-it-yourselfers. The basement had been reserved for storage and inventory spillover. And the top floor had been the family's living quarters for three generations.

As was the nature of buildings in towns sitting on the spine of the Colorado Rockies, it had been built to withstand the ravages of time. The builders had used native stone and steel girders for support of the main structure. Much of the original horsehair plaster and lathe walls had been replaced with wallboard but the remodeling had been kind. The walnut and walnut-veneer paneling, ornate door frames, trim, windows, wall skirting and baseboards were left intact and in good condition. The paint on the walls had been a pastel yellow with tiny hand-painted flowers. The flowers had since transmuted themselves into brown spidery stains.

Entering the old building was like walking into an ancient tomb, their footsteps hollow in the indifferent emptiness. Small cubicles for fitting rooms stood with their doors open reflecting oak-trimmed rooms. Mirrors where the fashionably dressed of the 1920's had lingered staring at their reflections lined the back walls. The only windows on the first and second floors were those, which faced Harrison Street and the alleyway. Other possibilities of exterior light had been eliminated when two buildings had been built on either side.

The building's expanse, measuring forty by 120 feet carried the unique character of front street middle America. It was the particular curiosity of such buildings to be brief of front and long into the alley with a definite purpose in mind. The builders and the owners designed the buildings to thwart the tendencies of taxation. Historically, cities taxed for their services and community improvements based on the storefront footage. Short fronted stores paid less than their grandiose wide-faced counterparts. A narrow-faced store could stand taller and stretch farther without losing the lion's share of its profits to the levies of the city.

Lynne checked the fuse box at the rear of the store and flipped a few switches experimentally. No lights. Happily, no sparks flew either.

"I thought you said you heated the building?" Lynne asked wiping dust from her hands.

"I did. I do, but its gas not electric. I'll give the utility company a call and have them switch the lights on." Charlie said as he reached into his jacket and pulled out a cellular phone.

"Right up town, aren't you?" Lynne said as she saw the phone emerge from Charlie's pocket.

"You bet. I might talk with a twang but I cannot afford to lose any deals. However, some relay stations are not as dependable up here as I'd like them to be," Charlie responded as he punched in the number for the utility company.

"I'm going to my truck to get some equipment I brought with me. I want to do a quick inspection of this place. Hope you don't mind?" Lynne said as she walked back toward the front doors. She glanced over her shoulder and saw Charlie waving her on as he spoke into the phone.

After confirming the turn-on with the utility company, Charlie had nothing to do but sit and wait for Lynne to return. He began to realize he should have talked to her attorney more. It was tough deciding whether to take her at face value or figure what values she was displaying. Patience, he chided himself. He could imagine what a crusty, testy, and cantankerous old fart he would become if he ever lost the love of his life. He shuddered, and dismissed the depressing thought. The possibility of losing his wife was too much to contemplate.

Lynne came back carrying a leather backpack. Charlie watched in amusement as she pulled out all manners of devices and instruments from its interior. She carefully laid the flashlight, two pairs of leather gloves, measuring tapes, clipboard with graph pad, and templates for building fixtures on a display case.

"Good grief," whistled Charlie. "Do you ever go anyplace unprepared?"

"Not so you'd notice," she said, and laughed at his bemusement. "Old habits. I took a building appraisal course once because I thought it would help me in investigative work. Did too," she said as she clipped the measuring tapes to her waist. "Ready?" Lynne walked toward the back of the building and the location of the maintenance elevator.

"Sure, why not?" Charlie sighed. He realized he was going to be spending more time in the walk-through than he had originally imagined. It was going to be one of those days and Major-retired Fhaolain seemed determined to make him earn his money.

It was after 4:30 p.m. before they managed to cover all the ins and outs of the two floors, basement, elevator conditions, and exterior of the building. Lynne had made numerous notes of Need-to-Do, Nice-to-Do and Can-Wait on the clipboard. Periodically, she had asked Charlie about prices of local supplies and hardware dealers as she inspected the wiring, plumbing, and heating systems. She had been relieved to discover that the furnace was a new forced-air model. She had been concerned that the building might be heated with an old gravity furnace built decades before her birth. The loading dock area was in fine condition. However, weather and hungry termites had victimized some extension platforms. It would have to be replaced and a complete termite inspection would have to be conducted for the building.

During the walk-through and inspection, Lynne realized how huge the old building was and silently wondered if she were biting off more than she could chew. She had looked at the list of materials, supplies and labor that would have to go into each floor before she could get her business up and operating. The timetable seemed to expand and stretch into the horizon. Weeks, not days, were suggested by the 'need-to-do' list. She would have to revise some of her original plans. Shelby had not realized the extent of work that the building would require. Lynne shrugged her shoulders and figured that he had the best intentions a college professor could offer and that she might not have been paying close attention when he told her about it. As she and Charlie walked back toward the front of the building, she slouched against the wall as the full impact of the work ahead caught up to her.

"Getting tired?" Charlie asked secretly hoping the Major's energy had become as flagging as his own had.

"What? Oh, yes, a little," she said. The amount of work she figured the building needed made her tired just thinking about it.

"It's an old building, but it is sound. It's more than capable of becoming whatever you want it to be…or should I say, whatever you can afford to make it?" Charlie asked, and waited for an answer.

"Money is not that much of a problem. Labor and time are," Lynne said, knowing she would gladly give back Shelby's insurance, sell everything she had or ever would have to changed back to the way it had been. But there was no one to make that bargain with.

They headed toward the elevator to go to the third floor. As they stepped into it, the lights winked out. Standing in the dark, she could hear Charlie's exasperated breathing.

"Just a minute," he said as he fumbled for the cellular phone in his pocket. "Yeah, Marge, this is Charlie. I am still down here at the Gellmore building. Yeah,…well someone just shut everything off and I can't see my hand in front of my face." He listened intently. "Great. Thanks. We'll be out of here in an hour. Tell Lloyd to stay away from that switch until you hear from me…Yeah, fine."

"Done deal?" Lynne asked, her voice floating toward him in the dark.

"Yeah, but meanwhile let's get off this thing. I'm getting claustrophobic simply knowing I'm on an elevator that might jump to life any second, gives me the willies." Charlie stumbled out of the elevator and toward the light of the afternoon sun coming thinly through the west windows.

"We could always take the stairs," Lynne said, and pointed to the back hallway.

"So we could. Hard telling how long it will take them to switch the lights back on," Charlie agreed as he made a mental note to have a little talk with Lloyd at the next Optimist Club meeting. Damn poor business to treat prospective clients this way. Lloyd could have soured the whole damn deal for him; he fumed to himself as he followed Lynne up the stairs.

Lynne picked her way along the staircase up to the third floor of the building. She wondered why or when the previous owners had decided to use the rear-half of the second and third floor as storage shed. She and Charlie scrambled over an assortment of damaged pieces of furniture, lamps, clothing, wood scraps, cabinet fixtures, and old newspapers. Lynne thought she was near her last straw when she stepped on the spade end of a long garden hoe that narrowly missed flying in her face.

"Good grief," she yelled back at Charlie. "What in the hell is all this crap?"

"You remember how your folks probably told you there was no accounting for some people's taste?" Charlie asked.

"So…what's your point?" Lynne shot back to Charlie as she let aggravation seep into her voice.

"The last generation of Gellmore's was a bust. After old Hank Gellmore III died, the property fell to his wife and her three boys," Charlie said as he struggled past the remains of a broken kitchen cabinet top. "Of course, there wasn't and isn't a brain, or at least a sober brain, amongst the lot of them."

"They leave this part of the country or what?" Lynne asked as she stood at the top of the stairs and waited for Charlie.

"No. Three are still around. Youngest boy is back east somewhere, under the care of a special agency or something. Doubt that you'll ever run into them, though," Charlie said as he reached the top of the stairs and tried to catch his breath.

"They don't get around much?"

"No. It's not so much that they don't get around; they are just not terribly social. Don't worry, you're not missing anything," Charlie said as he took Lynne's arm to steady himself and pretend to escort her through the third floor.

As they approached the open doorway of the apartment, crashing sounds came from within. Lynne stiff-armed Charlie automatically and shoved him down against the opposite wall. She flattened herself against the other side. Her hand had gone into the backpack and came out with the revolver, her breath running quiet and shallow.

"What, the..." began Charlie.

"Quiet," Lynne snapped in a sharp whisper. She knew they were safe from peering eyes but they were trapped in the narrow hallway.

The sound of movement came again from the interior of the living quarters. Lynne heard feet scrambling for purchase on a paper-strewn floor. She rose cautiously and moved toward the fleeing sounds. The fading light of day streamed in through the unblocked windows of the third floor as a shadow danced and loomed large on the other side of the open balcony door.

Lynne jogged toward the balcony and the overlook of the alley. Using the brick wall and doorjamb as a barricade, she quickly peeked around the corner. Nothing. There was no one there. Then the scraping, weeping sound of stressed metal was followed by a soft thud on the gravel below. She sprang through the doorway and bounded across the balcony barely skidding to halt at the low-bricked wall near the building's edge. As she looked over the edge, she caught a glimpse of blue-jean legs and the bottom of fleeing boots as they disappeared around the east corner of the alley.

"What was that all about?" Charlie asked cautiously as he joined Lynne on the balcony. The gun in her hand made him nervous. He did not want her to mistake him for whatever she had been after.

"Burglar, or vagrant, and he'd overstayed his welcome," Lynne said as she shoved the revolver into a pocket of her parka. "Well. If he feels anything like I do, he will not be back here without an invitation. That's a little bit more excitement than I care for," Charlie said as he patted his heart to emphasize his point.

"Me, too, actually. Give me a nice dead body anytime. This cuff'em and stuff'em nonsense is for younger folks. In the Army, I usually just came in the mop-up aftermath. Rank has its privilege. In other instances, I'd have a lot of good soldiers backing me up," Lynne smiled at Charlie as she sat in a patio chair. "This gun-slinger stuff wasn't generally part of it. So, were you entertained, Charlie?" she asked.

"More than you'll know," Charlie said as he sat on the balcony wall.

"So, the offer was for $ 335,000?" Lynne said, changing the subject.

"Yes. I do not know if that seems high or low to you. Maybe a high price for a building that's sitting empty but low for all this main street space." Charlie's breath was coming hard as he worked to hold up his end of the conversation.

"$ 300,000 firm. $150,000 up front and the rest to be financed. No charge for the entertainment, either," Lynne countered and glanced his way.

"$ 310,000 and what you said," Charlie shot back.

"Hmmm, that one I'll have to think on," Lynne said closing her eyes.

"As you wish, but, just out of curiosity, if money's no real problem, why would you want to drag out the payments?"

Getting to her feet, Lynne took a long look down into the eastern side of the town and to the mountains rising in the distance. "Let's just say it's my way of encouraging personal permanence."

"Well, that'll do. But, now to the real business," Charlie stood and cleared his throat. "I'd say by the setting of the sun that there's a long shadow cross the deck."

"Excuse me?" Lynne asked, blinking at Charlie's declaration.

"It is proper time for a drink," smiled Charlie, "I was in the Navy for four years. And seeing how we've had more excitement than we deserved in this bit of business, I'd say we owed it to ourselves."

"You know, I just think I'll take you up on that offer," Lynne said as she allowed her face to brighten. It might be just what the doctor ordered. She had been missing the communal feeling she had known in the service. Lynne looked at Charlie and noticed he seemed a little startled and pleased with her acceptance of his offer.

"Very good, milady!" he said, and half-bowed in a gesture of mock gallantry. He crooked his arm for her to take. "May I suggest we go to the most revered watering hole in Leadville?"

"Lead on, Charlie," Lynne said as she accepted his arm.

Out on the street he watched, lingered behind them, and waited in the shadows. Curiosity and hunger settled over him. He followed, sing-singing softly to himself. "Curiosity killed the cat but satisfaction brought him back," he said grinning as he walked past the Double Eagle.

8

The large windows stood low and close to the bed, offering a view of the western rise of mountains and Harrison Street. Lynne's eyes searched the wind-whipped confusion, the dancing of the hazy snow across the quietly deserted street. Her mind reluctantly struggled to pull itself up from sleep and toward the tasks of the day. Infrequent rifts and minute swirls of snow fell lightly throughout the clouded day. The tiny flakes crashed silently on the windowpanes, shattering their delicate structures, while luckier flakes floated to the deepening corners. The flurries danced and dizzied themselves in spiraling cascades, ordering and reordering their ballet on the shifting demands of the breeze.

The bed was warm and cozy. She felt as though it were a serious violation of natural law to have to crawl out from under the billowing comforter. She knew she could grudgingly admire winter's rally against the encroachment of spring where she lay. Her thoughts pulled along the same shifting meter of nature's silent song in the cascading crystals.

Closing her eyes, she turned her back on the sky and street to seek warm comfort beneath the mounted blankets. But she stirred uneasily as self-recriminations of duties and responsibilities forced her eyes open again. A small nudge of will power moved her hesitantly. She was afraid to stay in bed. The hauntings of a familiar sorrow wrapped around her heart. All else seemed to have been ripped from her, and her connection to the world and her heart grew more distant each day. She was running from the pain, the past, and into an uncertain future. So what! Her mind flared hot with outrage. The world did not make sense. Why should she try to make sense of the world?

Stuffing down recriminations, she hesitantly moved toward morning habits. She set her body into motion and knew her mind would have to find its own way as she burrowed through her morning rituals. Action, she thought hopefully, action could probably keep the hounds of futility at bay.

"Draw water," she said as she coaxed herself up from the bed and across to the bathroom. Her feet obeyed and her desire to give motion temporarily overcame her emotional fatigue. The water rushed into the tub and swiftly filled it within inches of the top. She gingerly poked cautious toes into the water and satisfied herself that, as steamy as it seemed, she would not be boiled alive. She sank gratefully under the hot water. In a few moments, the anger returned and she was at war with herself again. A tremor of anxiety shot through her shoulders and ran arrow sharp into her heart. Fear and longing played frightful pictures in her mind as she imagined her body floating in the blood-pinked waters of the tub. Her dead eyes stared back at her from the fantasy, crystallized and mocking. She saw her own dark desire and the truth of it caused sobs to break through her lips.

Lynne has treated herself to a stay at the hotel but knew she needed to make other arrangements the moment she concluded business with the

New York publisher. She found herself vacillating about what to do with the offer that they had made.

The water turned chill. She rose from the tub and began to briskly rub herself down with a large towel. She did not meet her own eyes in the mirror. Lynne did not know if she belonged to the world of the living, but she could not consign herself to anything else. She knew she would stay in the half-light between and let time decide. She shivered. Time was both her ally and antagonist.

At 8:30 a.m., Lynne emerged from the hotel holding her notebook with the lists of wants and needs in her right hand, and the truck keys in her left. She had managed to give she marching orders and was on her way to assault the towns with her notes stapled to the clipboard for a search and buy mission. She was determined to get the refurbishing of the Gellmore building underway. Holding the clipboard like a shield, she walked to the newspaper.

The Herald Democrat would provide her with an opportunity to find the skills and crafts of local folks to help her make the necessary repairs. A lot of clean up paint up and get ready was necessary of before she could open the doors of her new business. She hoped to attract a lot of strong, industrious backs from the local pool of unemployed. Lynne figured that with spring not yet having gained firm footing, the construction industry would be slack enough to provide her with a lot of people to pick from.

Tugging on the wood-framed glass door, Lynne heard a tin bell ring above her head as she entered the small lobby of the Herald Democrat. The front counter ran half the length of the building where ancient mahogany and deep-pitted walnut barred the way to the inner offices of the newspaper. She could hear the steady thud thudding of machinery as it churned out the afternoon's edition. Lynne glanced at the woman behind the counter as she reached for an advertising insert form at the counter's edge. She could feel the woman's eyes on her while she struggled over the wording of her message to local laborers. Lynne smiled to herself. She knew that as a stranger the newspaper's in-house guardian of the printed word was sizing her up. Lynne did not imagine that in this isolated community, either lonely hearts or alternate lifestyles, nor clandestine or erotic rendezvous of residents would ever get past the woman's red pen. And if they did, they would be subject to repeated discussion amongst friends with more detail than the printed page might allow.

Finishing her draft, Lynne approached the counter. The woman behind the desk rose to her full height and girth. Five-by-three and agile on her feet, the name-tagged Mrs. Adams pulled her glasses down to the tip of her nose and pursed her lips to read.

"General construction and apprentice laborers wanted."
Restoration of the Gellmore Building. Must have own tools.
Supplies provided. Wages dependent on skills and references.
$7-10 an hour. Inquire at Corbin Hotel lounge nine a.m. to
Noon, Wednesday this week only. Anticipated 4-6 weeks work."

"Honey," Mrs. Adams voice chided, "you know, if you write this up this way, you're liable to get every slack-jawed, lowbrow, layabout in a three-county area coming to get your money. And we have a poop-pot full of them hereabouts. It needs some fixing for economy too, unless you got more money than sense. This piece would run you over $30 just for Sunday's run."

Lynne blinked at the woman and peered over the high counter to where the advertisement was held in the woman's meaty hands. Half shrugging and amused, Lynne was firmly trapped by the woman's well-intended ministrations. Knowing when to duck and cover or charge ahead was one of Lynne's natural gifts. There were too many other battles to wage, and

Mrs. Adams dictates were of the kindly variety. Looking into the woman's face, Lynne imagined herself holding up a white flag.

"I see. What do you suggest?"

"Oh,…I'll tell you what," Mrs. Adams softened as her maternal instincts took over. "I'll see what I can do and keep it below 25 dollars for the three-day run. How's that?" Mrs. Adams smiled kindly up at the receptive student.

"Thank you," Lynne said, as she pushed her cash across the counter.

"Mind if I ask what you intended doing with the old Gellmore place?"

"Books. I am hoping to open a bookstore. Used books, new, rare, antique and such. I'm new to it but the idea appeals to me."

"That's a lot of room for a book store, especially in this town."

"Well, I don't intend to use the whole thing for a store. I'll use the top floor as my residence and see how it all turns out," Lynne said as she turned to go. She did not want to give more time than necessary and allow for any more questions or inquiries.

"Now," the portly Mrs. Adams called after Lynne. "If you get any scruffy types or questionable folks, you jest bring me their names and I'll put you straight about them."

Lynne turned back, a response poised on her lips.

Mrs. Adams continued, "My Frank and I have managed this paper over thirty years and his father for fifty before that. This town needs some developing and we don't want to have you scared away by any local miss-stepping," She said as she handed Lynne a receipt.

"Yes. Well, I certainly will keep that in mind. Thank you."

Outside, Lynne glanced at her list. She had a week of general cleaning and light repair to keep her busy in the building's living area while the advertisement did its work. Cleaning supplies, paint, checking account, savings account, lumber, stain, nails, screws, carpet cleaner, plywood, mops, broom, and a list of groceries on her long list promised a lot of busy work for the day. There was so much to do and she was grateful for the tasks that would help keep her focused on the future.

Fingering the money belt cinched across her waist, Lynne decided that the sooner the bank opened Monday, the happier and safer she would feel. She would have to get all of her accounts transferred and that would put her one step closer to the goal of settling.

"Next stop lumber yard," she said as she got back into the truck. Being busy felt good. Almost like she was real and connected.

By four o'clock in the afternoon, Lynne had exhausted her list and herself in activity. The sun was sliding toward the west and the anemic light of spring made little impression on the rapidly chilling air. Lynne carried the last of the supplies off the elevator and into the living room of her new home. As she put the parcels next to the kitchen counter, she turned around and saw the gentle refuge of an overstuffed chair. Without bothering to remove its dust cover, she fell into the chair and quickly sank into a motionless sleep.

The dreams came quickly. Lynne she saw herself walking down a long hallway wondering how it could stretch itself and recede rather than advance before her. Her steps ran ahead of her and seemed to ring louder and louder as she struggled to come to the end of the hallway. She looked down and noticed the heavy paratrooper boots on her feet. She stopped and stared at them, trying to imagine when she had put them on. Although she had stopped, the footsteps continued down the hall as she stared at the boots. The sounds of footfalls were behind her. And the watcher and the watched turned their gaze toward the sound ever nearer to her.

Lynne's eyes flew open as the sound of footsteps echoed hesitantly on the stairway to her apartment. The pitch-black interior of the apartment told her she had been asleep a long time. Her mind raced as she tried to decide if she had heard anything real or simply the reflected sounds of her dreams. She turned quietly in the chair and saw the quick flash of a light bounce off the walls from the depths of the stairwell. Just as quickly, the light vanished.

That was no imagining. Someone was in the building. The realization brought her to full alert. She slid her legs off the arms of the chair and was rudely warned by the spasms of muscles cramping across her knees and up her lower back. Painfully, crouching down low behind the chair, she reached into her waistband and pulled out a 45-mm semiautomatic. Caught in the double bind of tense anticipation and the tingling nerves in her arms and legs, Lynne waited in the dark.

The light returned. Higher on the stairs now, it bounced off the walls and was extinguished again. Lynne released the safety on the pistol, steadied her arm across the chair, and guessed at torso high for aim. The light had taken the night vision advantage she might have had. Her retina retained a memory of the light and sent confused mirages of shadow across her sight. Footsteps ascended the stairs and stopped as they reached the top of the landing. A heavy-footed thud told Lynne her visitor had expected another stair that was not there. She scrunched her body as low as she could and aimed in the direction of the intruder.

Suddenly, the flashlight came on again and flickered along the interior of the apartment where Lynne crouched. The lone figure at the head of the stairs was trying to get a fix on or the layout of the apartment. Lynne cocked back the hammer of the .45. In the quiet of the vacant apartment, the sound cracked through the stillness with deadly intention. Instantly, the light snapped off and pitched the room back into darkness.

"I'll shoot you where you stand!" Lynne warned huskily. She waited. A distant tentative foot started to drag itself across the floor near the head of the stairs. "Don't move or you're dead," Lynne asserted. She decided to fire at the next sound that was not surrender. Nothing happened. The only sound she could hear was her carefully controlled breathing. "Turn that light back on and point it at your face. I'm running out of patience."

A sigh. Cloth upon cloth brushed in the distance as Lynne felt cold sweat trickle down her ribs.

"Do it! Or I'll drop you." Three seconds and a lifetime passed.

Light broke the dark. It danced unsteadily across the floor and was raised with palsied motion up across a red flannel jacket and into the fear-widened eyes of a bearded man.

"Don't shoot, damn it!"

"Shut up. The only moving I want you to do is breathing. Is that clear?" Lynne said as she slowly stood up while keeping the frail cover of the chair between her and the stranger.

"Look, lady," he began, and took a step forward. He was a large man. The glow of the flashlight made his dark brown hair and cap pulled down covering his face made him appear sinister. The dark gray slacks sagged around the tops of his boots as he took another tentative step toward Lynne.

A shot rang out and plaster sprayed the right side of his face. Wincing and ducking he dropped the flashlight. He was trapped in the light in a half-crouch as his arms protectively covered his face.

"Next time, your belly button. Understand?" Lynne growled. Her voice gave no room for questions or mercy for error. Her original anxiety had been replaced by a self-contained self-preservation alert. Lynne walked cautiously forward. In the uncertain light, she could not tell if he had a weapon on him or not. She fell back on her training and twenty years of habits. She assumed him armed and dangerous.

"I'm only going to say this once…kneel down on the floor with your back to me and cross your feet at your ankles. Lock your fingers behind your head. Do it," Lynne said as she came to a halt less than ten feet in front of her unwelcome visitor. She watched his body rather than concentrating on what his face was doing. Faces lied about intent but the body rarely would. The untrained under skilled criminal generally telegraphed his moves in tiny and abbreviated body twinges. The message was in the body, not the eyes, and never the words. Eyes and words only teased the unwary.

She felt a twinge of recognition as she looked at him but could not remember why. He did as he was directed, and she noticed the smell of alcohol steaming from him. She fought her compulsion to hold her breath against his obnoxious odor.

"Do I know you?" Lynne asked uncertainly as she approached him.

"Sorta," he said as he knotted his fingers behind his head.

"Simple questions…first, who are you, and then, what do you want?" Lynne said as she flexed her toes and eased into a comfortable dedicated stance at his back. She aimed the gun at the middle of his torso and steadied the flashlight beam with her left foot. He loosened his fingers and leaned forward turning his body at his waist to get a look at her. A small and familiar voice warned her that the guy had the telltale attitude of someone who would try to get at her if he could.

"Put your hands behind your head and lock your fingers together," Lynne directed.

"You sound like a damn cop," he snorted at her.

"And you sound like someone who ought to know this routine by heart," she snapped.

He raised his hands far above his head and then settled them back on his head. As he clasped his hands together, he heard Lynne take a step and felt her knee press into the small of his back as she grasped and locked his fingers in place. He felt her use her weight to pull back on his fingers while she used her knee as leverage.

"Christ!" he swore as his back bowed forward and fingers strained in their joints. He had no balance except what she maintained for him by her grip. He wavered. If he flinched, he knew she would drop him with his unprotected face to the floor and ride his back down to a bone crunching impact.

"Again,…quick question, and quick answer…Who are you?" Lynne said as she holstered her gun and began frisking him. She could not detect any weapons but was not giving up her vigilance. She placed her right hand between his shoulder blades and pressed firmly.

"Greg!" he cried out as he felt his vertebrae wince under the steady pressure. "Greg Hanson." He cleared his throat and tried to sound less anxious. "I just saw your door open downstairs and your truck outside. That is all. Just thought I'd come in and see if you were all right."

"How do you know me or why do you want to do any of your so-called favors for me?"

"I saw you last night with Charlie at the Double Eagle." Greg tried to get comfortable by moving his feet. Lynne placed her right foot on top of the Achilles tendon of his left leg. "Christ on a crutch lady! You trying to kill me?" Greg cried out as he stiffened in pain.

"Not yet. Stay put and answer my questions."

"Fine. Just hurry up, this is killing me."

"We weren't introduced."

"No. But after you left, I talked to Charlie and he said you were fixing to take over this building. That you might be needing some help."

"Small town," Lynne mumbled to herself.

"What?" Greg cursed his inclination toward ladies. Damn fantasies. He had imagined he would find her up in the apartment in a big soft bed waiting for a real man to come along. Charlie had told him all about it, after he had drunk himself into his cups. He figured she would be really lonesome and bereaved after the way she had been widowed like. It made sense. His favorite fantasy magazines were always going on about how horny widows get and what you could get if they were properly primed. He cursed himself for daydreaming that she would take advantage of him. She had taken advantage all right. But not the way he had hoped.

"I said, small town," Lynne replied as her anger began to run down into cooler aggravation. Moving was supposed to be an escape from the past, and here she had to play cop again. She looked to her right, saw the shadow of a light switch, and decided to end the quiz session. She straightened herself up, let go of his hands, and pushed him away from her in a downward motion toward the floor. He landed heavily but managed to save his face as he crashed down on his right elbow.

Lynne nimbly jumped across his legs and flicked the lights on in the hall. She kept her weapon level at his prone body as he rubbed his aching arm.

"I suggest we get out of here, Greg," Lynne said as she motioned with the gun. "You first."

Humiliation and anger crept up Greg's unshaven neck and face. He began to open his mouth in protest.

"Can't you ever just do as you are told? I am tired and I want to go home. You do not belong here. Now or ever." Lynne motioned again in the direction of the descending stairs.

"I just wanted to know if there'd be any work here. I need a job," Greg complained as he began the long walk down the stairs.

"Shut up," Lynne said as she followed carefully behind him.

At the sidewalk, Greg turned back to Lynne. He would come up with what he hoped was clever repartee to recover from the ground he would lose. He started to say something but she cut him off.

"Lock up and clear out and I'll call it even," she said. Holding the weapon on him, Lynne tossed him a set of keys.

Glancing quickly up and down the street to see if anyone could see him or the predicament he'd gotten himself into, Greg turned back to lock the doors.

"I still want to talk to you about my helping," Greg said, his head bowed as he concentrated on locking the doors.

"You've got to be kidding?" Lynne scoffed as she retrieved the keys from his hand. He turned toward her and she saw him clearly under the streetlight. He was scruffy, unkempt and dirty. She was not afraid but she was very angry. Her pulse barely returned to normal. Huge shots of adrenaline had been pumped into her system and the clear night air was almost making her giddy with relief. What disquiet remained were twinges of knotted nerve ends.

"Well, the way I figure it, you'll be needing some help. This heap of rocks has been shut up for longer than you can imagine. Lots of stuff can go wrong in a building in that time. Making it livable again is not going to be a pretty job. Why the spider webs alone could take a month to clear out." He smiled weakly at Lynne.

"I don't believe it!" Lynne said in exasperation. She knew that human nature would never cease to amaze her. What did amaze her was how constantly people would remind her of that fact. "You trespass, scare me to death, try to intimidate me, and heaven knows what else, and you still have the gall to ask for a job?"

"No, seriously, I'm pretty handy with tools for any thing that might need fixing," Greg said. Feeling his courage stir, he winked at her.

His tone brought Lynne's eyes back to his face. She frowned. His face reflected the double meaning.

He winked again.

Son-of-a-bitch. Misanthropic bully, Lynne fumed volcanically. He had to be an idiot. She thought about shooting him as a small favor to the world, but rejected the idea. Lynne wondered how he had managed to survive to adulthood without someone putting out of his misery. She motioned to him to keep clear of her, backed up two steps and then turned away so she would not be tempted to do the fatal deed.

"Well?" he called to her as she walked down the street.

Lynne did not glance back at him. She listened for the sound of his boots and wondered if they would have to have another confrontation because he could not hear "NO."

Greg stood stock-still. He had expected and waited for bantering and flirtation to begin. It usually worked. Under the streetlight, his face narrowed in anger as he realized that he had heard her final answer. He started to go after her as an angry message formed for her in his mind. He stopped himself. She still had that damn gun somewhere near her hand. His shoulders drooped as he watched her back with increasing loathing. He mouthed soundless threats in her direction. Greg decided that he needed a drink. He picked up his pace and hurried towards the Double Eagle. Surely, one or more of them would have some money to spend on him.

As Greg turned toward the Double Eagle, he missed seeing the shadows emerge from the alleyway behind Lynne. The shadow watched Lynne walked down the dark street. She was small and alone. She was a minute shadow in the larger darkness of the night that moved between infrequent streetlights and the larger consuming night.

"Plenty of time for you," he said as she walked through the doors of the Corbin Hotel.

Inside the Corbin Hotel, the arching ache in Lynne's back seemed to relax. She would felt something nagging at her since she had left Greg standing by the store. She could not get a fix on the menacing feel. She was tired and hungry. She needed, wanted a drink but did not know what to do first. Then she saw the red neon lights announcing the Lounge in the Corbin Hotel. She decided to take it as an omen. In forty-five years she knew better than to ignore her instincts, it was too late to change.

9

Monday morning the rush of town folk grabbing an early breakfast had cleared out of the Double Eagle by the time, Lynne stood inside the door looking for a booth. She rhythmically tapped the newspaper on her leg as she noted the disaster areas of stacked dishes, cups and glasses in the booths. Sighing to herself, she walked to the cleanest looking table near the giant pot-bellied stove at the far corner of the dining area.

While waiting for a waitress, Lynne made short work of setting down the list of tasks and priorities, which would give her day form and meaning. The bank in Kansas City was to wire half her savings and checking account to the Leadville United Merchant's Bank before noon. It would make it possible for her to conclude her business arrangements with Charles Watson and establish some financial credibility as a new resident in the community. Busywork would keep her internal hounds safely at bay. Satisfied with her list, she settled into a feeling of accomplishment toward ordering her day. She flipped shut the notebook and placed it back in her jacket pocket.

The waitress left a menu and a fresh cup of coffee. Taking a cigarette out of her pack, Lynne opened up the thin newspaper to search for her Help Wanted advertisement. The front-page headlines leaped at her. From the moment she read the opening paragraphs, Lynne felt her mind stir into old habits as her eyes ran through the lurid details and reporter speculations.

The front page was filled with on-scene accounts and prose representing the high drama surrounding the discovery of a mutilated tourist. Lynne marveled at the story and cursed softly under her breath. There was too much information in the story. She felt an old typical twinge of disgust as she read the paper's account of the grieving husband. Based on experience, Lynne knew that the newspaper reporter would have reached deep into his wallet and out to the open hand of a cop to get much of the information. It was all there: the crime scene, investigative leads, and personal details about the victim. She wondered if it was greed or stupidity. The likelihood that local officials were dull-witted could not be totally ignored. Momentarily distracted from the meat of the story, Lynne drew a quick mental profile of the loose-lipped officer. She believed she could almost see him whispering to the reporter. He would be a small-minded, swaggering braggart of a man. He was the sort of man who was filled with his own importance and in-the-know superiority, the kind of superiority he needed to cover his personal and professional inadequacies. He had to be the worst of a breed to divulge the details of a case to rub elbows with local media. Just the sort to ruin an investigation.

Taking a pen out of her pocket, she made quick margin notes between the newspaper columns. She linked the details of the newspaper's account of the crime scene to statistical probabilities that existed between murderers and their victims. The puzzle pieces entertained her and drew her from her surroundings until someone's exaggerated cough brought her back to the world.

"I'm sure I could lend you some paper when you run out of margin," Charlie Watson said in an amused tone as Lynne focused on her unexpected visitors. "Mind if we sit with you?"

"Not at all," Lynne replied rousing herself from her concentration.

Charlie pulled a chair out for himself and gestured to the other man to take the place available on Lynne's left. The older man smiled courteously nodding at Lynne as he rounded the table.

"Doc, this is Major Lynne..." Charlie hesitated.

"Fhaolain, Lynne Fhaolain...Doc...?" Lynne shot Charlie a glance.

"Kennedy, Ms. Fhaolain," Doc said, as he extended his hand.

"Nice to meet you Doctor. Please, join me," Lynne said as she shook Doc's hand.

Retrieving his hand, Doc paused thoughtfully as he settled in the chair. "You got a good grip for such a little thing. Been a lumberjack long?" he asked as his face broke into an honest seamed jibe.

"Joker, aren't you Doc?" Lynne countered.

"She's quick, too," Charlie pointed out.

"Quite right, I can tell that. And, yes, I've been accused of being a bit of a kidder," Doc said with lighthearted begrudgement, as he tried to flag the waitress toward the table. "Been that way most of my life. Helps keep the riffraff away and my patients anxious to settle their bills."

"I can imagine. What brings you gentlemen here in the middle of the morning?" Lynne folded up the newspaper and pushed it to the far side of the table. It fell open again and Lynne watched Doc Kennedy's studious attempt to keep from looking at the glaring declaration of the headlines.

"Thought maybe I would try to nudge you toward a conclusion of our business," Charlie offered as way of explanation.

"My offer stands, Mr. Watson."

"You drive a mean bargain Major," Charlie asserted and smiled.

"How much should a white elephant cost?" Lynn chided.

"'Bout that, I reckon."

"Then, do we have a deal?"

"I'll draw the papers up but only cause you are such a pretty lady."

"You are so full of it," Lynne said as the waitress brought a fresh pot of coffee.

"My livelihood depends on it ma'am," Charlie nodded as though he were wearing a hat.

"You're the county coroner, aren't you?" Lynne asked and turned to meet Doc's eyes. She noticed how lightly he wore his dignity and authority. He was not over impressed with himself but he was not exactly humble either. Under the cardigan, a pocket bulged heavily under the weight of a pipe and small pouch of tobacco. His dark brown corduroy slacks were sensibly belted to a waist size that would have been the envy of many men half his age. Steel gray eyes matched the color of his thick widow's peak hairline and further distinguished him in or out of his profession. The eyes were not hard, but rather showed the reflected compassion some people gained through their acquaintance with life.

"That's the rumor."

"Seems more than rumor available in the newspaper," Lynne said as she maintained her eye contact with Doc Kennedy. His uneasy shifting in his chair told her he had a need to share his portion of the story. She decided to probe gently, and waiting was as gentle as she could be to get at what aroused her curiosity.

"Messy business. Awful," Charlie sympathized.

"No kidding," Doc said flatly.

"Autopsies were always my least favorite part of the investigation. The combined aroma of blood and formaldehyde made my head spin when I was a rookie. Don't think I ever quite got used to it, or wanted to," Lynne said as the waitress brought her plate of eggs and hash browns.

"Rookie?"

"Forgot to mention, Lynne here is a retired Major in the Army. She spent time apparently in criminal investigation. Came to our fair city for some quiet life," Charlie interjected.

"No kidding! I heard the title during the introduction but I guess it did not register. Well, isn't that something? Bet this whole thing kinda makes you wish you'd stayed in the Army?" Doc Kennedy raised an eyebrow and offered Lynne a lopsided smile.

"Well, I had hoped to be lulled into the security of small town warmth, if that's what you mean. But as long as you have people, things will happen," Lynne reflected philosophically.

"You ever do murder investigations?"

"Yes. Quite a few. I spent the last eight years at Fort Leavenworth and Riley, as commander of the homicide issues. Sometimes, my team and I were sent elsewhere to lend a hand. In the Army you see a lot of dead bodies and get to go to a lot of autopsies."

"Got any ideas or guesses about our local problem?"

"Can't say that I have. That would be a little out of line for me," Lynne said shrugging it off.

"Our Sheriff's department isn't bad. Leastwise for the normal run-of-the-mill crimes, we generally get. They're a fine lot for speeders, drunks, and our cabin fever domestic wars," Charlie insisted.

"True enough but that's hardly the point here. Now is it?" Doc snapped in irritation.

"What do you mean?" Lynne probed.

"Oh. It's just that...yesterday was like the blind leading the blind. Not one of us out there, deputies included, could figure how not to do damage. Bunch of stumbling fools if you ask me. And I was the head fool," Doc tossed back his coffee and waved the empty at the approaching waitress.

"Cripes, Doc don't be so hard on yourself. There has not been a murder in these parts since old lady Jeevers shot gunned that burglar two years back. She surely was a hell of a shot. But mostly the only things you get here are the remains of hapless hikers and a few misguided hunters who mistake their buddies for deer," Charlie defended.

"Maybe,...maybe. But, we surely got something special now, don't we?" Doc retorted. His voice had an uneasy, deprecatory edge to it.

"What do you think, Lynne?" Charlie quizzed her for support.

"I think there'll be a hell of a run on padlocks and dead bolts," Lynne offered.

"Excuse me?"

"Dead-bolts, padlocks, ammunition, dogs, and all manner of protective devices. Anything people can get their hands on to help them feel safer," Lynne said, checking the list off on her fingers.

"Little late, isn't it?"

"Not necessarily. You haven't identified the killer yet, have you?" Lynne quizzed.

"No, but the Sheriff figures he's at least two states away from here by now. Matter of fact, he is kinda curious about the husband. They got him in lockup down in Denver. Guess the Sheriff is going to Denver too, Tuesday and interrogate him," Doc offered.

"O.K. If he did it, that would put a close on it. But it's not very likely he'll find out much that will help him," Lynne said as she dropped an ice cube in her coffee to get it down to a drinkable temperature. She concentrated on stirring the cube down to size.

"Meaning?"

"Just that it's pretty unlikely a husband would do or hire such a thing to be done. Murder is one thing. My reading of the detail in the paper tells me that the husband would have to be one crazy son-of-a-bitch to do the deed. It'd take a rare bird to play that game to its conclusion."

"So,…even if it's not the husband, the man would be a fool to stick around here. Wouldn't he?" Doc Kennedy protested.

"Only if he doesn't live here."

"Live here!" Doc inhaled sharply as he locked startled eyes with Charlie.

"Home grown. One of your own. A neighbor," Lynne explained. "Doesn't have to be a marauding stranger. Truths be known, gentlemen, most communities have a full house of characters waiting in the wings."

"You've got to be kidding. Here? I cannot imagine…" Doc sputtered to a stop.

"I'd invest in security if I were you. You don't know what you don't know. It is that simple. And until this creep is behind bars, we just simply don't know," Lynne insisted firmly to her breakfast partners and silence reigned over the table.

Doc folded his arms across the top of the table and leaned over his hands as he stared at some mind's eye image dancing in the center of the rounded oak.

"I didn't exactly do a full autopsy. The boys from the Colorado Bureau of Investigation get that job when they get her back to Denver later this evening. Thank God," Doc said, and glanced wearily up at Charlie's face.

Lynne could see by his face that Doc Kennedy was working on what he did know and what he had seen. She watched as frowns played across his face and misgivings flickered across his brow. Finally, he exhaled slowly through his nose and settled back into his chair. He was ready to unburden himself of the images that had come to haunt him.

Lynne quickly glanced around the interior of the Double Eagle. This was not the right place for Doc to be talking. Through the benefits of the acoustics of the room, she easily caught bits and pieces of rancor between the waitress and cook. Her habitual curiosity was nudging her on, but she felt a twinge of guilt about trying to stick her nose into business that did not concern her. She knew better. The last thing she wanted was to become a hyped-up hobby cop.

Lynne had a store to bring into being, a house to arrange, and a life to get on with. The poor dead woman didn't need to become a thing of fixated curiosity or other device for Lynne to use to avoid taking charge of her own life. Life was too precious and uncertain as it was. She had had enough of death and dying. Groping and sneaking around this homicide would not help cure her of the discontent in her life. Lynne shivered at the maudlin streak running through her. Her bitterness made her wince.

"Well," Lynne said, suddenly pushing back and rising from her chair. "I've got a thousand things to do. And, Charles, you happen to be on the list of my list, too. I expect to have your money and sign papers this afternoon."

"Ah. Sure. 'Round two o'clock or so?" Charlie said as he tried to find his balance in the conversation.

"Great. See you then," Lynne said, and turned to leave. She reached out and lightly dropped her hand onto Doc Kennedy's shoulder as she passed his chair. "Nice meeting you Doctor Kennedy. Hope everything works out in the investigation."

Lynne was out the door before Charlie could bring himself to look at Doc.

"That was kinda strange, wasn't it?" Charlie asked as he turned toward Doc. "Quick on her feet, isn't she?" Doc replied. "Maybe we ought to take her advice?"

"Maybe," Charlie said, and turned his attention back to his breakfast. "Want to go over to the hardware store later?"

Doc grunted in agreement, as he turned the newspaper upside down removing Beverly's photograph from his sight.

10

Greg rolled over and snuggled up to the warm naked body. He felt the early morning hardness begin and wriggled his crotch deeper into the flesh next to him. A low moan broke from his throat, as his dreams seemed to mesh with reality. His companion did not struggle. Encouraged, he moved his arm though the covers to caress the slowly rising and falling breasts. He hoped she was waiting for his touch as much as he wanted to touch her. Thick matted hair met his hand. Alarm shot through his arm and up to his mind. His eyes flew open. He used the other man's buttocks as a springboard and catapulted out of the bed.

"What the hell?" roared the man under the sheets as Greg's butt bounced on the floor. An angry and bewildered face peered threateningly at Greg. "For the love of might! What are you doing in here?" The greasy-haired apparition turned into Jessup Gellmore.

"How'd I gotten here?" Greg said, trying to take command of the situation.

"How do you ever get anywhere, ass-wipe?" Jessup said as he ground his fist into his face to rough the sleep out of his eyes.

"Yeah. How's that?" Greg hopped from one foot to the other on the cold bare wooden floor.

"Idiot. We drink; we talk and get drunk, walk back to the nearest house and drink some more. Simple," Jessup replied as he sat up, tucking the blankets around him. He tossed papers off the nightstand as he searched for his cigarettes. Finding a partial pack, he lit one, offered the pack to Greg, and rested against the ancient headboard. Greg stopped his dancing long enough to accept the offer.

"Simple," Greg said, looking around the room for his jeans. He fumbled through a pile of dirty clothes on the floor but did not recognize any of them as his.

"Those are mine. You probably left yours on the couch cause that is where I left you last night. How'd you say you got in here, anyway?" Jessup asked as he took a long drag on the cigarette and eyed Greg through the smoke.

"I don't know," Greg complained. "Sleep walking I guess. It wasn't on purpose, I can swear to that." He wandered toward the bedroom door.

"Fraid you're a faggot?" Jessup laughed as the smoke streaming out of his mouth made him choke. "Well, even if you are, I'm not! Wait till the boys get a load of your wandering lust. I'll be sure to tell them not to turn their back on you next time you get to drinking with them," Jessup called after Greg. "Dip-wad!"

Greg's head swam in a sea of pain. The early morning shock crackled in torrents of lightning through his temples. He held his head; afraid the rising loaf of brain would leak out his ears. His mouth tasted like old gym socks to his dry tongue. He picked up his jeans near the couch and headed for the kitchen.

The refrigerator bulb was burned out. He searched blindly through the leftovers until he located the beer he needed. He grabbed the first can and downed it before he took another breath. Relieved, he sank into a worn plastic kitchen chair and tipped the beer back in gratitude. As he put the empty, can on the decayed Formica table top, he heard the sound of running water coming from the open door of a bathroom and the sound made his bladder ache. Not one to stand on formalities, he walked to the kitchen door and peed through the screen. Looking out the door, he saw the familiar rows of shotgun house construction blinking their vacant eyes at his early morning salute. He heard footfalls heading down the short hall toward him and hurriedly finished. As he tucked himself away, he turned to see Alan Gellmore stalk into the kitchen.

"A bit of the hair?" Alan quizzed Greg. Alan was the physical opposite of his larger, beefier brother. Jessup was powerfully built and carried a massive chest. Alan was slight of frame and inclined to be studiously reserved. Unusual in his family, Alan disdained the use of alcohol. The townspeople figured he had been switched at birth.

He stood slightly less than six feet but was supported by wiry muscle. His sandy gray-streaked hair made him look like a modern rendition of Custer shortly before the Little Big Horn. He always walked with quick, purposeful steps and a perpetual furrow in his brow. He looked like he was thinking about something, but no one had ever gotten close enough to him to find out what it might be. Allen was a humorless man, sulkily carrying the weight of the family's fall from prominence like a personal challenge.

"You two meet up at the Double Eagle last night?" Alan asked.

"Yeah. Must have had a good time, too," Greg said as he combed through his beard with ragged fingernails and farted.

"Christ! Take it outside, Greg. This is my house and you are a not too welcome guest as it is. Show some manners. Even if you have to make them up," Alan bellowed as he retrieved a carton of eggs and slab of bacon from the refrigerator. Alan wanted Greg out of the house and gone, but he knew if he said so he would incur Jessup's loud defense of his drinking buddy. Alan did not want to walk down the wrong side of that highway so early in the morning.

Jessup entered the kitchen and looked from Alan to Greg. He walked over to Alan and threw a heavy arm across his brother's shoulders.

"Say 'pard, Greg and I might go hunting up on the west fork of Rock Creek later today. What say you come with us?" Jessup winked conspiratorially at Greg.

"That's poaching, Jessup. There is nothing legal you can shoot this time of year, and I have not got money enough for your bail. Let it alone, both of you," Alan shrugged Jessup's arm away.

"It's not poaching unless you hit something," Jessup argued.

"Tell that to the game warden," Alan countered.

"Come on. Go for fun occasionally, Alan. All you do is work at that damn hospital. It's not like they pay you any kinda wage either, " Jessup said. He angrily pitched the butt of his cigarette at the tabletop and walked back down the hallway.

"What time?" Alan called after him, relenting.

" 'Round two or so," Jessup called, brightening.

"I'll think about it. Wake me if I'm sleeping."

"Mom?" Jessup called, knocking softly on the bedroom door. "Mom?" Hearing no answering call, Jessup strode back down the hall to the kitchen. "Alan, Mom's gone again," he said, looking tired.

"When did you see her last?" Greg asked, trying to be helpful.

Alan shot him quick 'butt-out glance'.

"Don't know. She took a six-pack and left out of here last night. She was talking about going to see some friends."

"The bed is still made, so I don't think she got back," Jessup said, sticking his head into his mother's room.

"Crazy old fool," Alan exploded, and tossed his breakfast filled plate across the table. "Call around. See if she's at Gertude's or Bernice's;…then, if not, we can probably guess where she might be."

"Where?" Greg whispered.

"Where do you think?…The store," Alan said as his voice dropped into thin exasperation. "She thinks we still own it or have rights to it. You know how she is when she gets to thinking about Father," Alan said, turning to Jessup.

"Yeah," Jessup agreed as he reached for the phone. He opened the local telephone book and looked at the numbers his mother had circled marking her friends. As he began dialing, he silently hoped she was with one of them.

Guessing the worst, and expecting it, Alan retrieved his coat from his room and signaled Greg to follow him.

Greg took advantage of the confusion of the moment to grab another beer from the refrigerator.

"Com'on, Greg," Jessup said as he hung up the phone. "No use in you going too, Alan, you might as well get some sleep. Greg and I can take care of this."

"You sure?"

"Yes, I'm sure," Jessup, responded as he hitched up his pants, waved Greg through the door, and walked out to a battered red pickup. "Be back in a flash."

They found her in the cool dampness of the basement; her old arms chilled like the whisper of death. Jessup gently wrapped her into the ancient quilt she wound around herself where she slept on the couch. She snored softly. He lifted the frail body into his arms and walked up and out the back stairs of the building. She stirred and smiled at him as she recognized his face when he lifted her into the truck.

"Just sleep, Mom. We'll be home soon," he murmured to her, and motioned Greg to drive on.

11

Early morning found Lynne fumbling at the front doors of the Gellmore Building. She placed her bags of assorted cleaning supplies and groceries on the ground to give her hands enough freedom to unlock the double doors. Her fur-lined gloves were too thick for the maneuvers and she dropped the keys twice. The second time she ripped the gloves from her hands. Hunching her shoulders to block the cool breeze as it tried to crawl down her neck, she concentrated on finding a key that would work the dead bolt. Her backpack swung heavily down on her arm and knocked the key's aim away from the lock as the chill wind bathed her bare hands in its ice. Muttering threateningly under her breath, she dropped the backpack and managed to get the last of the locks opened. As she dragged her supplies in after her, the resonant church bells chimed six o'clock. She touched a light switch but nothing happened. Somebody named Lloyd at the utility company had turned the switch off again. Resigned to the difficulties of the day, she groped though the interior of the building hoping she was headed in the general direction of the freight elevator.

When she found the elevator door, she fumbled in the dark for the button and pressed. Nothing happened. She felt for the wall plate, reassured herself she had pressed the UP button, and pressed again. Nothing. Not a rumble or creaking of motors could be heard. Dead. "Of course, the electricity's not on," she grumbled to herself.

As she sagged against the elevator doorframe, she considered dropping everything and heading to the hotel and her warm bed. Her resolve to work at cleaning up the apartment began to slip through her good intentions. Sighing in resignation, she turned toward the back stairs and tried not to think of the three flights she had to walk up.

"It's got to get easier," she promised herself as she rounded the second floor to the last flight of stairs.

On the top floor, she was grateful she had not forgotten to shut and lock the door to the apartment as she hauled her burden through the door. Swinging her grocery bags onto the kitchen counter gave her a momentary sense of accomplishment. She welcomed the soft light of the morning flooding through the patio doors as she arranged her coffee pot and other contents of the grocery bags on the cabinet top.

Lynne busied herself by starting a fire in the large wood stove in the corner of the living room. The paper and kindling bridge burned hot and bright under small remnants of dry logs. She called the utility company, used Charlie Watson's name, and told them to get Lloyd to turn on the switch again. After a few minutes, Lynne walked into the kitchen and flipped a light switch. It worked. The coffeepot gurgled, as the fire burned happily and sent heat through the open door. She added more logs to coax the growing warmth. Lynne pushed a dusty lounge chair near the stove, careful not to spill the steaming mug of coffee laced with Irish Crème. As she quietly sipped the coffee, her face softened and the lines imposed by the morning's minor displeasure began to fade.

Lynne decided to begin her day's work in the living room. She spread plastic drop cloths near the walls and carefully arranged them across the floor. Paint buckets, rollers, extension handles, brushes, and paint rags added to the preparation of the room. She spent several exhausting minutes tugging and wrestling musty remnants of furniture out past the patio doors to the roof. Lynne fantasized about pitching them over the brick wall and down into the alley below, but decided against it in consideration of her new neighbors. She did not want to get off on the wrong foot, not over some trivial matter anyway. If she were going to be in trouble it might as well be over something good.

The expanse of the floor was covered with an old dust-thickened carpet. It would be the first project she would give to the workers she hoped to hire.

"You are anal retentive," she chuckled to herself when she realized how futile it had been to cover it with the plastic tarp. She squared her shoulders and began opening the paint cans. At ten o'clock, she stopped to admire her work. Two fresh clean coats of paint covered the walls and ceiling from the kitchen to the patio doors. Her hair was tousled and showed signs of the light splattering of paint that had been thrown from thrusting the roller across the ceiling. Her arms ached from the unaccustomed difficult over-head work. She was pleased but tired.

Setting down the roller brush, she heard noises coming from somewhere inside the building. The muffled thud of a door closed somewhere in the distance. She shook her head, wondering if the sounds came from the street then became instantly more alert as the sound of voices carried through the patio doors and across the room to her. A vehicle roared into life in the alley. Curiosity drew Lynne across the open balcony.

As she stepped to the edge and looked down, she saw a red pickup truck trailing oil thick smoke drift out into the street. She gazed after the truck. Its filthy exhaust slowly dissipated in the alley, spoiling the clean smell of the morning air.

The street beyond the alley was busy with normal traffic, but a persistent sense of strange local nonsense settled over her. Lynne shrugged. Of course, it was strange. She was new to the community, unfamiliar with her surroundings, and unaware of what normal was in the new environment. She shrugged again. It was going to take her sometime before she got used to the comings and goings of what passed for normal in Leadville. She had developed a habit and comfort for new places a long time ago. All she wanted was to dig in and have things go quietly toward some form of mundane order. Leadville was the refuge she needed. She knew she needed to give Leadville and herself more time. Time was what she had to give.

She slid the patio door shut, but a small insistent voice tugged inside her head and urged her to check the security of the building. She acknowledged the voice, remembering she already had one unpleasant experience with a local interloper. Lynne was not in a mood to have a repeat performance and she hated surprises. She reached into her backpack, removed the semiautomatic, and placed it in the small of her back between her shirt and belt. Adjusting the weapon for comfort, she reached onto the kitchen counter for the flashlight. Not prone to paranoia but she did not want to be stupid either. Too much training, too many years of experience and hard, safe habits had developed.

A distant thin light met Lynne halfway down the basement stairs. She halted and crouched down to get a look. At the far end of the building, the door to the alley stood half opened. She strained her ears to hear the hint of any movement in the long hallway. A weak breeze concentrated its efforts along the walls and rustled scattered papers on the floor. She lowered soft-soled shoes to the stone floor and tried the light switch at the bottom of the stairs. It clicked ineffectually.

Silence and her own breathing filled the air as Lynne made her way cautiously down the hall. Rooms and the open expanse of the basement moved past her as she checked each new opening.

Suddenly, a loud hollow retort met her as she entered the door of the third room. The hairs stood up on the back of her neck as she swung the flashlight and gun up to meet the noise. She barely managed to stop herself before she shot the ancient furnace that was banging and chugging to life.

"Shit," she laughed out loud. She realized how embarrassing and expensive it would be to explain to an electrician why she shot holes in her own furnace.

Lynne stood up from her ready crouched position and walked to the open back door. She glanced outside and noticed how the wind had dumped remnants of leaves and trash down the exit's stairs. She shut and bolted the door. As she turned back to the hallway, she saw the framed paintings hanging on the wall. Her earlier distractions had prevented her from noticing them. Old moldy frames supported the stark disjointed oil-on-canvas images. There were melting flowerpots, pastel still life, and dark half-concealed images of poor Picasso's imitations littering the length of the hall. Near the end of the catacomb gallery, several gutted frames spilled out of a doorway and back into a room she had passed earlier.

She walked to the room, reached around the doorframe to find the light switch, and flicked it once without expectation. Light sprang from a weak bare bulb dangling from the ceiling. She did not know whether to be more surprised by the lights actually working or the mess in the tiny cramped room. Across the floor lay the empty containers for beer, bottles of cheap Scotch, food, and a dirty mattress piled high with tattered blankets. An old couch with a torn plastic slipcase slumped against the water-stained face of the basement wall.

"Good lord. A lover's nest…or rats nest," Lynne snorted, and kicked a beer can out of her way. "Kids or tramps?" she wondered aloud, but then remembered the red pickup and its retreat down the alleyway. Shuddering, she wondered if the intruders had been in the building all night or just this morning while she had concentrated on painting and cleaning her apartment.

"That does it," she declared as she stuffed the gun back in her jeans and marched back down the long hallway.

As she reached the first floor landing, she surveyed her territory with grim determination. "Dead-bolts, locks, and security alarm," she said under her breath. Her exasperation with the constant invasion by locals affirmed Lynne's decision to lease the most advanced security technology she could find for the building and her own peace of mind. Recalling the basement, she decided to have the pictures and junk removed and burned before they drew more rats.

As she started to ascend the stairs back toward her apartment, someone began knocking loudly on the front doors. She stopped and glared rudely in their direction. She took a long deep breath, and descended the stairs, daring the intruder to persist. Whoever was on the wrong side of the door was going to receive the wrong side of her attitude. Apparently, it was getting tougher to be left alone.

"What?" she barked through the door.

Nothing but silence echoed and returned to her.

"I said, what?" She barked and realized that in her present state of mind she could not remember how to spell patience.

"Miss Fhaolain?" a man's voice demurred.

"Yes?" Lynne searched for recognition.

"Lynne? It's Charlie and Doc."

"Oh…yes?" A sheepish looks dashed across her face.

"Do you have a few minutes?" Doc asked. "We just thought we'd maybe come to help you get settled in? O.K.?"

"Sorry…sure. Come on in. You're the best reception I've had all morning," Lynne said as she let them through the doors.

"Thanks," they chimed.

Flushing with embarrassment, Lynne turned her back. "Lock it behind you," she said waving them after her. "I've been upstairs painting until I had to check the basement for burglars."

"Burglars?" Doc asked as he puffed along behind her.

"Well, maybe not burglars. Maybe just kids practicing unsafe sex or an old wino dropping in for some zs. I do not know. And I do not care. There is a corner room down there that looks like someone has been using it for an adult-sized playroom. Whatever, I don't want them here again."

The two men followed Lynne in silence as they exchanged quick knowing glances. Charlie silently decided he had better speak to the Gellmore's' and for everyone concerned he had to do it in a hurry.

At the top of the stairs, Lynne opened the apartment door and spread her arms wide. "This is it, or at least it as far as I have got," she announced as she walked into the kitchen.

"Not bad. You've really been at it, haven't you?"

"Do you hire out?" Doc Kennedy tried teasing her.

"Yes, I have. And no, I do not. In that order," Lynne said, forcing her mood to soften. "But Doc, I'd think that a man in your profitable profession could hire anyone anytime he wanted to?"

"True enough, but first you have to decide where to start. I just can't get to start," he said as he wandered toward an available chair.

"He's been an old slug since his wife passed on. She was the only one who could really get him off his butt to work," Charlie whispered to Lynne.

"I see," Lynne said quietly, and moved around the kitchen counter to run more water for coffee. "Either of you want coffee? I'm going to fix more anyway."

"Not me, had more than my share already today," Charlie said, pulling a deck chair in from the patio.

"Same here."

"Too bad. I have some nice Irish Crème to go with it. It'd make a nice treat," Lynne said as she set up three cups on the counter.

"Well, now, that makes all the difference in the world. Doesn't it, Charlie?" Doc launched himself out of the chair and over to the kitchen bar-counter to watch the preparations.

"Yes, indeed," said Charlie as he abandoned his fussing placement of the deck chairs.

After pouring their coffee and trimmings, the two men returned to their respective perches. Lynne stoked the fire and added more wood before joining them. Several moments passed as they quietly savored the coffee.

"So. Did I hear you right? You offering to help around here today?" Lynne reminded them of their earlier hinted offer.

"Well," Charlie began, widening his eyes at Doc Kennedy and quickly nodded his head in encouragement. "Well, you don't know but Doc and I am on the town council and, well, ah…what would you say if that were a ruse, you know, to get you to open the door?"

"I'm listening," Lynne said cautiously.

12

The next day Lynne interviewed the men and women who had answered her help wanted advertisement. She had been a little surprised at the turnout of twenty job seekers but figured it said a great deal about the local economy and the reconstruction thaw of spring.

While working through the candidates, her mind wandered back to Tuesday morning and the conversation she'd had with Charlie and Doc. Reluctantly, she had agreed to look at the copies of the police reports and autopsy Doc brought with him. She knew better than to get involved with the situation, but she had ended up promising Doc to examine the material. The reports, and particularly, the photographs, had distracted her mind from the work at hand. More than once she had to ask an applicant to repeat some bit of information offered about their qualifications. The musing interfered with the organization she tried to put on her day. Grisly was the predominant word that circled her mind.

She had elected to do the applications and interview process in a by-the-numbers fashion, and had the hotel manager run off a couple dozen generic application forms for her. She had already prepared a list which described the various work skills and tasks she figured she would need to complete the preparations for the opening of the bookstore. As each applicant strolled in, she gave him or her a form and a list the list of tasks. The hotel manager had let her use a spare room for the interviewing office. Lynne had arranged for coffee, hot tea, and pastries to be available. Her long-term business needs and desire to get, and stay, on the good side of the community seemed to her to warrant those minor considerations. Her previous experience and preference as a supervisor had taught her that people were best led by example. She wanted to establish a positive example to get the best results from those who would work with her.

The early arrivals busied themselves at their tables with the details of the applications and refreshments. As they finished their form, they returned to the table where Lynne sat for the interviews.

By noon Lynne had managed to hire all the help she could use and thanked the rest for coming. She explained to those who were not hired that she would be keeping their applications. She intended to review them again as the work needs changed over the next few weeks. She invited the six men and two women she would hire to follow her into the hotel lounge, and encouraged the others to stay and enjoy the refreshments. In the lounge, she invited her work staff to sit and discuss the details of the repairs that she needed to have completed.

"I am aware of the wages in the area. The time and money available limit my need for your help. I want to be fair with you. In turn, I know I can depend on you being fair. I will set your hourly fee according to your level of verifiable experience and expertise. As I said earlier, I will be conducting that verification over the next several days by contacting your union halls or previous employers." Lynne felt stiff reciting her expectation experience

had been an exacting teacher. She never abandoned the practical or prag-
matic once she gained it.

"Any questions so far?" she asked, and looked around the room expectantly. No one uttered a word. They all were waiting to see what she might
do or say next. She used the silence. Waiting, she took the time to study
the faces of the people sitting with her at the long table. They were good
strong faces.

"O.K. The only way I know how to do this is by the book, so please
bear with me...Us, and I do mean us, will begin each morning at 7 A.M.,
sharp. Breaks will be from ten to 10:15 A.M., and again from two to 2:15
P.M. Lunch will be from Noon to one. It is not a paid break. Work will
continue at least 'till five each evening. Overtime, if necessary, will be paid
for each hour over the total forty hours accumulated during the week, not
on a daily basis. I must approve any overtime to be worked. Overtime will
be paid at time-and-a-half," Lynne said, and looked up briefly from the
notes she had been reading to see if there were any questions on the faces
that watched her.

"You'll get paid every Friday, at the end of the work day," she continued. "No advances, no day-to-day, or other unscheduled payments. No-
calls, or no-shows, will tell me that you have moved on to other things,
and a replacement will be found. So, call if you intend to be late, or cannot show that day. Just call me. It will reserve your job. Not calling will
end our agreement.

"So there'll be no misunderstanding, I have the details of this agreement for you to sign. You will have a copy and so will I. In that way, you
can hold me responsible for the agreement, your wages, and related
compensation, and I'll hold you responsible for the work," Lynne said
in conclusion.

"How do you pay?" The question came from the far end of the table.
The man had been sitting away from the table with his arms folded across
his chest. He had the look of distance about him.

"In check, through a local bank, Friday evening of each week," Lynne responded. "All the necessary taxes, insurance, and compensation will be taken out and dully noted on your check stubs. That way, I will be kept square with required employment laws. I like staying square with the law, particularly tax laws."

"Insurance?" asked an older man sitting to Lynne's right. She looked at him and tried to read his demeanor. Inscrutable, she thought. There was nothing to read on his face. It was a simple question, but he did not look like a simple man. She had noticed him before, in particular because of his age and sharp facial features. She speculated that a great deal of Native American blood ran through his veins, although she could not begin to speculate tribe or nation. She liked the looks. There were a strength and integrity in his eyes. Or maybe, she thought, it was because there was something about him that reminded her of her grandfather. He had also favored the bibbed blue-and-white-striped railroad workmen's coveralls the older man wore. Unconsciously, she smiled at him as she remembered her grandfather.

"Yes, insurance. I will make available some health and accident insurance. Part of your wage will cover 20 percent of the total cost, and pick up the rest. It will be in force for three months once you sign on with me. Even if there is no work after the first four weeks, I'll continue it for the remaining two months and pay the installments."

"Why?" the old man probed, leaning toward her questioningly.

"One, because it won't cost me any more for three months than one because of the way these plans are offered by the insurance companies. Two, although I don't have to offer any type of insurance, if any of you were injured on the premises, your recovery could cost me more than the total of the premiums I've set aside. And, finally, given an opportunity, I prefer to do what I feel is the right thing. Providing you with insurance is the right thing," she finished.

The old man leaned back in his chair, and Lynne noticed the other eyes at the table watching him intently. She wondered who he was and what he was for them. After a few moments, he nodded his head in acceptance of the proposition as he looked at to other workers.

"Will you be having us work for you longer than four weeks?" Asked the young woman sitting next to the man, who hugged his arms to his chest.

"Perhaps, but maybe not always in your current capacity. I have literally tens of thousands of books arriving here from warehouse purchases I have made and stock accumulated over the years. It has been in storage and I am anxious to get them on shelves.

"I have to have this building ready when they arrive. I need to have them up, on display, and ready to start business when possible." Lynne took a deep breath and decided to get to the bottom line. "It's simply this,...after spending a lot of money, I have to start earning some again."

"You're paying union scale, offering other benefits. That's fairer than usual. We'll be fair in return," the old man interjected, and sounded like the elder statesman he was.

"Thank you Mr.....?" Lynne glanced at her papers, trying to recall or locate his name.

"John Bowannie," he said as he reached down to flick the ashes of his cigarette into the cuffs of his bibbed overalls.

Lynne watched him in surprise and amusement. She wondered if all old men who wore bibbed overalls and smoked did the same thing. Her grandfather had, inside or outside his house. The little live sparks of hungry ash would slowly and surely eat at the pressed folds of the cuffs. In time, the hot debris would fray the material, leaving the cuffs shattered. It had caused her grandmother a great deal of aggravation to try to maintain a semblance of repair on her grandfather's besieged cuffs. Her normal inclination was to withhold judgment about people. But that was strongly countered by the memories he aroused. She knew it was silly and senti-mental, but she began to like the old man because of that one small act.

"Thank you, Mr. Bowannie. I appreciate your confidence," Lynne offered.

"No problem. My granddaughter is 'bout your age. She's a firecracker, too," Bowannie's eyes sparkled in reply.

"Firecracker," she mused, and she cleared her throat self-consciously. "Then I look forward to seeing you all Monday morning at the Gellmore building, soon to be the Fhaolain Book Loft," she said as she smiled at the people sitting around the table. She handed each of them a copy of the work contract containing the terms and agreements mentioned. They signed and returned the documents to her. She thanked them again and stood to signal the end of the meeting.

As they left the lounge, her new work crew filed out chatting amongst themselves. She noticed several younger men and women deferring to Mr. Bowannie. Lynne stored that piece of information away for later reflection.

As she turned her attention back to placing her copies of the contracts in her folder, she noticed Doc entering the lounge area. The sound of his footfalls caused her to look up. Smiling at him as he approached, Lynne noticed the lap-tied binder he carried.

"Hello. How are you?" She said, extending her hand.

"Fine," he said and handed her the binder.

"Is this all of it?"

"It's everything I have and a few extra notes I jotted down after our con-versation yesterday," he said as he sat in a chair. "Mostly, I just tried to answer some questions I remembered you asking. It is everything I can recall seeing, doing, or being done at the cabin. I even noted rumors, and I put little check marks by them so you won't take them for fact or gospel." He looked tired and fiddled with a pencil on the table left by one of the work crew.

"Good," Lynne said as she thumbed through the material in the folder.

"The Sheriff, let alone the state authorities, would have my head if he or they knew I'd given that to you," Doc confided in a hushed whisper. He was nervous, despite the fact they were the only ones in the room.

"I know. They would have my head, too. But he will not find out from me. Neither one of us need that kind of trouble. Are you sure you want me to do this?" she asked, and patted his arm reassuringly.

"Confidence is what I don't have in our local constabulary, even with the state boys lending a hand," Doc responded, shaking his head ruefully. "They're good boys, really. But, truth is, we are small potatoes as far as the state is concerned, and the Sheriff is way out of his league on this. Good man, but his pride can get in the way of his ability to make decisions. I've seen him do it before," Doc said as he tossed the pencil back down on the table. The gesture punctuated his determination.

"Saw what?"

"Little stuff. But you know, it's the little things that tell a lot about a fell."

"Yeah. Little things can add up to big things," Lynne said as she sipped her coffee and watched Doc's face firm his jaw in resolution. Doc and Charlie seemed to make quite a pair. But a pair of what she did not know. Lynne wondered what she was getting herself into with these two well-intended old friends.

"Mind you now, he's the type that figures he's in charge and the only one with ideas. Been that way since he was a boy. 'Course that attitude has bit him in the butt more than once over the years. Unfortunately, he's managed to ignore the implications," Doc confided.

"I don't make any promises on this, Doc. I said my inclination is to stay out of it."

"I know. Charlie and I both know and understand. But we've lived here a long time and, well, I guess when something crazy like this happens, we just want to see everything done that can be."

"This may not be the best thing for any of us. I am trying to make a new start here. This is like going backwards. Curiosity and habit are my worst enemies," Lynne said as she felt tension growing. "Anything I find, or even guess at, I intend to turn over to the locals, somehow. I was in the military and a cop too long not to make sure I mend any fence I might be breaking here. I really don't want to get into a muddy mess or go to jail for interfering in an official investigation."

"We appreciate it, and will keep it to ourselves."

"That has to be an absolute," Lynne reemphasized.

"It is." Doc scraped back his chair from the table and without another word walked out of the lounge.

Lynne looked at the folder. It brimmed over with documents, Sheriff's reports, more photographs of the crime scene, transcripts of the partial autopsy, and a hefty addition to the papers he had given her Monday. She wondered how Doc had gotten the copies out of the office, but decided it was probably best not to know. Someone had been there stalking, waiting, and ready to act. Everything she guessed, Doc had confirmed when he described the crime scene. Her instincts and training focused on the possibility that the killer was still in the area waiting to act again. He found himself a new hunger and the way to satisfy the appetite.

"Well," she said quietly, "into the breech again."

13

Lynne woke feeling as though she had been working much too hard. Saturday morning, the end of her first hectic week in Leadville, and the altitude plagued her ability to feel motivated. Sluggish and easily tired by the thinner atmosphere she felt puny and insubstantial. The geographic realities and her own sense of incompleteness conspired to ruin her best intentions. Altitude and attitude spawned listlessness and confusion as her emotions sapped her ambition.

Leavenworth had been only 523 feet above sea level. Leadville reached up to a dizzying 9,450 feet above the comfort zone. She recalled Shelby remarking about how the differences in altitude and climate would require getting no little effort and adjustment. It had seemed preposterous then to Lynne that every thousand feet of altitude could represent three degrees in temperature variation. But Shelby had been right, every thousand feet of climb weighed on her like an additional five-pound weight gain since her arrival. She hoped that so-called adaptation would not be far behind.

"And miles to go before I sleep," she quoted from the comfort of her bed sneaking a look at the morning sky and noticed the sun beginning to glint through the thinning patches of clouds. The day began to promise a real change from the gray and oppressive days she had suffered since her arrival. With sun-inspired hope, she swung her legs out from under the covers and willed herself across the room.

Freshly showered, she ordered breakfast in her room as a deserved luxury and settled down to the table where she had scattered the homicide report file. Pencil in hand, letting it hover over the notebook, she began to read the file again. Habit settled in as she reviewed the sheaf of papers and photographs. She operated by training, instinct, information, and what she called her "back-burner-method."

She had learned the techniques twelve years ago after attending a four-week training session on serial homicide investigation, Quantico, Virginia, at the FBI Academy. The skills had been later supplemented by intensive training through the Justice Department. But at Quantico a capable but quirky field-agent had conducted the lecture on the "viability of routine investigation requirements and necessary habit of imaginative leaps" or simply 'investigator intuition'.

Lynne spent the first three hours of the lecture at Quantico believing the training staff had played a practical joke on the students. She had heard the grumbling of other trainees rise and fall around her in the crowded amphitheater. She exchanged raised eyebrows of quiz, questions, and almost comical disbelief amongst the officers. They had been bound together at their desks by their general respect for the FBI, but uncomfortable with the lecturer's proposals. She had dutifully taken notes but continued to glance around the amphitheater trying to find the cameras recording the gullibility of non-FBI initiates.

When the lecture concluded, she approached the agent with her concerns. He listened to her consternation and the inferred suspicion of his slippage in logic with quiet patience. He had smiled and offered coffee in the trainer's break-room while he helped her clarify or resolve her misgivings.

Lynne had found him to be earnest and insistent in the appropriateness of his philosophy. He confided in her. He said he believed in, and attempted to enhance, what he knew was the capacity of the human mind when truly focused on a difficult project. He believed that an insistence on logic was a cultural basis for simple linearity of thought. And that it tended to stiffen or stifle the creativity necessary for a successful conclusion to an investigation. He admitted that he routinely practiced what he preached.

The instructor's genuineness helped Lynne to suspend her disbelief and repugnance for what smacked of investigative mysticism. The suspensions allowed her to memorize the "not-so-secret habits" he said he had developed. His eyes had danced as he spoke about the rituals of the mind he had found useful. His intensity, intellectual integrity, and humor encouraged her attention. Finally, he had suggested books to read a course of study to pursue dynamic techniques, scientific instrumentality, and the use of standard intensive investigative processes. In those few hours, he became the best mentor she would ever know in her career. Lynne came to depend upon the "back-burner" and let it operate while she slept or otherwise allowed her mind to relax. In those moments the information, images, and details of a case would form and reform relationships in the realm of her trained imagination. Over time she had expanded on agents' tools but had not forgotten his insistence that, "If it works, use it," as an axiom to dispel doubt.

Breakfast arrived as she plowed through the processing of the papers spread before her. The aroma of fresh baked bread, hot cocoa, and sliced sweet fruits temporarily recalled her from the questions and analysis of murder.

She glanced at the clock on the nightstand and was surprised to see that she had spent two hours lost in concentration and reflection. She had gleaned all she could from the material. There was nothing more to be gained by rereading it again. Although she might review it again later, she needed a walkabout. She wanted to get out of the room and away from the Sheriff's assumptions that glared throughout the reports. Lynne knew she needed to do something else if she were to comprehend the essence of the crime and the mind of the murderer. She knew she would have to visit the murder scene, but not today. Today she decided to take care of other business. There was a potential travel book publisher out there waiting for her first few tentative chapters. She owed them a little of her time and a lot of effort.

Lynne poured herself another cup of coffee, walked toward the window in the room, stretched as she tried to switch her personal reflective gears from homicidal miseries to mountainside comfort. A foolish grin reflecting the disjuncture of purpose and process dashed across her lips before she turned to fetch her travelogue notes.

She hoped she was not wasting ever one's time. The bookstore had been Shelby's dream and Lynne wanted to see it manifest itself. But now with Shelby gone the dream held little more than a need for completion, more like a promise than a prayer.

The New York publisher had fallen across a copy of a travel piece Lynne had written for the Army Vacation Times when it had been brought to his attention by a retired military staff member in his officer. She had written it as a lark discussing the beauty of the Ozarks and wooded lake country after she had visited Fort Leonard Wood in Missouri. It had been a tongue-in-cheek article with serious information about the variety of vacation sites in and around the immediate area. He had found her style bright, rich in detail, and intriguing. The initial contact had come through the publishing board of the Army Vacation Times and the serious negotiations for travel book authoring had begun in earnest shortly after Lynne announced her pending retirement. She owed him a reading of the contract and a re-write of her first proposal. She always kept her promises if she could. This was an easy one. The terrain, climate, multi-access resorts, and multifaceted entertainment possibilities year round in the area would make her proposal development easy.

Turning her attention to the proposal Lynne felt her heart lighten as murder and mayhem slipped from her consciousness.

14

By the time he got home, the idea of a stiff drink seemed like a good idea. His day was not going as he had planned. He decided to pretend it had not happened and start over. Grabbing a bag of potato chips off the top of the refrigerator, he sat wearily at the kitchen table. The brine of the chips made him thirsty. The warmth of the house and the lightness of his head made him feel as though all his movements were heavy and dreamlike.

He had the rest of the day to himself. He would have another beer, and then maybe figure out what to do. He lingered over the second beer and let it wash the irritations and discontents from his mind. He began to imagine the sweet havoc he wanted to create when a heavy fist began pounding at his door.

"Hey? 'Pard? You in there?" the familiar voice cried.

"What the hell do you want?" he opened the door.

"You gonna drink alone?" Greg said as he eyed the beer in the other man's hand.

"My house, my beer, guesses so."

"Come on 'Pard. Have a heart. You know, they say it's a sign of alco-holism if you drink alone?"

"Do tell. Way I hear it, it's a way of saving money, too." He reluctantly waved Greg through the door. "And quit calling me Pard."

"Come on, man, you know everyone's my partner, Pard. I don't mean anything by it." Greg's feelings smarted from rejection.

"I know," he said, knowing Greg was too easy a target.

"Kinda surly for so early in the day, aren't you?" Greg said as he walked toward the six-pack. "So, and what the hell did you want, anyway?"

"Nothing. Just, no one's around downtown. So I thought I would look you up. I always enjoy talking to you, you know?" Greg said plaintively. He did not have friends, no family, or anyone else outside his beer mooch-buddies. Greg understood that most people suffered his company, but he did not know how to change things. He had been the class clown in school. It was a cute act on a boy. But the same behavior was not the least bit charming on a grown man when the clowning act had not matured. It made finding and keeping jobs more than a little difficult. He slowly but surely wore out his welcome on most people.

"It's been a long day already, Greg," he sighed deeply.

"You'll miss all the fun."

"I don't mind. I came home because I was thinking about a nap."

"A nap? A grown man like you?"

"I'm tired. Been feeling run down lately," he said, and grabbed a third beer in hopes it would help him sleep more soundly.

"Come on, Pard. Daylight's wasting. A man doesn't live by working his life away," Greg said as he tipped back the beer. He opened his throat and let it pour down the open chute. Four seconds later he sat the can down on the kitchen table. Empty.

"You still making money pulling that stunt?" he asked, recalling when Greg first learned the trick. Greg could down a beer faster than any man alive could. He could open his throat and pour it down. He was betting on that fact and it earned him a little cash every now and again. Greg had told him it was the quickest way to a cheap drunk.

"Nah. Just some dopey tourist here and there," Greg said, and raised his eyebrows in a question.

"Go ahead, I have two more six packs in the cupboard," he waived Greg toward the refrigerator, figuring Greg was not too bad for company.

"So, what do ya say?" Greg asked as he carried the second six-pack back to the table.

"About what?"

"About hunting. Let's you and me go do a little light-fingered freezer filling."

"Poaching? Last time you did that it cost you thirty days in the steel bar hotel when that game warden got you."

"I know but I got stupid then. 'Sides, I could really use the extra groceries now," Greg urged.

"Let me think about it."

"Look, those other state birds are really busy taking over that investigation. You know...that killing out near Peavey's'," Greg said pointedly, remembering a detail he thought could help the other man make up his mind. "They haven't got time for anything but running their asses off sniffing in circles. They've got no time for looking for poachers. We won't get caught, and you have nothing to worry about. Come on, I'll share with you."

"I've seen you shoot. Remember? It's more likely I'll be the one doing the sharing."

"Yeah! That's right," Greg laughed.

"All right. Let's go show those deer whose boss," he said as he got up from the chair, stretching noisily. "Arrghh! By the way, you got any money?"

"That a joke?" Greg responded.

"Not necessarily. What with only one six-pack and a-half, we're about out of beer, and you know how dry it gets waiting for deer to come by."

"Yeah. But you know I've been out of work for two months," Greg complained. "Only chance I've had lately s'been with that snooty tight-ass bitch who bought the Gellmore building," he fumed.

"She wouldn't hire you?"

"Let's just say, I'm probably too much man for her," Greg laughed and grabbed at his crotch.

"You get fresh with her while asking for a job? That was stupid."

"Hell, from what I saw of her attitude, I figure she hates men. Rather shoot'em than screw'em. Probably frigid bitch anyway." Greg pulled at his crotch again imagining a remedy for his fantasy.

"Probably. But that doesn't solve the beer problem," he said as he fished into his hip pocket for his wallet. "Go get your gun. I'll get the beer and pick you up over at your place."

"Sure thing, Pard," Greg said, bounding happily out the door.

"Simpleton," he called at Greg's back. He went to the living room and retrieved his Winchester 30-06 from the gun cabinet, checked it and loaded it. He put an extra box of shells in his coat pocket on his way out to his truck.

An hour later, they had made their way into the hills looking for a place to stop. The 4x4 churned thawing mud and gravel packed ice as it struggled up the road. A few miles on, they crossed South Willow Creek and came to a rest.

"This looks as good as any other place."

"Suits me," Greg nodded as he looked at the loose-spreading limbs of tea fir, yellow pine, and oak shadowing the forest floor. He wondered if the walk along the creek might be difficult with the mountain scrub and dog birch gathering in greedy packs along the edge.

"Don't know why you had to bring that mangy cur. He's more likely to scare the game away than do us anything like good luck," the man said as he got out of the truck and pulled his rifle after him.

"Fred? Fred here's my buddy. He's like family. In fact, he's the only family I got," Greg, said in protest as he hugged the yellow Labrador-Golden Retriever mix fondly around its neck. Fred's jaws dropped and showed a foolish doggie grin of appreciation.

"The family resemblance is remarkable," he said to Greg as he checked the rifle sights.

"He never gives me any grief, no back talk, no complaints. Do you, Fred?" Greg said as he rubbed the top of the dog's head.

"Whatever."

"Come on, Fred," Greg called as he climbed out of the truck. Fred followed eagerly.

For two hours the men and dog moved together quietly through the trees, keeping each other in sight, and watching for game. Fred moved easily and attentively at Greg's side. They worked their way back and forth along the creek hoping for thirsty game. Moving along the weaving back-tracking deer trails, elusiveness of the game and the muddy spring runoff began to wear their patience thin. They circled back near to the place they had started as resignation overtook them. The sun was high overhead.

"Hold up a minute," Greg said as he leaned against a tree to relieve himself. "What say we just sit, think, and drink for a while? Maybe the deer will come to us."

"Fine."

"I'll be right back," Greg said as he zipped up and bounded the fifty yards back to the truck. Returning quickly, he saw his hunting buddy tipping back a long draw on a bottle of bourbon.

"Hey! Where'd that come from?"

"Same place the beer came from. Care for a little Widow Maker's?"

"No cups."

"Don't need cups. Just take a pull and wash it down with the beer. Simple," he said as he handed Greg the bottle.

"They always said you were smart. Now I know you're downright brilliant." Greg tossed an extra six-pack at his friend and made sure he kept a pack for himself. He found a comfortable log, balanced himself on it, leaned his back against the tree, farted, and sighed in relief. "Here's to friends, Pard," Greg toasted, and rose the bottle hungrily toward his mouth.

"Same to you. Pard."

The sun neared its zenith as they swapped drinks and tall tales of past hunting prowess. Fred loped near the creek and worried the neighboring shrubs eagerly looking for small animals to harass. Conversation slackened and the silence between the men grew longer and more punctuated as each found himself deeper into the bottle and the noise of his own thoughts.

Long stretches of silence made Greg uneasy, even when he was by himself. The past, and present, were too filled with regrets and missed opportunities to let him rest comfortably with his own company. The sound of his voice was the only way he had of assuring himself of his place in the world.

"Say," Greg slurred, and cleared his throat. "What'd you think about that woman gettin' chopped up? Wasn't that sumpin'? Did you see her picture in the paper? Can you believe someone could do that to something as fine as that?"

"Yeah, I saw her," he responded. He cast his eyes in the direction of the looming peak of Mount Massive but the alcohol made the image tilt uncertainly.

"Yeah? Oh, yeah. Shit man! What a waste! If her old man was tired of her, he could have just given her to me."

"What? What did you say?"

"I said…that fool that killed her, he could have given her to me," Greg repeated slowly for the other man's benefit. "He screwed up a perfectly good piece of ass."

"You knew her?" he asked Greg.

"Knew her? Hell…not hardly. But if I had of, I surely would've ripped one off for myself," Greg massaged his crotch for emphasis. "I'd have pushed ole 'pard here up her so far she never would've wanted to go home."

"No way…no way to talk 'bout her, Greg," he said as indignation spread across his chest, burning him.

"Like shit. All them snow bunnies' want something special. You know they come up here looking for strange. She just got it a little too strange and ugly."

"Enough!" he screamed. He could hear his blood beginning to pound heavily in his ears. His breath came in quicker gasps as he listened to Greg defame her. Talking about her like she had been a slut. That wasn't the way it was. Not at all. "Did you touch her?" he asked Greg as anger and betrayal flared through the haze of alcohol.

"Touch her? She's dead, man. That's stupid. Did you touch her?" Greg fixed his eyes uneasily on the other man. "Shit, look,…I'm talking about a dead woman. I don't touch dead women. I'm just talkin'. She was bitchin', you know, sweet meat, but dead-ass now. The only thing

new in town now is that cunt I ran into at the Gellmore place. Ya gotta
meet this one!"

"I couldn't give a shit, either way."

"Ah, man. She's alive and I bet she would hump up good. Not like putting your pud just anywhere."

"You don't know anything about her! You don't know crap about anything," he roared and struggled to his feet.

"Like you did, dick-wad," Greg sneered at his hunting partner. It made
him mad. The alcohol emboldened Greg. He glared at his friend. "So
much for smarts," he snorted. "Big man, you're Damning drunk. Standing
there, swaying around, slouched over trying to keep your balance. You're
just like any other slobbering drunk," Greg hammered at him. He had
seen him like this before. Sympathy was cheap. His buddy had been
taunting him so he figured turnabout was fair.

"I said, stop it."

"Go Damn yourself. Go Damn her. She's just one piece of dead piece
of meat. There's plenty more where that came from," Greg retorted,
screaming. The scream hurt his throat and he finished his beer to cool its
raw edges.

"She was,…she was…" confusion and anger ran their course through
his mind. She had been beautiful, commanding, beseeching. And she had
been his. Greg was defiling his memories.

"Alive, but not anymore,…" Greg said, warming to the ranting harassment. He imagined himself getting even for all the times the man made
him feel inferior and stupid. "Now she's worm bait. Get over yourself, and
give me a hit off that bottle," Greg said, and reached for the bottle care-
lessly clasped in the other man's hand. The big man was nothing more
than a sniveling soppy bastard.

He jerked the bottle away from Greg and stumbled back to where he had dropped his backpack. He fell to his knees, searching for it furiously; he knew he wanted her close to him again.

"Listen. You think what happened to her was bad…you know what Doc did to her?" Greg's eyes sparkled with malevolent intent.

"Doc?…What's he got to do with it?" he puzzled at Greg. "An autopsy fool! You know that. You must know what they do in autopsies don't ya? Doc explained it to me," Greg said, reeling out the line and hook.

"I know…I don't want to hear," he insisted as his frantic hand found her.

"See,…first they start by cutting open the chest. Zip, just like that, then he takes some fancy looking wire cutters and snips open that bone stuff that holds your ribs together. Pulling her open would have spread her breasts all the way back under her armpits. Bet that was ugly. Yeah, now that I think about it,…then, he would have just…" Greg hesitated in his story as he tipped up a fresh beer. He was enjoying himself, but it was hard thirsty work.

The first bullet struck Greg in his left shoulder and caused him to drop his beer as he slammed against the tree. The second one caught him in the chest, raised him off the log, and dropped him back down again, hard. Four more were added randomly to his legs, head, and crotch.

Standing over the body, admiring his work he was suddenly slammed hard with ragged pain as Fred sunk his teeth into his arm and dragged him to the ground. Dog and man fell on Greg. Struggling frantically, they rolled over Greg and onto the snow crusted ground. The man grabbed his knife as Fred tried to chew his way through jacket, sweater, shirt, and into his soft flesh. He stabbed two hard desperate strokes into Fred's chest. Fred yelped and dropped away.

Scrambling over the tree trunk, the man grabbed his rifle and fired at Fred. The first bullet missed the dog by inches as Fred danced away from the exploding spray amongst the leaves and ice. The man aimed carefully and fired again, hitting the dog in the left forefoot. Fred yelped and lunged through the brush, out of sight. He continued to fire at the dog's fleeing back.

The man turned and looked back at Greg in his trembling rage. He was not finished with him. Not yet, not by a long sight. He owed Greg something special and himself something special to remember.

"Ole 'Pard," he murmured, "that's a nasty tongue you got there." He knelt in front of Greg's body, wiped the dog's blood from the knife, and pulled the dead man toward him. "Must be something we can do about that?" he said leaning closer to Greg's face.

15

Lynne turned her truck south onto the snow-sloshed highway. The directions' Doc had .given her suggested the cabin she was looking for would be about two and one-half miles northwest off old Highway 4. He had been precise, but only because of a lifelong familiarity with the area. Lynne longed for street signs, landmarks, or even posted house numbers. She clutched the note in her hand as she drove, and cursed the rural byways disguised in landmarks. The whole process was irritatingly cryptic and obscure for an outlander.

Traffic was infrequent so she took advantage of the pace and worked her way slowly along the snowplowed roadway, eyeing the borrow-pits and ridges for discarded items. Sometimes criminals would discard weapons after leaving the scene, and she wanted to check for the possibility. When she finally found the turn for Half Moon Creek road, she noted the truck's odometer and turned back to town to complete her search of the other side.

Lynne covered both sides of the highway as it made its way from Leadville to the Half Moon Creek turnoff. Time and patience, she thought, and resigned to the idea that the recent scattering of snow and blowing winds had become deep enough to cover anything that might have been tossed out of the murderer's vehicle. Turning south again, Lynne watched the calibration of the odometer to help her spot the unmarked exit. She did not want to miss the turn off onto Half Moon Creek from the highway.

The late morning sun added warmth to the engine's heat in the truck and took the chill from her as she drove down the gravel road. She found it hard to concentrate on the borrow-pits as she struggled to control her truck on the intermittent patches of ice and slick mud softened by the sun. The patches threatened to pull her truck toward one minor disaster then another. She found the Pevey's mailbox with the name painted in bold red letters on its side. Doc had said the cabins were a way's past the Pevey's tiny ranch and hoped she would not miss them and get herself lost in the mountains.

A few hundred feet past the Pevey's, Lynne spotted a small run of split-log fence and what seemed a driveway entrance leading to cabins. The driveway was a churned mess of chunky ice and melting snow. Lynne looked down the continuing stretch of Half Moon Creek and decided she wanted to see where the road led but would wait to do that later.

"More mud," she fussed to herself as she put the truck into four-wheel drive and entered the cabin's meadow.

Six cabins sat scattered over the large cleared meadow. In the distance, trees forested the knees of the mountains and hunkered down at the rear of the clearing. A hundred feet or so of sparsely scattered wild grasses, pine and fir trees ringed by scrub brush separated one cabin from another. Lynne thought it looked as though it would have been a nice arrangement for vacationing. It seemed to her that the placement of the cabins would offer a sense of solitude or at least some noise-muffling distance from other enthusiastic vacationers neighbors one would have to share the meadow with.

Nice in the summer but the lonely stretch had been too far from help for the hapless Beverly.

Lynne stopped the truck and surveyed the surrounding area for perspective. She saw a sagging, whitewashed shed crouched at the back of the meadow, with an almost perfect line of Douglas fir curving around the far reaches of the distance field. The line of trees did not seem to abide by the laws of nature and seed scattering, but strongly hinted of a road-hugging design. She would have to investigate the trees and the shed to satisfy her suspicions.

She looked behind her toward the Pevey's mailbox and saw the top of a chimney and sharply sloping roof. Smoke poured out of the chimney. The wind drove it down toward a house hidden by the gentle curve of a rolling hillock. The quarter mile distance Lynne estimated between the properties might as well have been light-years away for all the good it would have done Beverly if she had tried to call for help. Any quieter noise than the roar of a cannon would not have found its way to the house.

She started the truck again, drove it through the entrance, and parked under the masking cover of several elderly Douglas firs. The old fir stand was challenged for space in their tiny grove by a few spare mountain maples, and satisfied Lynne that her truck would be obscured from the possibility of prying eyes. Underbrush of buffalo bush with a clustering of juvenile bull pine gave additional shadow-speckled concealment for the truck. She didn't want to be seen traipsing around the area, and knew it would be better not to have to provide creative responses to questions of any law enforcement officer who might catch her on the property.

Reaching for her Russian fur hat, Lynne checked her parka pockets for the tools she had brought with her. Stepping out of the truck, she zipped

her parka closed to protect her against the chill wind that came slipping
down over the mountains and nipped the warmth of the sun from the air.

As she walked toward the cabins, Lynne observed the deep rutted vehicle grooves leading to a cabin at the farthest edge of the meadow. On the
ground, here and there, the vehicle tracks had been crisscrossed with signs
of foraging wildlife. Closer into the cabin tires tracks and the hooves and
paws of wildlife mingled with the imprints of heavily booted feet. The
exterior of the crime scene was a mess of crosshatched business. Its scrabbled condition told Lynne all she needed to know about the lack of skills
and cautions applied by local and state investigators.

The old sinking feeling of lost opportunities settled over Lynne as she
surveyed the damage done to the site. The crime scene had not been managed. Rather, it had been a bungle of inept curiosities. Incautious exuber-
ance revealed itself at every turn. She had expected as much. The
photographs Doc had given her had suggested the uncontrolled impatience of the investigators, although she had remained hopeful. She was
not hopeful any longer, and worried what errors had been committed
inside the cabin.

Lynne slowly she inhaled the crisp mountain air and held her breath to
a slow count of four before exhaling slowly. By calming and centering, she
gentled herself away from useless disgruntlement of a botched job and
tried to refocus on her errand. She relaxed, opened her eyes, and started
to walk to the cabin.

A muffled air-puncturing sound spilled down a mountain ridge, star-
tling Lynne. The rifle shots and retorts splintered off the hills and echoed
in the trees around her. She ducked and reflexively reached for the .45 on
her right hip as her eyes searched the meadow. Distance? Direction? The
rarefied air and interfering contours of mountains and tree-packed slopes
bounced the menacing echoes around her in confusing array. She waited.
The firing stopped.

How many shots? Four? Lynne's mind whirled as it tried to recount the flashing events. From her crouched, uncovered position, she laughed derisively at the way being shot at tended to break normal concentration and refocus it significantly. She bunched her leg muscles and propelled herself forward. She ran to the porch of the cabin making her as small a target as possible. She bounded up the stairs and flattened herself protectively against the wall.

Under the shadow of the porch eaves, she breathed a little easier but did not relax. Straining her ears, Lynne searched for stray sounds across the expanse of the meadow, and waited. Nothing. Silence, and the whisper of the timber's nodding resistance to the breeze, was the only sounds that met her ears. Habit and caution held her. Half an hour passed as she maintained her vigilance.

Dropping off the south side of the porch, Lynne moved warily toward the rear of the cabin. The snow and ice had been churned up and frozen over several times during the week. Snowmobiles and boot tracks muddied the ground and made her footing hazardous as she circled the cabin. Nothing and no one challenged her. She relaxed her wariness a tiny degree, and looked closely at the area surrounding the cabin and toward the shed against the tree line. She saw a curious wavering stain receding into the distance, marring the windblown expanse of the meadow. She walked toward the blemishes and knelt down beside a set of the stains for a closer look. Her eyes narrowed as she raised her head to follow the trail. Lone snow-dusted, man-sized boot prints suggested themselves across the western expanse of the clearing. One pair of boots. Going out and back the same way.

"'Perp,'" she said, and cocked a wry grin at the vanishing line of tracks. Uncluttered by other boot prints, she was confident the investigators who had destroyed the other impression evidence in the yard around the cabin had not caused them.

"That's one," she whispered to the tracks. Her penchant for reciting the child's game while investigating homicides rolled off her tongue. There were thirteen steps up the gallows walk to the hangman. She counted the murderer on the first step of the short final walk. She went back to her truck to get her camera. "Some fine day," she chanted as she felt herself drawn into the chase.

As she finished photographing the footprints and exterior crime scene, she walked back to the cabin's porch. She stood facing the door and tried to imagine herself as the perpetrator on the night of the murder. Lynne closed her eyes to slip into the mood and talked herself through the feelings.

"I'm not random. I know what I am doing. I know where I am. I parked my vehicle on the far side of the meadow and walked here in the dark. The cold night covers me in comfortable expectation. I live around here. That's how I know about the road and these cabins. I heard in town that a woman was staying out here alone. I've been thinking about it for days and finally got my nerve up to come out here." She closed her eyes and leaned against the door. It felt right. A stranger would not have risked his neck crossing the frozen field. A stranger with murderous intent would have pulled up to the front of the cabin or a short distance into the drive.

Whoever the murderer was did not want the Pevey's to notice his vehicle. A local vehicle would be easily identified by familiarity. And a passing stranger would have needed luck to find someone staying at the cabins in off-season. A local stalker would only have to pay attention and make inconsequential inquiries among unsuspecting acquaintances. Information would have been shared as part of the local gossip. Inquiries from a stranger would have met with curiosity. Curiosity was not something normally wanted by even the most opportunistic murderer.

"That's two." She opened her eyes on the count, and turned around to try the cabin's door. It was locked. There were no signs of forced entry.

Nothing on the exterior suggested to her that the murderer had forced his way in. His victim had allowed him to walk into the cabin. She wondered if Beverly had known her assailant or if he were as smooth a talker, as he was homicidal.

Lynne peered into the window on the right side of the door but delicately patterned curtains obscured her view of the living room. The window on the left side offered her a slightly better view of the kitchen. The latch had not been firmly set. She grabbed the sides of the window and shook the frame to test the tightness of fit. Satisfied, she reached into her pocket, retrieved and opened a thin blade knife. She slid the blade between the edges of the trim until it met the latch in the hasp.

Before crawling through the opened window, she withdrew a rag from a parka pocket. Lynne cleaned off her boots carefully removing the clinging snow and dirt. She did not want to leave any tracks for others to find or confuse herself with her own imprints inside the cabin. Once inside she saw that she had no reason for concern. Snow-dried dirty boot prints littered the kitchen floor. She noted that the table had been cleared but telltale powder circles faintly outlined the previous locations of a dish, cup and spoon. She would have to luck upon fresh and unadulterated prints elsewhere.

"Now,…where would I be," Lynne, said and hummed to herself as she eyed the kitchen cabinets and sink counter spaces, "if I were coffee?" As she walked over to the cabinets, she pulled on a pair of light plastic gloves. She reached up and opened the first cabinet door.

"Bingo," she said as she looked at the coffee can. "Can't have coffee without the grounds, can we?" She left the can where she found it with the intention of retrieving it later. "That's three, Bucko." She hoped that the can would hold good prints. She smiled to herself enjoying, as always, the little things she encountered in an investigation. It was the expected and the unexpected, which revealed the lifetime of the crime. They were keys to murder. It would have had a rhythm, an order, and expectations set within the broad framework of normalcy of human behavior.

Nothing about human behavior was abnormal. Anything could and would happen. If it could be imagined, it could be done. The range of possibilities was almost unlimited. The only thing's, which would limit and throw boundaries up around behavior, could be seen in the details. But one had to know what they were looking at, what they were looking for, and recognize it when they saw it. Devils were in the details. Details present and missing. Details were her expertise. She knew the devils that haunted and tormented. They would reveal themselves in what should be present, what should be absent, what should have been done or left undone within parameters of bounded human rationality claimed every criminal.

Things that did not fit had to be accounted for added up and reshuffled until it balanced as a whole. The small inconsequential beginnings and endings of actions like the large and easily visible left their traces throughout any human undertaking. Lynne had learned how to understand the combination of human actions and intentions from the simple to the profound. It was not just a matter of learning how to think like a thief to catch a thief, but learning how to live with consciously and purposeful intention rather than to conduct one's affairs through an unexamined life.

Reaching inside her parka, Lynne pulled out the package of black and white photos taken by a deputy and examined them and the room in which she stood. She walked into the living room and rested on her haunches to look back across the linoleum floor. Underneath the table, two elongated black marks made faint comma-like streaks across the polished surface. No other part of the flooring contained similar marks. She crawled forward and gently touched the closest mark. Her index finger detected the smudged ridge welt on the surface. As she moved her finger across it, a tiny chip of the black rubber came away in her fingernail. Black-soled boots had scuffed the floor, revealing the signs of a possible struggle. She photographed the marks then removed some residue with her thin-edged knife and placed it in a small glass vile.

Nothing further called for her attention in the kitchen or living room. Lynne moved down the hallway. The spare room was unremarkable. The bathroom door stood open and she eyed the interior. A touch of gray fingerprint powder had been dusted across the porcelain of both tub and sink. A hint of thin wavy lines clashed with the geometric regularity of the floor pattern. She turned on the bathroom and hallway lights for more illumination. The marks were the same type of scoring as those found in the kitchen.

"Curious," Lynne whispered to herself as she got down on all fours to examine the floor and fixtures more intently. Looking up, she noticed the exterior of the commode and decided to be compulsive and duck her head into the small space between the tub. A splash of color contrasting with the sparkling white of the commode surface immediately drew her attention. Under the rim and bowl of the commode was the oxidized smear of dried blood. Lynne sat back and retrieved a penlight from a pocket in her parka. Lying down on the cold floor, she squeezed herself back into the tiny space.

With the light from the penlight, she noticed that the faint trailing edges of the blood smears never gained the edge of the front of the commode. Her light followed the trail down the back and side of the bowl. Back there, behind the bowl, the dried blood clarified into the recognizable shape of a partial palm print. Lynne whistled softly to herself. The side of a palm, mound of the thumb, and the spottily smeared forms of the two smallest fingers from a large hand streaked across the porcelain.

"That's four, Rube, and we're getting real close to you on this count. Lynne spent the next fifteen minutes adjusting her camera, film and position. She patiently framed the pictures in flash, without flash, and other minor adjustments to ensure the greatest likelihood of obtaining readability of the print. She used a roll of film just in case the state investigators would not be able to lift it for examination at a lab. Lynne hummed to herself as she worked, and wished she had brought more of her equipment.

When she stopped and tried to rest back on her knees, she discovered that the cold of the cabin floor had crept into her joints. Dull streaks of pain stung across her kneecaps. Gingerly, she stood up.

"Baseball or criminalistics, the knees go first," she mused as she hobbled down the hall to the bedroom where they found Beverly's body.

Lynne stood at the door looking at the disarray of the room. The bloodstained mattress was still there. It had been photographed from a variety of angles. The photographs she did not have were those she had originally brought her camera to take. Blood splatters on the walls, over the headboard of the bed, and flecked across the ceiling were not represented in the photographs' Doc had given her. She corrected the oversight. She took out a tape measure and notepad. Working carefully, she recorded the detailed size and direction of the splatters. The creation of an accurate scaled representation and analysis would depend on her exactness. She worked intensely and contentedly during the next hour.

Glancing at her watch, she realized she had been at the cabin over three hours. It was time to leave. Patting her pockets to make sure all her belongings were present, she secured the snaps and Velcro closures on her parka to ensure the safe journey of the contents, and crawled back out the kitchen window.

"Four steps up, boy-yo, four steps and rising," she breathed into the fresh air. Lynne looked around again at the road rising toward the cabin and tried to make sure she was still alone.

Back in her truck, Lynne turned north on the Half Moon Road to see where it would lead. She was not surprised when it made a wide ellipse to the far side of the meadow and along a tree-lined road behind the cabins. She drove until she lined her truck up with the slanting shed and the direction the heavy boot prints had made across the snow. She peered at the clear-cut between the tree line and road.

"Its a count of five, darlin'," she said as she pulled her truck forward and found the boot prints between the trees. She climbed out of the truck and made short work of photographing the prints, the tires tread impressions in the still frozen snow, and the rear view of the cabins in the distance.

The murderer had been successful, smart and calculating. So far, his calculations had paid off in his continued freedom. She knew his success would only serve to encourage him. He had driven in, walked to the cabin, done the deed, and drove out with no one the wiser.

Distracted by her own thoughts as she drove back to town, Lynne almost did not see the dog limping beside the roadway. As she slowed her truck, she saw that the left side of his golden coat was splattered with blood. Holding one paw in front of himself, he hopped determinedly down the road.

She stopped the truck and walked slowly, behind him, calling softly. He studiously ignored her. Lynne walked back to her truck and opened the passenger side door.

"Here boy, come here," she called.

He stopped, sat, and eyed her suspiciously.

She was caught between wanting to help and feeling wary of him. She knew an injured animal could be a dangerous thing. As much as she wanted to see that he got taken care of, she did not want to get bit. Lynne called to him again as she got back in the truck and slowly drove to where he was sitting. He did not move. They looked at each other through the open door. When she called to him again, he whined anxiously but hesitated at her offer. Lynne patted the seat next to her and clicked her tongue softly in encouragement. He leaped into the truck and lay down on the floorboard, his head near her foot. Lynne spoke gently to him as she reached over and closed the door.

16

Sunday Lynne took the whole day and used it for herself in necessary and comfortable rituals. She felt the need to escape after days and nights of steeping herself in the quizzes of the murder with its sparse clues. All the issues would percolate, sift, and grind against themselves beneath the mundane burdens of life. She let herself become absorbed in the mindless life-sustaining activities of paying bills, doing laundry, and cleaning the apartment at the Gellmore building. The small mercies of routine and convention breathed life back into her.

When all the required duties had been complying with, she returned to the Corbin Hotel and rummaged through a box of books she had brought in from her truck. She counted them among her treasures. The books drew her to them as the afternoon marched on. It was an eclectic mix of curious titles in fiction, criticism, and psychology that invited her to give them further inquiry and examination. It was a smorgasbord for the mind. Each book well wore or new, held fresh and refreshing possibilities. She spread them out across the floor of her hotel room and poured over them, picking a chapter here, an indexed topic there and a paragraph when it caught her eye. She read for sport, perspective and as an investment in herself.

At six, she made hot tea in the diminutive kitchen of the hotel room, and took the delicate black pot to the table. She glanced at the clock. She had a little time before her guests arrived. Time enough to pop into the shower, invigorate her mind, and leave behind the self-imposed lethargy of the day.

Promptly at seven-thirty, she heard a light rapping on her door. Leaving the coffeepot to its business of perking a fresh brew, she answered the door.

"People will talk." Charlie glanced mischievously from Lynne to Doc as they stepped into the room.

"People always do, even if they have to make it up. If we were seen, we just gave them something new to story about," Doc said as he glanced about the room, removed his coat, and headed for the oak kitchen table.

"Of course. But in the telling, the two of you will probably gain some status and I'll be cast as the fallen woman," Lynne said as she shut the door behind them.

Lynne unplugged the coffeepot and brought it and cups to the table. As she watched herself perform the ritual, she had to smile. The casualness with which they began the evening made it seem like a social call. But it was all business.

"What do you think?" Charlie hesitantly asked.

"The place was a mess but that's what you were getting at, wasn't it?" she said as she looked over at Doc. He nodded in agreement.

"A mess?" Charlie said, as he raised an eyebrow over the steaming cup of coffee.

"I told you," Doc said shooting a glance at Charlie and back to the file folder Lynne had placed on the table. "They had ten or twelve people out there running all over the place. Gradey must have called in every off-duty deputy he could get his hands on. You would have thought he was the sheriff the way he strutted around poking his nose into everything and bellowing orders at people. Anyway, after he got through calling in the Mounties, he called the para-meds and state police boys. By the time I got there the place looked like revelers at a convention for all the lack of control and coordination."

"The place was pretty well tracked up. But the cabin wasn't too bad. It looked as though someone had been in to do some tidying up. That was a little strange," Lynne said, sifting through her notes.

"If they did tidy up, it must have been after I had them load the body into the para-meds van. To credit Deputy Gradey some, he did try to keep most of his folks out of the cabin. But between him and the state boys, there were at least five or six people in the house at one time. All of them were climbing over each other and generally getting in the way," Doc said as he remembered that afternoon.

"When I got there, I heard someone shooting."

"Shooting at you? Do you think the killer came back?" Charlie said, looking anxiously at Lynne.

"I don't know. I don't think so. It was close but I could not really tell where it was coming from. The shots echoed off the hills and bounced around a lot."

"Poachers or someone out playing with their toys for fun."

"Could have been? But it did make me a little jumpy. I mean, there I was sneaking around where I did not belong and then, someone starts shooting. Raised my quotient of enlightened self-interest about a hundred percent!" Lynne said as she refilled her coffee cup and stirred in an ice cube thoughtfully.

"Did you see anyone?"

"No. Nothing. Just shots. Four or five, I think, and then nothing. But I did find a dog on my way back to town. He had been shot. He might have been what they were aiming at."

"Someone probably mistook him for a deer, or were trying to run off a stray pest," Charlie reasoned. He had seen more than a few strays dropped off on his property, and knew that they could become wild and attack weakened or young livestock. He had lost several lambs last spring to a pack of wild dogs.

"Not a stray. At least I don't think so. This one had a collar, but I guess that does not prove he's not a stray. Anyway, I took him to a vet. Cost me fifty Double Eagles to have her look at him. Maybe she can locate the owner."

"He has a tag?" Doc asked.

"Yes. It said Fred. No owner's name or address."

"Fred? Fred is Greg Hanson's dog. You remember that mutt, don't you, Doc?" Charlie said, pouncing on the name.

"Greg or the dog?" Doc laughed. "Yes, on both counts. Be just like Greg using his dog for target practice. Boy never had respect for anything. It's not like you'll get your money back either."

"Doesn't matter. I just didn't feel like leaving him out there. Maybe, if he, I'll see if this Greg wants to sell him or give him away. I could use a watch dog in the store after all the unwanted foot traffic I've had in it lately," Lynne speculated. She had not owned a dog since she was in high school. He might not be much of a watchdog but he might be company. And he might be in the market for a new owner if his master had been the one doing the shooting.

"Don't let him know you got money. He'll try to steal you blind for the mutt," Charlie advised.

"Whatever."

"You had some day," Doc observed.

"Certainly did. There were some interesting things at the cabin. Maybe some things you can turn over to the state authorities or sheriff to have them look at."

"You found some things?" Charlie asked.

"Enough," Lynne said. "What I found may be a key to the guy's identity, but we won't know until it's all been through analysis."

"What?"

"Well, I found a bloody palm print. Actually a partial."

"You're kidding!" Charlie interjected.

"No. No, I'm not. Its location was unusual and I'm betting they missed it because it had not been disturbed."

"How in the hell could they miss it?"

"Well, it's likely they just didn't expect the guy to be grabbing the commode. I don't know if he were upchucking, or what but he had to have been on his knees and hanging onto the thing to get his hand back there."

"Then we've got him," Charlie said cheerfully.

"Not necessarily, but we may have a better chance."

"What do you mean?"

"It doesn't do any good to have any kind of print unless you have something to compare it against. If the guy has never been arrested, there will not be print one available for comparison. And a print is a print. You can try to match it here or send it off to the FBI, but unless you have some clue, they will have to check it against the millions of prints they have on their system. That's for starts and, unfortunately, it was only a partial palm print. Even the FBI doesn't have palm prints on file." "So, either we match it here or the Feds do? What's the problem?" Doc said in agitation.

"Let me explain," Lynne began slowly. 'The public has some pretty high and unrealistic expectations of investigations and forensics. Sometimes, we are at fault for making the real hard work look like magic and its neither simple nor magical. But the public's higher expectations ultimately lowered its confidence if we do not do as well as they think we should."

"We may have a possibility. But the palm print has to belong to someone who has been printed before. What I found was a palm print with no fingers or partials that might be used for comparison. Our boy had to have been arrested for a felony, applied for a security job, or has been in the armed forces to have his prints on file with the Feds. That still won't get us anywhere if the partials aren't readable or have too few points for comparison." She wanted them to know how daunting even the most foolproof appearing clues could be.

"So we won't know?" Charlie said, looking defeated.

"We can hope. First things first. Doc, you've got to take these rolls of film to the Sheriff and have them developed. You also need to tell them where the print is so they can lift it. The rest of the film has boot and tire track photographs. They could probably get clear resolution for additional detail. I have made a few notes so they can go locate the places where I photographed them. They can go and cast impressions. But they should hurry. The snow and ice could begin to thaw or other vehicles may run over them. If that happens, their usefulness will be lost," Lynne said as she pushed a package across the table toward Doc.

"Me? How'm I going to explain what I'm doing with this stuff?" Doc asked, and moved his hands away from the package. "You know what you are doing. You can explain it to them."

"No. I can't. Leastwise not like you can. You're the coroner. Tell them you went back out there because you were snooping. You've got an excuse. I have no legitimate reason for being out there. If I go to the Sheriff's office with this, they are more likely to throw me in jail as a suspect or for interfering with an investigation," Lynne insisted. She knew how she would have reacted if someone had ever had the audacity to get in the middle of one of her investigations. She would have thrown them in jail and thought about what charges to file later.

"But, look at what you've already done. You found more than anyone else did. Seems to me they would be grateful. You could help us wrap this up before the town gets crazier than it already is," Doc encouraged and pushed the package back toward Lynne.

"I don't think so. I just stepped into someone else's nest. And no matter who you are, you are never grateful for having your faults pointed out. Very few people are that mature and if we say we are, sometimes we're just kidding ourselves." Lynne shoved the package back to Doc and held it against his reluctant hand.

"All right, Doc. Do what the lady asks. She's done what we asked her to do. The least we can do is see to it that what she found gets made use of," Charlie interjected.

"It's everything I can do. I have got a business to put together here, and I have got to get on with it. I cannot afford to get hooked into this. Have a little faith in the folks who still do this for a living. I'm sure it will work out for the best," Lynne said. She was done with it. She was concerned that she had let her former life slip back in on her but she was determined not to let it overtake her. But her interest was peeking and a small war waged quietly inside her.

"O.K. I'll keep you out of it," Doc said as he picked up the package.

"There's another thing," Lynne said quietly. "I feel certain he's a local, or someone very familiar and comfortable with the area."

"You'd mentioned the possibility before. What makes you so certain?"

"It's the time he took to do the deed. The reports and the photographs of the scene suggest that he knew he had time, was sheltered from prying eyes, and confident in his comings and goings. If you do not know an area, you cannot get comfortable. There would be too many unknown chances you would not want to take. That is why I am certain he knows the area. I found his tracks leading to where he parked his vehicle behind the cabins. He would have had to walk across that field in the dark. That is not something I would chance, or any other stranger. He had had coffee and breakfast in an interlude during or after the murder. He leisurely smoked cigarettes, cleaned up the kitchen, and took his souvenirs. All that takes time and confidence born of familiarity."

"What souvenir?" Charlie interjected.

"I didn't mention it before," Doc said, glancing quickly at Charlie. His face paled with the memory. "I didn't mention it because it's not the sort of thing you want to remember."

"Worse than cutting her head off and propping it in the window?" Charlie asked.

"Not worse, but just as bad and an indication of how sick this puppy is," Lynne offered. "He cut off her right breast. It was not found at the scene. I can only assume he still has it. He also took the bedspread and sheets after he had washed her down. I figure he was trying to remove any trace of evidence related to the rape and sodomy."

"Good Lord," Charlie said, shuddering.

"Let me assure you that God has very little to do with this. This guy enjoyed himself, took his time, experimented, got comfy, and had the presence of mind to clean up after himself," Lynne expanded. "He's not just a little dangerous. He is very dangerous. He has his own reasons for doing what he is doing. And he probably feels very competent and confident right about now."

"Meaning?"

"Meaning, he'll do it again. Trouble is, we do not know when, where, or who. The only thing I can be certain of is that he will find someone else. He went hunting once. He'll go hunting again."

"We've got to find him. He needs to be caught," Doc said as he grabbed hold of the package Lynne had given him as though he thought it would try to leave on its own volition.

"To say the least,…to say the very least."

17

The afternoon had been hard in coming. Although the sky had remained clear for most of the day, it now seemed to signal an intention to change. A blanket of moisture-laden clouds had begun to threaten the peaks of the mountains. From his office window, Sheriff Brett Callison could see the first tendrils of fog sneaking down the high slopes, and gray leviathan clouds nosed their sluggish migration toward town. He hoped they would spend their load of snow before they reached the wide gulch that held Leadville. He was tired. The call he had received from Deputy Gradey had interrupted his vacation. He was tired of the clouds that bore down on his mood and converged like all the questions surrounding the murder.

He stood watching the heavy clouds, as his eyes searched the veiled horizon. He stood with his hands behind his back, his legs resting at an unconscious parade rest. Callison shoulders and chest fit snugly in the tailored dark hunter green uniform shirt. The creases of his matching trousers had not been ruined by the morning's desk duties. His eyes moved across his reflection and he smiled at the muscular six-foot tall

double in the window. A head of close-cropped hair and a practiced rogu-
ish grin nodded back at him.

He had turned to the window to seek relief from the photographs scattered across his desk. The ruined images of the young woman had been
all too well captured in the black and white mat finish. The stilled reflection tugged at the corners of his eyes. Stark and paralyzed facsimiles of
the woman's last hours perverted his interest in the day. He decided to
take it personally.

"Tourists," he snorted. Someone had been out there. Brett Callison
knew the hordes of tourists had finally brought their own homegrown
beasts with them. He hated tourists. It did not matter that they were the
economic lifeblood of the region. He hated their intrusion on the sanity
and sanctity of the valley. They nudged, pushed and shoved their condos,
ski slopes, snowmobiles, and chain saws into the defenseless tree-filled
ranges. Worse, the murder had happened in an election year, and Callison
knew from experience that there was nothing worse to undermine the
confidence of the county in general and the Sheriff in particular, than an
unsolved murder in an election year. That was how he had gotten his job
six years ago. A local boy made good and returned with moneymaking
expertise intact. Then the murder had gone unsolved and the former
Sheriff had gone on to sell insurance in Aurora.

Sheriff Callison had to solve the murder. He was too set in his career
to have it all fall away now. As bad as it was, she was a tourist and not a
local. There might be some positive mileage there. She had brought the
seeds of her own destruction with her. Maybe he could sell the idea that
someone followed her. The husband, a lover, a pickup between transients,
anything of that sort would calm the citizenry. Until then, he had to try
to straighten out the cobbled investigation and pray for luck. Turning

from the window, he saw Deputy Gradey standing in the doorway staring at him.

"What?" Callison asked as he sat back down at his desk and dared the day to get more difficult or aggravating.

"Katherine Ward, the vet, called from over at Pine Creek Veterinary Hospital. Wants you to come over right away."

"The vet? Why?"

"She wouldn't say. She just told me to get you over there. Sounded like she thought it was important."

"Great! Not like I have anything better to do!" Callison blustered, and threw his pen. It flew toward the deputy and landed at his feet. Gradey quickly shut the door and fled.

As Callison pulled up in front of the low squat buildings of the Pine Valley Veterinary Hospital, he heard the varied complaints of dogs and other large animals confined in their runs. He absently wondered how anyone could get used to the constant calliope of noise, all too common to vet clinics.

"Hello?" Callison called as he entered the empty front office. The aromas of tinctures, medicines and animals assaulted his nose.

"Back here," a woman's voice responded.

Walking behind the counter, Callison picked his way around a small corridor of interlocking offices.

"Keep coming," the voice encouraged to Callison.

He entered what was an operating theater and found a tall, angular, ruddy-complexioned woman wearing a bibbed canvas apron as she sutured the dog on the operating table. She was bent studiously to her work.

"Be with you in a jiffy," Katherine Ward said, glancing up at him. "Have a seat."

"What's this all about?"

"Keep your britches on. I've got to close Gertie here before she comes around," Katherine said, without looking up at the Sheriff.

Callison settled onto the cool surface of a metal stool and tried to hold on to what little patience he had.

"There you go, girl," Katherine said as she tenderly patted the dog's head. "She's had too many pups, too soon. Her poor insides were about to fall out on the floor. But that's all over now, isn't it? You can play now but not have to pay the price." She unhooked the locks on the operating table wheels and rolled her charge over to a recovery cage. Sliding the roller tabletop into the cage, she deposited the dog gently onto the blanketed surface.

As Katherine Ward stood at the scrub sink, she directed her attention to Callison. "What I've got to show you is over here." She motioned with her elbow to a second cage. "Came in yesterday. A woman brought him in. Said she'd found him on the highway outside town."

"A dog?" Callison asked as he stared into the cage, wondering what he was supposed to do about the dog.

"Of course it's a dog. But he had human blood smeared all over him and smelled like a brewery. Someone has spilled booze all over him," Katherine said pointedly.

"Human blood? How'd you know?"

"Curiosity, mostly. He was a real mess when he came in. He had been shot in the foot and stabbed in the chest. The bullet separated his toes but missed the bone. I almost lost him 'cause he'd lost so much blood," she said as she opened the cage door and stroked the dog's head. The tranquilizers had him out cold. "Whoever shot and stabbed him didn't get good aim. The knife wounds tore across the plate of his sternum and ripped down into his chest muscle. He'll be sore as hell, but he ought to recover."

"What about the human blood?"

"Oh, yeah. I was cleaning him off and, like I said, he'd lost a lot of blood. Maybe got a piece of whoever tried to kill him? I know I surely would have tried if I'd have been him," she said as she walked over to a long cabinet filled with testing instruments and microscopes.

"See here," she said, peering into the microscope. "These red blood cells and platelets on the left are his. The ones on the right are human. You can tell by the shape," she explained, and gestured to the microscope.

Callison stared through the lens. Shapes swam before his eyes. Round globules and softer looking, nearly transparent things floated on the viewing glass.

"I can't tell the difference, not even if one side barked, Miss..." Callison hesitated.

"Doctor Ward, not Miss anything, Sheriff Callison," she corrected him.

"I bet not,...Dr. Ward," Callison said under his breath.

"Not much and not often. Way I see it, you've got someone out there with a big whole or two in him."

"Why him and not her?" he countered.

"For one, the dog's not rabid. Two, I said a woman brought him in. Dogs aren't fools. If she or some other woman had tried to shoot or stab him, he would have tried to kill her as simple matter of reflex. She would never have gotten near him. When he growled at my Hank, the woman and I had to carry him in here. He wasn't going to have anything to do with a man."

"Hank?"

"My husband. You don't get around much, do you, Sheriff?"

"Apparently not enough. Tell me about this woman," he said as he took out a notebook from his shirt pocket.

"Don't know much to tell. I think she said she was staying at a hotel in town. Drove a blue pickup truck with a camper on the back. I think she had out of state plates. Kansas, maybe," Dr. Ward said as she cupped her chin in her hand and stared at the smooth cement floor trying to remember.

"She tell you where she found him?"

"Best I could get was she found him south of town. Said he was limping his way along like he was headed into Leadville and home."

"Do you know what hotel she's staying at?"

"No. She didn't say. I didn't ask. She did paid fifty Double Eagles for his care. That was decent of her. Most people wouldn't do that sort of thing. 'Course, that's about a hundred or so short of the expense of transfusion and surgery."

"Right," Callison said absently. "Did the dog have any identification?"

"Yeah, a tag. But all it says is his name's Fred. Could be the owner's name? I have never had him in here before. I know that. If you find out, let me know so I can send them the rest of the bills."

"Could be,...could be he killed his owner?"

"Serve him right," Dr. Ward interjected.

"Hold on to the dog. If he did kill a man he'll have to be destroyed," Callison said as he closed his note pad and turned to leave. He made a note next to the dog's name and underlined the name Greg Hanson. Callison frowned at the note wondering if Greg had survived the attack.

"We'll just have to see about that, Sheriff. Even an animal has a right to defend itself. No dog should be treated that way," Dr. Ward asserted at Collision's retreating.

"Sure, sure." He waived back at her, and walked out the door. He had two people to locate. Greg and some woman from Kansas in a blue pickup truck who liked to pick up strays.

Nearing his patrol car, he kicked the tire. Callison did not believe in luck, except his own bad luck. He got in the car and grabbed the mike. "Sue," he called into dispatch.

"Yes, Sheriff?"

"Tell Gradey to call the hospital and check around with the other doctors in the county. See if anyone has had a report of a gunshot or vehicular injury walk in the last twenty-four hours. After he does that, tell him to meet me over at Greg Hanson's residence."

"Right, Sheriff."

"You can be a big help, too, if you would, Hon," Callison's voice encouraged Sue.

"What d'ya need, Sheriff?"

"Call around to the hotels and motels in town and see if there are any blue pickups from Kansas registered to a woman or a couple from Kansas." He liked getting all the balls rolling at once.

"Sure thing."

"Hold what you find out 'til I get back to the station."

"You got it," Sue said cheerfully. She liked working for him. He had hired her straight out of VO-tech School when she needed a job. Getting pregnant out of wedlock had set her at odds with her family. Callison had not judged her and never asked any questions about the absent father.

"Good girl," Callison said as he headed the patrol car to the East Side of town, the proverbial wrong side of the tracks, where Greg's ramshackle house would be found.

Sue beamed at the microphone as she handed Gradey the message. "Sweet man," she said softly, thinking of the Sheriff as she dialed the first hotel listed in the telephone book.

Half a block from Hanson's house, Callison waved Gradey over to the side of the street. Gradey got out of his patrol car and got into the Sheriff's car.

"What's up?"

Callison gave Gradey a quick rundown of the events. Gradey eyed Hanson's house for movement while the Sheriff shared his speculations.

"Could be someone's killed Hanson instead of his dog finishing him off. Could be he's at home trying to lick his own wounds. Whatever, we're going to play it by the book until we know for sure."

"What do you want me to do?"

"Be backup. I want you to take your car and go down the alley behind his house. Wait for my signal and then approach the back without getting spotted. I'll take the front," Callison said as he picked up the mike.

"Why the big deal. Why don't we just go in and get him?" Gradey interrupted.

"Because," Callison took his finger off the mike, "he may be drunk and he may be involved in more than we know for sure right now. One thing we do know, he's got guns in there. Other than that, it makes good sense because I told you so. That clear enough?" Callison said in exasperation. Gradey's impatience wasn't a flaw Callison could help him with.

Callison had been trying to help Gradey smarten up. After three years, he felt he had almost nothing to show for it. Training episode after training episode at the academy and Gradey still had trouble putting it together. Callison knew what the problem was. He knew that all the training in the world would not make up for poor selection. The previous Sheriff had hired Gradey. A good 'ole boy with good intentions. He was stuck with one of his more misguided attempts at good intentions. A good carpenter never blamed his tools, but he might question the quality of materials.

"Sue, run me a registration on Colorado tag NRH 437. That's on a white and green trimmed Ford, looks to be about a 1986, 150 model."

While Callison and Gradey waited for Sue to run the registration, they watched the house and neighborhood silently. The tiny gray-washed house was not much larger than an apartment. The front porch sagged precariously under the weight of a discarded burgundy recliner. Callison figured the recliner was Greg's attempt at lawn furniture. Most of the houses in the three-block area made braver attempts than Greg had and showed a semblance of repair. Callison knew that poor was poor. It did not necessarily follow that a trashy and mean appearance was required.

"Sheriff?" Sue called over the radio.

"Go ahead."

"The truck belongs to Greg Hanson. Tag's expired. We don't have any wants or warrants currently."

"Thanks," Callison said, and turned to Gradey. "O.K. Go ahead. Just remember that we don't want him getting out the back. Cover yourself. Remember we only want to ask him a few questions. He may not be alone. You know he's got a lot of drinking buddies."

"Too many," Gradey said as he climbed out of the car.

Callison waited at the curb until he saw Gradey drive down the alley. When Gradey parked near the dumpster in the alley, Callison moved his car within three houses of Greg's house. He got out of his vehicle and proceeded on foot. As Callison moved toward the front door, he saw Gradey jogging through back yard and position himself behind an electrical pole behind Greg's house. He watched as Gradey drew his gun and held it at ready down along his leg.

On the porch, Callison moved lightly, trying to avoid loose boards that might signal his presence. He listened at the door for a moment but could not hear movement or indications of life inside. He drew his gun and used the barrel to knock on the door. Using the doorjamb as best available cover, he tried to make his body into a smaller target.

"Greg! Greg Hanson! This is Sheriff Callison. I want to talk to you. You're not in any trouble.

"Greg, come on. Open the door. I want to make sure you're all right," Callison called as he shifted his feet and crouched in tensed readiness. "We got your dog at the vet's. He's been hurt bad. Vet says he'll be all right, though. Are you all right in there?" Dogs in nearby yards took up alarm at the sound of the loud, strange voice and passed it around the neighborhood.

"Gradey," Callison spoke into his walkie-talkie. "I'm going to go in. Get ready." Two clicks on the mike told Callison that Gradey had heard and understood.

"All right, Greg. I'm coming in. Don't do anything stupid," he warned, and punctuated the last word by throwing himself against the door. It yielded immediately and he rolled into the darkened room. No one challenged his entry. He rose and walked cautiously through the house. Trash, beer cans, dirty clothes, and other remnants of Greg's scant belongings were strewn about the house. When he reached the back door, he radioed Gradey to come inside.

"Any signs?" Gradey called as he loped through the door.

"No. You see any thing in the back?"

"Nary a thing."

"Open some of these shades. Let's nose around. See if we can come up with anything."

"Messy bastard, ain't he?" Gradey asked, looking around the rooms.

"You Suzie Homemaker now?"

"No, but I live better than this," Gradey insisted.

The search was fruitless. No blood. No weapons. There was nothing inside to conveniently link Greg with the murder or the injuries to his dog. The only sign of Greg had been his truck. The engine had been cold for a long time. There was no way of telling where he might have gotten.

"Any luck with the hospitals?" Callison asked as he walked past the dispatcher's desk when he got back to the office.

"Nothing so far," Joe responded.

"How 'bout you, Suzie Q?"

"I got three hits," Sue said brightly.

"Good girl. What have you got?" he asked, and leaned closer to her as he tried to read from the notepad she held.

"I found three Kansas staying in our fair city and vicinity. Two have cars, so I eliminated them. The third one is a woman who has a truck, like the one you described. Her name is Lynne Fhaolain, I think. I had them repeat it three times to me. She's been in town a week, or so, and is staying at the Corbin. But she's not there right now. She's over at the old Gellmore building. The desk clerk told me she's bought the place and is fixing it up," Sue finished out of breath, and beamed up at him.

"You're a marvel," he said, and patted her on the shoulder. Taking the notes she offered, he turned and looked around at the other officers in the station. "She makes us all look bad," he warned them. "A little more time here and I'll have to hire you as one of my deputies." He winked at Sue and strode out of the office.

"You want me to go with you, Sheriff?" Gradey asked, calling after him.

Callison turned around and eyed Gradey. Deputies near Gradey recognized the look on Callison's face and hurriedly found some busy work to do.

"No. I don't think so. You could stay here and help Joe with the calls. I think I can talk to this woman all by myself," he said as he watched the backs and shoulders of several deputies moving in muffled spasms of laughter. His anger flared as he realized that his reputation of hot and cold luck with women had become a point of general office conversation and amusement. Most people avoided the slightest hint of knowledge that the ladies of his acquaintance came and went. Some more quietly than others. The ones who stayed longest had been of a type: dependent, dependable, and satisfied with an infrequent pat on the head he might give them. Others, made of stronger stuff, were rebuffed by his condescending behavior and long out of sight almost before anyone knew they had been around.

"You think the rest of you could get out of here and go protect our county?" Callison asked in a commanding tone from the door. At the rebuff, he heard desks and chairs grate into quick motion as they headed for their patrol cars.

He found the truck parked in front of the Gellmore building. He noticed workers gathering up their tools and cleaning up their work areas as he entered the building. Callison recognized several workers who watched him as he walked through the debris of their endeavors.

"George," Callison called to the man nearest him.

"Sheriff." The man barely acknowledged him and continued to put his tools away instead of looking up.

"George," the Sheriff said pointedly. The man turned and looked at him. "Where might I find a Lynne Fhaolain?"

"Fhaolain,..." George pronounced it slowly. "She's upstairs in the apartment." He slowly turned his back to the Sheriff to finish placing his saws carefully in the toolbox.

The old man's brush off infuriated Callison but there was no law against ignoring a Sheriff. Callison fumed his way up the stairs of the store.

"Hello? Anyone home?" Callison called up the stairs as he approached the third floor. There was no answer. Only the soft melody of jazz strayed through the door.

As he reached the top of the stairs, he saw a woman at the end of the room gesturing enthusiastically to John Bowannie who stood by patiently nodding his head. They made an interesting silhouette against the sliding glass doors. The woman speaking to Bowannie made small gentle gesturing to emphasize her points. The old man was apparently absorbing the instructions and the intent with easy tolerance. She was intense and straight as a ramrod. Bowannie was taller, age bent and patient. For a moment Callison felt as though he'd interrupted something personal and compatible, and that he should beg pardon and leave. He shook it off. He had business to conduct with the woman.

"Hello!" he called sharply, and strode with a reluctant purpose toward them.

"Hello?" the woman asked, and turned to look at him. Callison could almost read her eyes, and apparently, she did not know whom he was. As he watched, he saw her take in his uniform and her face flash a momentary speculation. Then, seemingly having taken his measure, she appeared to grow a little taller by changing the look in her eye and ever so slightly tilting her chin. It made her appear suddenly challenging. It was an attitude he did not care for in men, and could not tolerate in women.

"I need to talk to you," Callison said, not looking at Bowannie.

"Yes?" Lynne smiled easily at the Sheriff, dismissed him, and turned to Bowannie.

Callison saw something pass between them.

"We need to talk later, if you can. I'd appreciate your help on designing the rest of my apartment," she said as she took Bowannie's hand into hers. "Thank you."

Lynne turned her gaze back to Callison. The Sheriff had the odd sensation that he had been reprimanded for an impropriety. She ignored his interruption and refocused on old Bowannie.

"What can I do for you, deputy?" she asked as she turned back and smiled sweetly at Callison. She saw his epaulets and the small silver-colored star resting on his shoulders. Lynne wanted to know his personality. His sudden appearance made her feel a little cornered, but refused to let it show. She wondered if the Sheriff had connected her with the information, she had given Doc.

"Sheriff," he corrected with an edge to his voice.

"I'm sorry, what can I do for you Deputy Sheriff?" Lynne heard his tone and persisted in her best soft southern tone as she walked over to Callison holding out her hand for him to take. Nothing worked so well as the dizzy-blond routine if you really wanted to jerk around with someone. If a title were part of his psychological makeup, she knew he would pull the big-man-routine. And she would know the depth of his character. If he were not, then she would know she was playing in a different ballpark and have to be careful.

"Sheriff Callison," he doffed his hat, shook her hand, and was surprised by the firmness of the grip.

"Nice to meet you. How may I help?" Lynne asked, having taken his measure.

"May I sit?"

"Certainly. But please excuse the mess and my own, sir. I promise I clean up a lot better than this." She smiled and showed him to one of the two lawn chairs she had rescued from the patio.

"Of course..." Stalling, Callison tried to remember how he'd intended to approach the questioning. Lynne seemed to have changed ever so slightly. Callison felt a little off balance as he tried to reconcile her gentle demeanor with the flash of steel he thought he had witnessed. "I understand you found a dog by the side of the road yesterday. Can you tell me how that happened?"

"Surely," she drawled. Her heart was racing, fearful that the good doctor had given her away. Steel bars leaped before her imagination. Even the shortest time in jail for interfering with an ongoing investigation would complicate her other plans. She could not, would not, have that. Lynne took a deep breath and tried smiling emptily at him again. She needed to distract him, throw up smoke and mirrors.

"You were driving?" he prompted.

"Yes. I had gotten tired of being cooped up in my hotel room. The workmen," she swung her arm lazily about the room, "they weren't due to arrive until today…You know I've been here all week because of the dreadful weather?" she asked, and touched his hand sympathetically.

"Yes…I understand. So you went for a drive?" he asked as he tried to extract his hand from her touch.

"I'm sorry," she said, lowering her eyes demurely. "You just don't know what it's like. I mean, to be cooped up here for days on end, nothing but papers to sign, contracts to agree to, and waiting to get a new,…fresh start in life." She felt him tensing under the pressure of her hand.

"Yes,…" he said as he stood up and moved away from her.

"So," Lynne said as she turned her back to him to reach for the cigarette pack on the makeshift table. She did not want him to see her smiling ear to ear. "So, I went for a drive. The afternoon was so pretty. Finally, there was a sun after so many days of clouds, fog, and snow. Don't you get tired of it, Sheriff?" she asked as she walked toward him. Lynne let her voice drop an octave into what she hoped was a seductive timbre.

"You can get used to 'bout anything, ma'am," he said, beginning to desperately want her to simply finish the story so he could leave.

"Yes. So you can. Anyway, I drove up the highway, no particular destination in mind. It was just trees, trees, and more trees. You know I'm so used to the wide-open spaces that I was beginning to feel claustrophobic. But I couldn't get away from the trees." She smiled at him distractedly.

"Where did you find the dog?" he asked, feeling his patience slip. It was clear she did not know anything. He wondered how she had made it through the mountains without getting lost.

"Oh! He was practically sitting underneath a snow bank. All bloody and mangy looking. I couldn't leave him there like that. Did you know, he'd been shot?" she explored gently. She lowered her eyes. Raising them, she looked at his body in a slow suggestive stare. He fidgeted under her gaze.

"Yes. The vet said he'd been shot and stabbed." Callison backed slowly to the door, wishing he could rush to the safety of the street. His shoulder blades were itching with the desire to get away from the heat in him that the woman was creating. He wanted to keep their meeting professional. Later, he thought, later he might be interested in getting to know her.

"Well, I was afraid of him, but he looked so helpless. I coaxed him into the truck and took him to the first vet I found." As Lynne finished, she knew she was enjoying the playacting too much. She decided to cut it short. She did not want to over do it. The point had been to get him out of the building. "Do you think he'll be all right?"

"The vet thinks so. You have been very helpful. Thank you," Callison said as he touched the tip of his hat and took several backward steps toward the door. As he spun on his heels, he almost ran over Charlie Watson.

"Careful, Brett!" Charlie barked as he protected his toes.

"Excuse me, Charlie. I was just leaving. Didn't hear you sneak up on me."

"See you met Major Detective," Charlie said smiling at Lynne. Charlie's smile disappeared as he saw Lynne cast her eyes hopelessly toward the ceiling.

Callison stopped in mid-stride. "Major? Detective?" he asked as the color of rage slowly crept up his neck.

Lynne prepared herself for the full brunt of the anger his voice warned her about. "Charlie?" Her eyes flashed plaintively. The Sheriff turned a purpling face toward her.

"Actually, Major Fhaolain, late of the United States Army. Investigative work in the service. I am retired now. Was there anything else...Sheriff?"

"Not right away. Let's just say I've got your number." Callison remarked as he stomped out the door.

18

At the end of the week, Lynne felt wrung out. Even getting back to the habit of running in the morning had not helped revive her flagging energy. There had been so much to do. Although she realized that she had barely gotten started, she could not help wondering if there was ever going to be an end to it.

The utilities had been switched over into her name Monday and she had had phone service by Tuesday. Repairs were going well on the first and third levels. The second level would have to wait for real renovations. Meanwhile, it would simply be cleaned and painted. It might be sometime until she would require it for more book space. She did not want to get ahead of herself.

Getting a giant dumpster delivered made it possible to finally pitch out all the garbage from the basement. The general laborers had worked two days lugging foul-looking furniture, decomposing fixtures, and boxes of ancient business papers from all the nooks and crannies of the poorly lit catacombs. Once cleared out and cleaned, Lynne believed the whole building seemed to heave a quiet sigh of relief. Even the air seemed fresher. Feeling a little silly and superstitious, Lynne hoped that the bad luck and ghosts of misfortune that had been attached to the building had left with the trash.

Everything seemed to keep happening all at once, and she found out that she needed more of everything. She struggled under the idea that more supplies had to be bought, more materials for repairs put in place, and more decisions had to be made. It was not like any of the work she had ever done before. Worse, yet, she knew there were two or three more weeks of work staring her in the face. She had thought she was physically fit, but nothing had prepared her for the stooping, bending, lifting, standing on toes, and stretching she found herself doing. Her body ached in places she did not know she even had.

She speculated fleetingly about feeling older and rudely dismissed the idea. Lynne decided to blame the altitude, the weather, and the uncharacteristic spurts of domestic drudgery as the culprits and vowed to avoid the latter as much as possible once things were in their proper order.

"Lynne?" a voice called behind her.

The head of her hammer slammed into the wood, missing the nail she was aiming at. A small startled yelp escaped her lips as she barely grazed her thumb with the fast dropping hammerhead.

"Sorry," Charlie Watson said sheepishly.

"You ought to be," Lynn carefully lowered the hammer. "You really have a bad habit of sneaking up on folks, don't you?" she asked accusingly.

"Never noticed before," he said as he fought to keep the smile from his face.

"Come on. I think there's coffee and Irish Crème, and I could use a cup," Lynne said, and motioned him toward the kitchen door.

"Splendid idea."

"What brings you 'round here?" Lynne poured the coffee into large mugs and added the promised treat.

"Not much. Time on my hands mostly," Charlie, said as he sank into the new sofa.

"Business slow?"

"Not really. I thought I would let the other folks make my living for me today. Martha and I spent some time with the grandkids earlier. Girls, ten and twelve, nice to have them, and after they wear me out, nice to have them leave. Kids at those ages have more energy than they know what to do with."

"I've heard that." Lynne tried to sound appropriately appreciative and sympathetic because she knew that grandparents could be formidable if aroused by lack of appreciation of their grandchildren.

"Have you got plans for this evening?" he asked.

"No. What do you have in mind?"

"Oh, I just thought how maybe you, Doc and I could make our way over to the Double Eagle for a meal and more. Sound good?"

"What about your wife?"

"She doesn't care much for hanging out with the boys."

"And I'm one of the boys?" Lynne asked in amusement.

"Only if you play your cards right," he said as he looked at her over the rim of his cup. "'Sides, don't you think you deserve a break. You were going at it pretty hot and heavy."

"That's all you got in mind?" Lynne asked, digging a little deeper.

"Pretty much…I, we,…well, O.K. Doc and I were talking, and he said the Sheriff's heard back from Denver about the stuff you found and some other things."

"And…?"

"And, aren't you interested just a little?"

"Double Eagle seems the right place to do this?"

"Right as any. It gets noisy enough in there most nights. No one is likely to pay any attention to us anyway. On top of that, Sheriff is probably still got his eye on you. I don't think he bought into the idea of 'ole Doc being the one who'd been at the cabin scrounging around playing detective."

"Might have,…but for you," Lynne reminded him.

"I already apologized about that."

"I know. Doesn't cure it though, does it?"

"Not much. So, you coming or not?"

"Sure. What time?"

"Make it seven-thirty. I'll buy the first round. You can catch us up on your big adventure here." He said and rose to leave.

"You got it," she said to him as he headed for the door. She found herself looking forward to visiting and spending some of her evening with Charlie and Doc. They were a couple of strange town characters. At the rate she was going, she figured that would be what the town would be thinking about her in the not so distant future.

At a quarter till eight, Lynne walked into the Double Eagle and quickly found the table where Charlie and Doc were seated. She wound her way through the other tables.

"Fashionably late, I see," Doc, said, as he and Charlie rose to greet her. They waited for her to be seated before sitting again.

"Old manners, I see," she said as Doc held her chair.

"Old men, old manners," Charlie asserted.

"Right enough," Doc agreed.

"What might we order for you?" Charlie asked as the waitress approached their table.

"Miller, bottle, with a glass. Not frosted. Please."

"As the lady said. Doc and I'll each have another one of these," he said as he raised his bourbon glass.

"So, tell us what you've been up to since we've gotten everything back down to a low roar in this town."

"Sure you haven't got anything else on your mind, Doc?"

"In a little. I do not want you to think I'm antisocial or uncouth. We can get to the other soon enough...for now, tell me how you've been doing in that barn of a building over there."

"All right," Lynne said, sitting back in her chair. She told them about the work, and found many weeks' events amusing at a distance. It seemed to help to be among these men who felt like old friends. She enjoyed their inquiries, and tried to make sure she spun the truth with the right amount of humor. As she told the stories, she felt the tension begin to break its grip on her. She was amused by the verbal jabs and light sparring Doc and Charlie tossed at one another. They were like finding a matched set of comfortable old shoes she'd forgotten.

"Hello Charlie, Doc...and hello there, strange lady."

Doc smiled and nodded up at the man. His face said the man was a well-received acquaintance. Lynne tried to reduce her at-attention level, but he was standing at her shoulder, hovering like some strange bird of prey.

"Ray! Sit and meet the new townie," Charlie encouraged, and waved him to a chair at the table.

"Thanks, don't mind if I do," Ray said as he stretched his leg over the chair. He propped himself back and balanced with the chair's front legs dangling off the floor. "Who's your friend, Charlie?"

"This is Lynne. She's the proud new owner of the Gellmore building." Charlie beamed at Lynne.

Lynne nodded hello to the new arrival and tipped back her glass. She let the amber liquid flow down her throat. It hit her like a slowly widening fire and reminded her that she had not eaten since noon. She realized she would have to eat soon or end up staggering home in the dark.

"Finally got that dump off your hands?" Ray teased.

"Bite your tongue, man! She practically stole it from me!" Charlie shot back.

"Lynne what?" Ray asked.

"Lynne what?.... Oh! Fhaolain! This is Major Lynne Fhaolain and Lynne, this is the honorable Herr Doctor Raymond Billings."

"Major, a pleasure."

Lynne grinned and shook her head at Charlie. She turned back to Ray and said, "It's nice to meet you, Dr. Billings."

"Ray, please, just call me Ray. It's a pleasure to meet you, although I find the company you keep suspect. I feel it my duty to warn you about this pair," he said as he waggled a thin blunt-ended finger at Doc and Charlie.

"Warning noted, Ray," Lynne said, and turned back to Doc. "We should probably try to conclude our business at some other time."

"Your suggestion is well taken, seeing how this has turned into more of a party than we could have hoped," Charlie said, chucking Ray on the shoulder.

"Fhaolain? How do you spell that?"

"F-h-a-o-l-a-i-n. The family is something of a motley mix. Scotch Irish is the strongest line." Ray's eyes were a deep gray with great long lashes and the way he hunkered over the table made him seem like some rapacious bird. It was a picture that would stick with her.

"I'd say the Irish won out, what with that fair skin and those blue eyes," Doc said as he studied Lynne's face.

"Is Fhaolain an Irish name?" Charlie asked.

"Well," Lynne began. She was not actually sure, but she would willingly repeat what her grandfather had told her but she need not have worried, Ray did not give her a chance.

"It's the same thing, no matter. Your forefathers were a clan of wolf hunters. The name is spelled precisely to designate the duty of the clan," Ray said leaning across the table as he nestled his beer in his crossed arms.

Lynne felt a discomforting accusation in his assertion and his stare made the hair on the back of her neck stand at attention.

"Lynne?" Doc touched her sleeve. "You all right?"

"Yes, I'm sorry. What were you saying, Ray?" she smiled and cleared her throat. "A wolf hunter. I do recall some mention of hunting two legged wolves. It's just the sort of story you'd tell to children."

"Two legged wolves?" Charlie asked skeptically.

"The wolves who are men," John Bowannie said, moving toward the table. He moved to stand between Doc and Ray.

Lynne was not aware he had come into the bar. She swore silently to herself that she would never again sit with her back to the door. Her night had become less comfortable. She had interior bells sounding their alarm all over the place, and wanted a wall at her back and the opportunity to get her bearings. She was getting too much noise and input to read correctly, what the night and its environment were trying to tell her. It set her teeth on their edges.

"The men who are wolves?" Ray asked, and glanced curiously up at Bowannie.

"No, the wolves who are men," Bowannie corrected.

"The Europeans called them werewolves," Ray said, catching Bowannie's meaning.

"Yes," Lynne interjected. "But they didn't mean real werewolves. They meant the men who behaved worse than wolves ever could. It is all legend, of course but it means my ancestors hunted those who slaughtered others for sport and amusement. We, rather some of my ancestors, were like the early police in the region and tried to keep people from simply running amuck," Lynn said, and realized that she needed to change the subject.

"So just what makes you so smart, Ray? How'd you know about Lynne's family name?" Charlie asked.

"That's what they pay me for," Ray replied matter-of-factly.

"How much have you had to drink? Charlie, I'm a sociologist. I do research and teach. It just so happens I have an inclination toward social anthropology and ancient cultures. Names, even European names, have a particular meaning. Just like our Indian friend's here," he said as he nodded in Bowannie's direction. "We've just mostly forgotten them, that's all."

"That's true. I did a little research of my own in heraldry back at the University. Just for entertainment, you understand. It was a way of getting out of doing my real studying," Lynne said.

"What did you study?" Ray asked.

"I finished masters in sociology and psychology. It took forever, but I enjoyed it." Lynne remembered it had helped her earn her oak cluster and Major's pay.

"Really? Well, maybe I've finally found someone in this lowbrow town to sub in my classes at the college," Ray said cheerfully.

"Oh, I don't know about that," Lynne hesitated. The idea of teaching had never appealed to her.

"Maybe we can talk about it later. That is, if you like?" Ray asked hopefully.

"Maybe," Lynne said as she finished her beer and looked around for the waitress. She desperately needed something to eat.

"So, you're an educated werewolf hunter?" Charlie joked.

"Something like that. But, only if I had been born a thousand years ago. Never found any in the Army," Lynne assured him. Looking about, she could not find a free waitress. It was getting late, the drinks were beginning to get to her, and the weariness of the day was settling in her bones. She noticed the waitress had finally seen her waving arm but misinterpreted her signals and was bringing another beer. Lynne sighed in resignation. Apparently, she and Doc would not be able to discuss the matters that they had intended to in the Double Eagle that evening.

"They were savage times," Doc said, sensing Lynne's discomfort.

"We are still in savage times," Bowannie interjected.

Lynne looked up at him again uncertainly. "I'm sorry, Mr. Bowannie. Please, would you care to join us?" Lynne asked hopefully. She looked forward to sharing her side of the table with him. The conversation had taken a strange turn and his presence made her feel more at ease.

"It's late. I must go home," he said and inclined his head at her. He sat the beer on the table and left the Double Eagle.

Lynne saw her opening. "He's right, you know," she said as she rose from the table and put on her parka. "I've got to get an early start tomorrow, too. I will take a rain check on supper, gentlemen. Call me, or I'll ring you," Lynne promised. "Goodnight."

As she walked down the street to the hotel, Lynne hoped the feeling at her back was Mr. Bowannie's paternal eyes. But she locked and double-checked the door and windows of her room before going to bed. Not trusting the sanctity or impenetrability of locks, she slept with her gun under her pillow as an added precaution. She slept fitfully.

19

Saturday morning Charlie and Doc called Lynne and arranged to meet her at the Corbin Hotel. They could talk in her room without running the risk of being elbowed or overhead by the enthusiastic bar-goers they would run into the night before.

The results from the lab had been as Lynne expected but hoped against. The forensic lab at the Colorado Bureau of Investigation had been thrilled with the photographs of the partial palm print and other items collected, but they had not revealed any answers. To Lynne's amusement, Doc told her the lab had sent a salutary letter to Sheriff Callison for his persistence in accumulating hard physical evidence. Callison had been in a foul mood when he'd shared the information with Doc. Unfortunately, the lab had also noted their attempt to match the print with anything on file had met with failure. Without a suspect, it was hopeless to attempt comparisons. The lab had been able to show good intentions and secure the evidentiary material for later use, but nothing more. Good intentions, unfortunately, rarely solved murders.

"It's all right, Doc," Lynne said sympathetically. "Sometimes we just can't get as lucky as we'd like. That doesn't mean we can't narrow the field down some."

"How's that?" Charlie quizzed.

"Well,…the best way is statistics."

"Lies, damn lies, and statistics," Doc snorted.

"Sometimes, but it is a place to start," Lynne insisted.

"O.K.? How do you start?"

"The Behavioral Science unit back at the FBI has one of the world's largest collections of books on crime. All manner of crimes, which have been cataloged, cussed and discussed by learned, and speculator alike. Their library contains a very impressive collection of books on sociology, psychology, and the bizarre in human nature. They had tons of data patiently and continuously collected and processed over the years, from Europe and, of course, the United States. They've been collecting psychological profiling information based on extensive interviews with murderers, particularly serial murderers, for the past ten years."

"And…?" Doc interjected.

"And that's how they begin. They try to make statistics work for them. They compare and look for motives, motivation, techniques, and detailed points of behavior. You see when it comes down to it what limits a criminal is 1) what they want to do and 2) the skill they have to do it. Even crimes take a bit of skill. That includes murder. It's based primarily on three things: time, motive and opportunity. The three things are, the time to commit the crime, the motive for doing it, and the feasibility or skill to commit it.

"See, these things are available but restricted by the capacity and perception of the person's intent," Lynne, said. She was working on building a foundation to build her suspicions on. She needed their help, their eyes, and their knowledge of the community if a suspect list could be gleaned from the residents of the community and then narrowed into anything meaningful or manageable.

"Committing crime takes skill? You mean to say you think this bastard was skillful?" Charlie asked, looking appalled.

"In a sense, yes. Everything we do as a human being requires a skill, and skill is part of the opportunity I'm talking about. Humans have to learn everything. At least everything beyond basic survival, for all I know…Anyway, it's not that we learn murder, although sometimes that does apply, but more often we learn how to use tools, applies techniques, and carry through the action in our own unique style. It's all the same, whether we're talking about learning how to patch someone up like Doc or make a real estate deal like you, Charlie. We learn. Learning, and then the environment we live or work in, creates opportunities for us. An opportunity is nothing more than a perception of favorable circumstance or set of circumstances we use to our own purposes. Criminal and non-criminal alike, its what we do every day. We take advantage of the circumstances life presents to us."

"I don't think I care for the comparison," Doc said, and squirmed uneasily in his chair.

"Me either. You make that butcher sound commonplace," Charlie retorted. He and Doc exchanged uneasy glances.

Looking at them, Lynne could imagine what they were thinking and why. They were uncomfortable with the idea that a murderer was anything like the good people they believed themselves to be and the people they knew. Crazy people, vile people and their terrible inclinations were supposed to be easy to spot because of their strangeness and not members of the *real* human race. Doc and Charlie wanted to cling to the belief that evil was something, which permanently marks those, possessed by it. But it was an unrealistic and superstitious preference that rationalized that ugly behavior would somehow show and mark the possessor in some grotesque physiognomy of personality or detectable behavior. It was an easier belief than remembering the sage admonishment of how one should never judge a book by its cover.

"Well, like it or not, that is pretty much how it is," Lynne said, not knowing if she were getting through to them. "But let's not argue. Let me use it as a launch point."

"All right, I'm with you," Doc said.

"Me, too. For a while anyway," Charlie said.

"O.K." Lynne struggled with herself and wondered how much further and how much detail to go into, and remembered her grandfathers' warning not to confuse people with too many facts. She did not need to tell them how to make a clock if they just needed to know what time it was.

"Let's do this instead…everything I've been taught and the way I've been taught. I used it when Doc gave me the reports, and I combined them with the things I discovered at the cabin. That, along with the latest reports from the CBI, gives enough pieces to let me start to narrow down the field of suspects to a manageable profile base. With me?"

They nodded in agreement.

"The likely groupings of 'who commits and how they commit crimes' statistics based on known offenders and the other things I mentioned allow me do some guessing. It is educated guessing, but guessing nonetheless. So, my guesses and reasons for the guesses are," Lynne raised her left hand and began counting off issues on her fingers. "He has a long stride. I measured it, so I would put him at six-foot or six foot two. The way he walked was slightly splayed when he left the house. Part of that may have been from walking in snow, or because he was carrying something heavy. We have a tendency to bend under weight and shift our stride to achieve balance under the burden of whatever we carry. But his straight-footed walk tells me that he was or is an athlete. Caucasian, male, and a tendency to land hard on his heels. When he walked away from the cabin. He was not running. The depth of his boot print and stride suggests he is not bulky. No duck waddle. He's right-handed and has a strong upper body. The blood splatters in the bedroom gave me his strong arm by the way the blows would have had to land and arch for those splatters to occur.

"The firm, sure way he pressured the knife through her neck gives the strength. He did not waste effort slicing through the spinal column. That suggests he's something of a skilled hunter," Lynne said as she continued to tick off the points of analysis.

"Hunter?" Doc interrupted.

"Yeah," Lynne insisted looking out from under her eyebrows at Doc. "He's used to field dressing his prey and making short work of it."

"You have a way with words."

Charlie shuddered visibly. Lynne seemed to know a great deal about a gruesome science.

"You use what you know," she reminded them.

"Great."

"He hid his vehicle. That could mean that if the Peveys' had spotted it, they would have recognized it. So, he's a longtime or well-known resident here. He knows that area like the back of his hand, hunting again at night sometimes. But it was a full moon, so maybe that helped him. The familiarity with the area and his own relaxed way of staying since he did in the cabin makes me want to put him here in town or up to two or three miles in any other direction. Oh, yeah, I almost forgot. His strength and victim type tells me he's pretty much a contemporary of mine, what I mean is that he's a man somewhere between the age of thirty-five and fifty-five years old. The age thing works pretty well with his stride and strength levels too."

"Thank God. That leaves us out. Doesn't it, Charlie?" Doc said. His head was spinning at the issues' Lynne recited through her calculations.

"Apparently, we need something to be grateful for," Charlie added sarcastically.

"You can tell all that from the reports?" Doc asked, and looked at Lynne with renewed curiosity.

"The reports and other statistical probabilities you don't need to worry about right now. It's a combination of training, research and a whole lot of experience. But remember these aren't facts; they are merely likelihood based on comparative probabilities. These are firm but still just guesses."

"That it? That all we got?" Charlie asked and sat back in his chair in exasperation.

"There are a couple of other things. They have more to do with who he did and how. So don't jump until I'm finished."

"All right, let's have it."

"To begin with, murders like this do not make any sense."

"No kidding? " Doc shot back.

"Really. But that is the point. From what the reports say, the husband is not a good suspect. There were no lovers. There is no external motive we can attribute to the murderer which would have made Beverly a good target for him."

"Say that again," Doc requested looking perplex.

"No money, no robbery, no personal relationship gains. Sex was an afterthought and that after she was dead. Necrophilia says a lot about his need for total control. As far as we know, Beverly had no enemies to speak of, nothing we can firmly put our finger on that would show the murderer was someone she knew. Nothing we can say with any confidence provided a standard external motivation," Lynne emphasized quietly.

"I thought you said he just walked in, like she let him in. Doesn't that mean she had to know him?" Doc asked.

"It could mean any one of three things,…she knew him, wasn't afraid of him, or she was simply gullible or naive. You ever let anyone in your house or place of business you don't know?" Lynne asked pointedly.

"Yeah, but I'm not a woman alone in a cabin," Charlie retorted.

"Your biases are showing, Charlie. No one, man, woman or child ever expects to let death walk through his or her door. But it happens and happens all the time. An unguarded moment, sympathy for the devil disguised as an amiable stranger, or the simple act of charity will not interfere with the intent of the wolf you let come near to you. She could have been a spur of the moment…his moment. Nothing personal, available and he was in the mood. Stuff happens to nice people all the time. I know that for a fact and personally. You don't have to go looking for trouble, Charlie, sometimes it finds you." Lynne said as her throat constricted.

"So the motivation had to come from the assailant, something inside him, his mind, the way he sees his twisted little world," Doc said, and leaned forward. "He's crazy. All that really means is he's crazy."

"Yeah. But he was not crazy last week or the week before. Not so, you would have noticed anyway. He has been on his way to getting crazy for a while. It may have been showing up in lots of little ways. You may have noticed it, seen it happening and if you knew him, you might have chalked it up to his having a bad day. But you wouldn't have put it together or imagined where it could lead."

"My God. You mean we could know him?" Doc asked horrified. Charlie moved uncomfortably in his chair.

"Sure. But, it might be as well as we ever really know anyone. See we never know people as well as we think we do. It could be someone with whom you have passing contact or maybe you know him or her fairly well. That is what I have been getting at here. He's someone from around here, and although he may have been suffering from the beginnings of a psychotic episode, that's really not something he's been wearing on his sleeve."

"But you just said we could have seen something," Charlie insisted.

"Yes. Yes, I did. But I'm also telling you that he may have temporarily averted his full-blown descent into psychoses. He has stuffed it back down again. It's back under the surface of his mind and itching at him like a demon. That is why he will do it again. He will have to. It's the only way he'll feel can maintain his security, his sanity, and his peace of mind."

"When, where, who?" Doc said urgently.

"Depending on his psychosis?" Lynne mused. "It could be someone like Beverly again. But unless it's driven by a fancy for women, it might be anyone who is standing too close to him when his compulsion rages out of control."

"Great!" Doc fell back into his chair. Exasperation and hopelessness mixed on his face. "I think I'm going to need another drink."

Later, lying in her bed, Lynne knew how helpless they felt. She tried her best to give them some way of thinking about the murderer and cast a little light into the dark foreboding. She drank with them until eleven, by which time they would all gotten heavily 'into their cups'. They had parted with her asking them to think about the people they knew. She had tried to encourage them and remind them that between them and their professional callings, they had to have met and talked to most of the people in town. She assured them hopefully that it was a matter of thinking about it and putting the pieces together. Lynne hoped they had enough time, and did not have to wait for a fresh body to show up.

Lynne felt compelled to do something, anything, even if it was useless motion. She would go back to the cabin area. Maybe take a run there.

Maybe, she wondered, what if she was looking at the thing all-wrong. As her vision swam in the dark, she knew she had had too much wine. Her head felt thick, and she needed to clear out the cobwebs before she could get it going again. Charlie and Doc liked their drinks, and she wondered if they were going to be a bad influence on her. With that thought, she drifted into sleep.

20

Lillian Peavey liked to think of herself as a naturalist, an amateur, but a naturalist just the same. She loved the high mountain valley she and her husband had moved after his retirement seven years ago from the Seattle-based banking firm. They had bought their home, the resort cabins and land, immediately after they arrived. It had seemed an ideal supplement to Harold's retirement income. In the summer, they had guests at the cabins, and during the winter, she and Harold spent their time creating their crafts, which kept some regional shops filled with various sizes of their hand-woven white oak baskets. But the murder at their resort had deeply disturbed them. And Lillian felt that the last two weeks had barely begun to let them come out of the fog that had settled over their lives.

Saturday appeared a promising day. The sky was robin-egg blue with a bright sun warming the mid-afternoon. Harold had left earlier to make his rounds among the shops in Leadville, Buena Vista, Salida and Gunnison with the truck filled with their winter's labors. Lillian usually did not mind being alone, but the terrors of murder continued to make her uneasy. The large ranch style house and yards did not offer her the sort of comfort she wanted. She knew she needed to shake it off her distress, to get over it, and not to let it claim more of her sense of security than it already had. Lillian was a realist. She intended to take back the sense of security that had been fractured.

She dressed warmly. As she looked at herself in the mirror, she noticed that the winter seemed to have added a few bounds to her small robust frame. Harold would never mention it to her. He was too kind. But she did not want another pound to sneak up on her. Lillian was sixty-seven and there was no need to let the years and gravity beat her just yet. She put a small .22 in her coat pocket. The heft of it made her feel somewhat more secure as she carefully locked the door to her house. Lillian called her companion for a walk.

Bandit, her black and white Husky, raced around the side of the house and bounced eagerly at her side. Bandit loved his mistress and loved to wander with her over the hills and through the woods of Half Moon Creek to discover the secret smells and promises of flowers and wildlife. Dog and woman climbed into the jeep and headed down the lane. Both were eager to explore the early snow-fed flowers that could be expected to be pushing up through the sun spotted snow and daring the cold runoff of the clear mountain streams.

Lynne arrived a little after three in the afternoon and drove along the winding circular lane of Half Moon Creek. She pulled off the road and brought her truck to a stop inside the lane. Locking her truck, she stripped down to a black Spandex suit, windbreaker, night-watch cap, and a pair of jersey gloves. She used the side of the vehicle for leverage as she stretched her muscles into warmth. Her head pounded. She did not know whether to blame her condition on the nap she had taken after Doc and Charlie left, or the alcohol during their last meeting, or both. But she promised herself that she would be wary of both in the future.

During her last visit to the location, when she'd been snooping around the cabin, she'd gauged the circular lane to be a little under four miles round trip back to the place she now parked. She hoped it would be a good run, invigorating stretch of the legs, and help her shake off the ache inside her head. As she controlled her breathing into deep-relaxed waves, she concentrated on the increasing flexibility of sinew, joint and muscle. The deep breathing and enforced regime of the warming exercise focused her attention on the present and removed all thoughts of past and future. Lynne centered and concentrated on the moment. She slipped through time using the motion of her body. Everything else became scenery and backdrop for the run. Finally warmed and ready, she quick-jumped in place a few times and set off at an easy pace.

The air was fresh and clean as it poured into her lungs. She let herself become motion. Breathing easily, she felt herself move along the road. The altitude and the rutted road challenged her to maintain footing and pace. The dense forest of slender lodge pole pine sprinkled with Douglas fir moved lazily past her as she wove her path down the lane.

Small-unexpected clearings flashed into and out of view as she rounded the lane toward the meadow and the Peavey cabins. She ran past the snowplowed banks of snow that partially obscured the wooded fence. A thin line of gray smoke rose from the Peavey homestead and melted into the air. Everything was silence except the crunching of her shoes against the gravel and thin crust of snow on the road, and the labors of her breathing. Robber blue jays eyed her curiously from their perches while rough-legged hawks above rode updrafts and watched the clearings for stray vermin's snacks.

A half-mile on, as she rounded the sharp bend in the road, Lynne noticed a blue mud-smeared jeep parked next to a turnoff. The turnoff had apparently been widened by a snowplow as it had banked wide to take the corner. As she passed the jeep, she laid her hand quickly on the hood and felt its warmth radiating beneath her gloved hand. She jogged on, knowing she had company somewhere in the remoteness of Half Moon Creek. She ran on unconcerned. Not everything need be a threat, she thought, as she acknowledged the right of others to be in the area and eased herself away from her internal alert.

A hundred feet farther her ears brought the sounds of huffing and panting snorts coming from the woods and underbrush of the thickened forest. A fast-moving animal was keeping pace with her. Its footfalls dashed up the range of the hill and returned suddenly nearer to her. She stumbled as the sounds of its tracking her and she lost her concentration. Distracted and slightly alarmed, she recalled stories about mountain lions and fervently hoped for deer.

Lynne stumbled again and struggled to keep herself erect but tripped over a rough piece of ice and dove headfirst into the frozen roadway. She let out a small cry of amazement and dismay as she twisted her body, falling toward the cold hard ground, and felt muscles strain in her back.

The animal that had been pacing her burst through the brush line as she landed. Alarm spread like a hot jolt of adrenaline through her neck and she twisted around in an attempt to meet the onrushing animal. She fell. Her left arm and leg skidded across the road until she lay crumpled in an awkward sitting position. The animal was on her in a flash and knocked her viciously to the ground.

The Husky fell over Lynne in the excitement of his welcome. He licked her face, nuzzled her arms and neck, and greeted her as his new playmate. His large feet stepped on her legs and his tail beat her at every turn. His wide mouth and lolling tongue seemingly asked her why she chose to sit to greet him. He dashed off, turned around, and scampered back to her. Abruptly, he sat next to her feet and seemed to wait for a reply. His foolish grin and pounding tail could barely contain his excitement as his solid body quivered in elation at the new sport.

Lynne laughed at him and moaned as her body yielded to the punishment of the rough landing. Her back muscles felt as though they had been pulled dangerously close to the edge of endurance. She frowned at her new companion ruefully and sighed helplessly. As she patted his head, she heard the faint cry of a woman's voice calling to someone in the distance. Lynne looked at the dog and then strained her ears to hear. The dog turned a nervous head to the voice echoing through the woods, and then turned back to Lynne anxiously.

"Is that your mother?" Lynne asked the dog, and he rose quickly to run back into the woods. At the edge of the trees, he turned around, crouched down on all fours, and wagged his tail at Lynne enthusiastically. He seemed caught between duty and his new playmate's attention him.

"Bandit?" the voice called, closer and louder. "Ban...!" the call abruptly cut off and was followed by a shrill scream.

Lynne and the dog jumped to their feet at the sound. The dog bounded hastily through the trees leaving Lynne to struggle along behind. Another scream. Low miserable tones wafting through the air. Up and running, Lynne grappled with the brush and made her way through the close growth of trees as she tried to ignore the twigging of pain in her back and bruised side. She jogged determinedly in the direction the dog had taken and the last place she heard the woman's voice.

Her aching back slowed her pace and the stumbling, half-walking, half-running efforts frustrated her as she ran. The woods were silent around her. There was nothing but the sound of her own feet pounding the ground and the scraping of her clothes grabbed by outreaching brush. She stopped and listened intently for the trace of any sound. Then to her left she heard the echo of hurried footfalls across dead leaves and softening snow. Lynne turned toward the retreating sound and reached for a weapon. Her hand clasped her key ring and came back empty.

"Damn!" she breathed. A lapse of common sense, she cursed to herself as she realized she had left her revolver in the truck. She ran on until the brush cleared to an opening surrounded by a compacted growth of Douglas fir and lodge pole pine. Lynne scanned the area and spotted a figure moving in quick darting motions between the trees. She saw that the person's path would take them back to the roadway and pushed into a charging cross-country run. She stumbled and caught herself on the hard coarse surface of a lone pine.

As Lynne shoved off and rounded the tree, she saw a small stand of clustered trees. Their bows had collapsed under the accumulated weight of winter snow. Through the trees, Lynne saw a frantic woman bolting through the brush as a dog trotted beside her. Lynne dug in her toes and raced to catch up to the woman. She was behind her as the other woman reached her jeep.

"Excuse me! Wait!" Lynne yelled, and gasped for air as her bruised ribs fought for attention.

The woman spun around. Her eyes were wide with fright and a scream broke through her lips. The dog turned on Lynne, recognized her, and bounded back playfully toward her. The scream lingered on the older woman's lips. Then as she watched her dog bouncing around her pursuer, she stopped and replaced it with a look of relief.

"Bandit!" Lillian called to her dog in a shaking voice.

Lynne tried to smile and wave to the woman as she jogged toward her. Bandit trotted beside Lynne as she approached the woman. Lynne figured she had to look a frightful sight to anyone. Her running clothes were splattered with mud, her hair was disheveled, and her arm protectively clutching her ribs impeded her loping stride.

"Well!" Lillian Peavey gasped as Lynne trotted up to her.

Lynne stopped running and bent over to catch her breath. Her chest felt like it was on fire. She held on to her knees as she tried to breathe normally. She weakly raised a hand and asked Lillian to wait until her pains subsided.

"My Lord! What are you doing out here?" Lillian asked. She had not expected anyone to be behind her. She did not want them to be there. Not after what she had seen. It had been too much. Lillian wanted to get away from the area and get away now.

"I...I...heard you scream," Lynne said as her breath came in sharp spurts against her abused ribs.

"Yes," Lillian said her tone dropping and a sob breaking from her. "Awful," she whimpered, and sagged against the jeep. Bandit stood protectively and quizzically at her side. "I thought for a moment, when you yelled, you were after me."

"No. I'm not. Is someone after you?"

"Yes. No. I don't know," Lillian quivered.

"What happened? Are you all right?"

"Oh, I'm fine. But there's a...a body back there. Horrible..." Lillian repeated as her voice drifted.

"Body! Back there? Where?" Lynne turned and looked back toward the woods she had run through. The hair on her neck stood up at attention. She had the uncomfortable feeling of unseen eyes watching her and the other woman.

"'Bout 200 yards back in, near the roadbed, that clearing...across the stream. I was looking for flowers and herb bunches...for teas...I lost Bandit," she stuttered, and held the dog's head close to her for comfort. I almost walked on him," Lillian gasped.

"He?" Lynne felt confused.

"Yes, he. My God, I thought he was a pile of brush. Didn't look real."
Lillian was beginning to visibly shake again.

"Where do you live?" Lynne asked the woman as she sank down the
side of the jeep. She had a nasty shock. Lynne sympathized. She knew
about unnatural shocks.

Bandit nuzzled Lillian's hand. That seemed to revive her to the present.

Lynne walked over to the woman and put her arm around Lillian's
shoulders to support and comfort her.

"Where do you live?" Lynne repeated softly.

"Back there," Lillian directed with a nod of her head.

"You're Mrs. Peavey? All right, you go home. Get inside and lock your
doors. You'll feel better if you do. Just go home, now. Call the police after
you catch your breath and tell them how to get here. I'm going back to
the body," Lynne gently commanded, forgetting she was a civilian. She
patted Lillian's shoulder and urged her inside the jeep.

"Who are you, and what are you going to do?" Lillian asked, suddenly realizing she did not know the woman who was taking charge of
the situation.

"Oh,…tell them Lynne Fhaolain is out here." Not that it would mean
anything to anyone, she thought to herself. "I…I live in town. I'm just
going to make sure nothing happens to the body. Go on, but safely,…you
look like you need to rest," Lynne said as she looked into the gray
blanched face in the jeep.

"I'll be fine. I need to go home. But I'll call the Sheriff and tell him
you're here," Lillian promised.

"Good," Lynne acknowledged and moved back toward the woods.

"Here, here," Lillian called, remembering. "Take my gun. Whoever did
that might come back."

Lillian handed the .22 to Lynne and waved as she turned her jeep
down the road to her house. Lynne looked at the tiny weapon, smiled

weakly at Lillian and nodded her thanks. Lillian climbed into the jeep; Bandit bounded across the passenger's side, and sat at attention next to his master. The dog rode back with Lillian, swiveling his head at full alert. Lynne watched the jeep until it was out of sight before going into the wooded area.

Lynne paced off the distance back to the area where she had first seen the woman running. She figured if she kept going in the direction the woman had pointed that she might stumble across the creek. Stumbling was what she felt she was doing best now. Ten minutes later, she found him or what was left of what had once been a man. He had become a crumpled, animal-ravaged mass of flesh and weathered cloth. Between the slump animal-roughed posture, and his hunting clothes of browns and grays, he had begun to blend into the environment. More specifically, he looked as though he was becoming part of the environment. Lynne thought it was little wonder the poor woman had almost walked on him. He was just another mound of forest decay.

Lynne carefully walked a wide circle around him as she examined the ground. She carefully avoided other tracks, and the beer cans that lay scattered across the ground. Most of the trash was cluttered around the victim. The scene looked disproportional. Either the man had a hell of a thirst, or he had help finishing all the empties scattered around. Had he drunk himself to death, or drank till he passed out and died of exposure? She checked the ground around the body and saw the smudged impressions of another set of boots. She circled the area in a wider arch and found the trace of boot heel dug in near a fallen log. Someone had been sitting with his feet stretched out in front of him; crossing and uncrossing his legs as time went by. The area around the log was free of trash and booze debris. Lynne wondered if he had policed the area before leaving it. She did not want to ruin or contaminate the area of a potential crime scene. But she wanted to see and note every nuance of the scene before the Sheriff arrived.

Lynne walked over the area behind the log. A beer cans' silver and red label flashed from underneath a clump of leaves. It lay crushed a mere twenty yards from the body, as though it had been tossed off prior to the assault or by someone waiting for an opportunity. Lynne gingerly put a twig in the flip-top hole, picked it up, and placed it in a pocket of her jacket.

She walked back to the dead man. His face was a ruin. Scavengers had victimized the soft exposed flesh but the cold mountain air had preserved the flesh that remained. The mouth was stretched wide with the jaw dangling from its hinges. Ravaged as it was, something else seemed amiss about the exposed features. Reluctantly, Lynne peered closer and shivered involuntarily when a creeping feeling snaked along her limbs. It was not the chilled air under the shadows of the trees that made her shiver. It was the pity she never failed to feel when faced with the aftermath of ruined lives. She stared into the cavern mouth.

"Incredible," Lynne whispered to herself as she attempted to control a nauseous response. His tongue was missing, and it had not been taken by a woodland scavenger. She could see the clean line of stubbed root. It had been neatly severed. The sure sliced edge could not be hidden by the swelling decay. Lynne pulled at his jacket his torso was lifted off the ground. It was then that she could turn the body and see the ragged hole at the back of his head. No animal had done that. He'd been shot and mutilated. Hate-spawned or psychosis triggered.

"Collector," Lynne breathed. She lowered the body and backed away. Her eyes fixed on the ground; she searched the area for other bits of prints and debris that might give clues to the murderer's identity. Lynne's head swam in speculation about the brutality of the injuries. A collector had marked the dead man, and souvenirs had been taken. A crazy man's attempt to silence the dead. Lynne gave the 'hangman' the count of five.

The lonesome whines of distant sirens sounded through the trees. The Sheriff officers and others were on their way up the Half Moon Creek road. Lynne backed away and sat waiting for them.

She eyed the area and tried to put together the scene of the man's last hours. She imagined them sitting, drinking, talking, and sharing time before the attack. Had he been brought out here against his will? Whoever the murderer was, he had known this man, intimately, as a companion. But something had gone wrong. Somehow, he had been sparked like a keg of gunpowder, and exploded in a murderous rage. He had killed an acquaintance, a good friend, or partner in crime. Last time it had been a stranger. And if the murderer was the same man who had killed Beverly, all holds were off. The last shred of civilization had been stripped away. He would be raging now and no one would be safe from his flashover. He would live in the psychosis while it ate him alive, and anyone else he might cross. Lynne wondered what the dead man had threatened him with. Exposure? Collusion? Blackmail? None of it made sense right now. She sat quietly as a host of questions and possibilities raced in her mind. Slowly, she got up and walked back through the trees to meet the sheriff's officers a little further away from the grisly scene.

Lynne felt herself being pulled back into the world she had thought she had walked away from. Lynne was not happy about the turn of events. The predator as a collector was an alarming thought. He would have no boundaries now. No event would be without its potential danger. Sheriff Callison reached her first. His quick pace through the trees had left his deputies and Doc Kennedy scattered in his wake. Lynne saw the look on his face, and knew a wicked storm front was bearing down on her. She leaned against the nearest tree and waited. Her idyllic afternoon run had been ripped away. Her headache was coming back, and by the looks of the Sheriff, she knew things were not going to get any better.

"Mind if I ask just what the hell you think you are doing here?" Sheriff Callison asked as he brought himself within three inches of her face. He hovered over her like a grizzly bear. He intended to unnerve her. He was having a bad day and she was in the middle of it, if not the cause.

Lynne smiled up at him. "Why, Sheriff, how nice to see you again," Lynne said. Her eyes never left his face. The flexing jaw and bunching muscles under his coat signaled to her that he was thinking about grabbing her. Lynne had not provoked him, but she could tell he was looking for anyone to blame for his day and give him a reason to vent his irritation. She could hardly blame him. Two murders in two weeks were not good business.

"Don't 'Hi' me, Lady. I know what you're about," he said as his hands came to rest on his hips and clutched at his gun belt.

"Excuse me?" Lynne asked simply. She had embarrassed him unintentionally last week. But now she wanted to deflect him back to his reason for being there. All she wanted to do was to go home, find a nice fire to sit in front of, and sort out the afternoon's events.

"You. You nosey bitch. Just who do you think you are?"

"Look, Bubba," Lynne breathed slowly through her anger, and washed away her good intentions. "It's Major to you. Retired, but Major nonetheless. I'm out here minding my own business. Or I was trying to. It's not my fault your county has bodies scattered all over it."

"Bubba!...Bubba! I ought to lock you up!"

"Yes, Bubba. You're the one that started with the 'B' word stuff. And you can lock me up, but you will have a hard time explaining why calling you Bubba would be a felony. Additionally, I'll sue you for every dime you and your grandchildren will ever make," Lynne countered, and looked over to see Doc and the deputies hanging back in the distance. None of them wanted to get too close to the Sheriff. They looked like people who knew his attitude might spill over onto them.

"You…" Callison bellowed.

"You are wasting precious time, Mr. Sheriff. There is a body over there, and Mrs. Peavey to talk to. I am standing here marking the spot so you do not miss it. So get out of my face and on with your job." Lynne turned and tried to step around him. He blocked her way. Lynne felt her chest constrict as she realized that nothing in Leadville was turning out the way she had hoped. All she wanted was a quiet retreat from life, and forgetfulness. A place to bury herself.

As she turned, Callison took the opportunity to reach out and grab one of her arms. It was a mistake.

Lynne's right foot snaked out and twisted behind Callison's left ankle as she raised her elbow and sank it sharply into his chest. He fell in a heap at her feet and made a grab at his holster.

"I wouldn't do that if I were you. 'Cause I'll just take it away from you and knock your dick in the dirt," she whispered at him. "You don't want that to happen in front of your friends, do you?" she asked. She had had all the annoyances she could tolerate. Lynne waited for his decision.

His hand halted and stayed poised above the butt of his pistol. His fingers remembered the rigidity of flesh and muscle under his grip when he grabbed her arm. His ears refused to believe what he had heard her say, and he faltered in apprehension. He wanted to slap the look off her face but hesitated when he saw her relaxed self-possession.

Callison's hesitation was the break she had waited for. He would not move against her now, and she knew it. She nodded at him and stepped away toward the place where Doc Kennedy was standing.

"I'll be at my store if you need me," she said to the Sheriff as she walked toward Doc.

"Come on," Sheriff Callison said coarsely to his deputies. He glared at her as he stood up and strode away toward the location of the body. His deputies hurried behind him, and cast quizzical glances in Lynne's direction.

"You two are bound and determined not to get along, aren't you?" Doc grinned at her as he shook his head.

"Don't worry, Doc. It's nothing personal," Lynne said shaking her head.

"Sure seems personal. You all right?" he asked, noticing her holding her ribs.

"Fine, or at least nothing that a good long soak won't cure."

"The Sheriff didn't hurt you when he grabbed you, did he?"

"No, nothing like that. I fell while running in these damn woods. The Sheriff is a walking attitude problem. Hard to figure. But some things you simply can't figure, or cure. Has he always been like that?"

"You mean the bad temper?"

"No. I mean his problem with women," Lynne said as she felt muscle spasming in her back. She moaned and limped toward a tree and leaned against it.

"You think he's got a problem with women?"

"I know he has a problem with women. You can smell it on him. An overabundance of macho-crotcho crap," she asserted. She wanted to get back to the hotel and let hot steamy bath water soak her bruises.

"Think so?" Doc chuckled. "And what do you have?"

"My reflexes didn't retire when I did. Other than that and my aching rib. But the Sheriff is probably one of those dinosaurs who figures women have their place...somewhere like on his bed or under his thumb. Gets worse I imagine when he's under pressure. Has he been married much?"

"Twice I know of, and runs through the ladies pretty good too, if rumors are to be believed. Fancies himself as a ladies man. He is a good-looking cuss," Doc said grinning at Lynne.

"Not my type, Doc," Lynne laughed at him.

"Doc! Come on!" Callison bellowed from the distance. Docs' head jerked up and he smiled sheepishly at Lynne.

"You better go before he figures out I'm a bad influence on you. By the way, you got a plastic baggy on you in that kit?" Lynne asked as she reached under her windbreaker.

"Sure. What have you got?" Doc responded as he reached into the kit and pulled out a quart-sized bag from amongst the clutter.

"Evidence. Maybe prints. See it gets sent to a lab, and let me know if it matches anything I found at the cabin. O.K.?" Lynne asked as she transferred the can from her parka to the plastic bag. "Just tell the Sheriff you found it while checking the area. He'll think he missed it and then no big deal."

"Sure. He'll be pissed at his deputies and himself then."

"Better them than me. 'Sides, you're the Doctor. Take him down a peg or two. He needs you in on this and not so much the other way around."

"What do you think happened over there?" Doc asked as she turned away.

"Somebody's worse nightmare. The same somebody who killed the woman. And the same someone we've got to find really soon, Doc." Lynne patted Doc on the back and limped past him. "We'll talk later. Maybe the Sheriff, too, if he gets off his high horse," Lynne promised as she headed back to where she had parked her truck.

21

Tuesday at the Gellmore Building the first call Lynne received came from the moving company. They said her belongings would be arriving the following Monday afternoon. She had not expected them until late the next week, and her apartment was far from ready. There were minor repairs, painting and a lot of wall papering to be done. They offered to store it but she did not want to imagine the trouble of trying to get it out of storage and having to pay to move it again. She conceded to delivery Monday and dashed away from the phone to find Mr. Bowannie.

Lynne found him on the bookstore level supervising the construction of the shelves she had designed. She wanted to make the isles accessible to anyone in a wheelchair, and to do so the isles would have to be at least thirty-four inches wide. The decision created a problem of shelf space that she finally solved by creating pyramid like shelving units that had edges that would meet at the top. The angle would give the impression of greater room and allow ease of reading for the browsers. The shelving against the walls would be attached and upright to the floor.

196 Murder in Cloud City

The shelving units in the middle sections would be six feet tall while the wall units would soar to ten feet and give the last four feet for storage of duplicated or triplicate books on the easier to reach shelving below. Storage was not going to be one of her major concerns for some time, but she wanted to be prepared. Several wall units were shorter and would allow her to hang artifacts and pictures she had gotten at auctions in Kansas City. They would add warmer touch to the interior of the store.

The isles would be interspersed and staggered rather than continuing a full complete line as in most libraries. She wanted to give people the opportunity to flow through the space rather than being regimented to direct lines. In three open areas created by occasional wall jutting, she would place comfortable chairs and reading lamps. It would encourage browsing, relaxation, and hopefully encourage purchases.

She recalled the bookstores she had enjoyed and would combine the things she admired into her own store. She wanted warmth, comfort, and the feel of a private library, which the chain stores could not offer. Lynne wanted to create the feeling of respect for books as their own special form of art that would share the various features of all aspects of the human experience.

After years in the service and studying several different disciplines in college, she was convinced there was only one quest in the university and the world. People. Each question was personal. And each issue was central to the questions of why we are here, what does here mean, and what shall we make of it and ourselves? It was egocentric, but it was the question and the quest that had not been satisfied.

She wanted her bookstore to respect that quest in whatever small way it could. The essence of a library, ready assistance, comfort and space for reflection, with shelving reaching to the ceiling and books from as wide a net as she could cast. She would not limit her potential customers any more than she wanted to limit the possibility for them of finding their own answers.

Eggshell white walls with mahogany-stained shelving would provide the feeling she wanted to work in, and it was beginning to take shape. She was reluctant to remove Mr. Bowannie and his crew from the picture they were creating, but with her furniture due in a week, she needed help to get ready.

Bowannie was talking to his crew about smoothing the raw stains on the wood with cloth to soften the effect. She had been pleased with his work. He had taken her ideas for shelving and transformed them into solid reality. In a few days, the walls had been lined with the shelving units. Two sturdy tent-like structures, his practice pieces he called them, stood proudly to one side. There was so much open space in the store, the tall shelves looked a little forlorn and small.

She remembered that halfway through the construction of the first unit, he had stopped and asked her if she were concerned about the floor load. She had been puzzled. But when he explained to her that each unit would weigh 600 to 800 pounds, she began to understand.

Hardback books of even standard proportions would weigh over a pound each. The shelves would hold twenty-five to thirty books each. Each unit contained five to seven shelves, depending on the height of the books. The shelving units for the soft-back books would have eight shelves each, as soft-back books were generally not very tall. In paperback, it would take three or four books to equal a pound and each shelf would hold fifty to sixty books. Soft or hardback, the units were designed to be the double side of a triangle held together by a triangle shaped brace board. A little quick figuring and Bowannie found that each unit holding hardbacks would weigh somewhere between 600 to 800 pounds over each shelf-tented are of floor surface. By using the design, there would be no need to reinforce the floor above the basement.

If she had gone with the traditional design of shelving, the straight up and down models, the surface of support would have been reduced significantly. The design would have meant incredible pressure on a smaller floor space. Four rows of such structures angling down the building space would create thousands of pounds of pressure on the floor. It would not have been a safe combination. Additionally, traditional design would have meant that the shelving would have had to be reinforced at the top to reduce the need for expensive foundation struts.

Bu using the triangle design, the weight was spread over an eighteen square foot surface that was hardly a challenge for the structure of the building. Mr. Bowannie had told her how much better the new design would work and she had been pleased with his approval, and relieved that there would be no need to add expensive reinforcement to the floor above the basement.

"Yes?" he responded politely. He turned to Lynne and motioned to the men to continue with their work.

"I have a small problem," she said, approaching him. "It seems the moving van with my furniture will be here Monday, and I need your help with my apartment."

"All right."

"I would like you and some of your assistants to help me paint and wallpaper the rest of the upstairs. I may also need some additional help in some last minute carpentry." She thought of the things that needed to be done and tried not to feel overwhelmed. "This is probably going to mean some overtime. Will that work all right?"

"Let me ask…For myself, I can say I am willing to help you, but I must ask the others."

"If you could let me know by tomorrow, it would help me plan my week."

"Of course. We'll do everything we can," he said and waited patiently for anything else she wanted to add.

"Thank you. I think that should cover what I need to have done."
Lynne nodded at him and left. She was not angry or upset, just wondering what else could prove to make hash out of her plans and good
intentions in Leadville. It seemed that every time she struggled to get a
thing her way, the world became a trickster and showed her how much
she needed to let go and let be. She needed patience, but knew it was
the one thing she was least practiced at. She resigned herself to the fact
that the world would probably continue to remind her until she got it,
and got it right.

An hour later, she was waxing the floor of the room she planned to
make into her study when Mr. Bowannie arrived.

"Three of us will be here until you have done what you need."

"Thank you. And thank the others. I appreciate your help."

Lynne was in the apartment's living room having lunch when she heard
heavy footsteps coming up the stairs. Thinking it was Mr. Bowannie or
another worker, she waited while washing down her sandwich with cola.
She was more than a little surprised to see Sheriff Callison, Charlie, and
Doc come through the open door.

"Lynne?" Doc asked.

"Gentlemen," Lynne said hesitantly, waiting to see what the congrega-
tion was about.

"Charlie and I have convinced the good Sheriff to have a bit of a talk
with you," Doc explained, and glanced at the Sheriff.

Lynne looked at the Sheriff's face and noted that he appeared as though
he had been more than a little reluctant to follow Doc and Charlie into
her apartment. He stood to the side of the other two men, looked at the
refurbished rooms, and glanced back to Lynne with a hinted glare.

"I see," Lynne replied. "How might I help you gentlemen?"

"Well, we thought,…" Charlie began enthusiastically.

"Do you have any coffee, Lynne?" Doc interrupted.

"Sure. Why don't you make yourselves as comfortable as you can and I'll get cups," she said as she motioned the three men to the chairs and an oak table she rescued from the basement.

Charlie and Doc sat waiting for the coffee. But the Sheriff wandered to the patio doors and stood with his hands behind his back while Lynne brought the coffeepot and cups to the table.

"Sheriff, your coffee is ready," Lynne ventured, trying to break through the coolness that surrounded him with a small gesture of goodwill. She understood they had gotten off to a shaky start and wondered if he were a big enough man to let it go and get on with things. She was hesitant to guess what Charlie and Doc might be up to. Lynne had her suspicions, but she did not want to get ahead of them in case she was wrong.

The Sheriff came back to where the others sat and took the offered cup from Lynne almost as reluctantly as if she had handed him a hot iron. He settled into the remaining old chair and gingerly tested its ability to hold his large frame.

"We've been talking…" Doc began.

"Yes, we have," the Sheriff interjected.

Doc shot the Sheriff a glance. The Sheriff shifted uneasily in his chair and became silent again.

"This is ridiculous," snorted Charlie.

"Not yet, but it will be if we keep acting like we're circling the wagons. Look,…here's the deal…Charlie and I decided we needed to talk to the Sheriff about the things you told us the other week,…" Doc began.

"Particularly considering those other fingerprints," Charlie interjected.

Lynne was trying to follow and watched the Sheriff drink his coffee in silence. His face showed dashes of crimson that said to Lynne that he was biding his time, or biting his tongue, with what he had on his mind.

"Yes. Apparently, your suspicions were correct. The beer can have a set of partial prints on it. They were smudged but good enough to suggest they may have come from the same person who committed the first murder. Also,..." Doc started.

"Also, Ms. Fhaolain," the Sheriff began, "we've had them run through the Colorado Bureau of Investigation without finding a match. I'm afraid there were not enough points of comparison to provide an identity of the killer. But you probably already know that," he said and glanced accusingly at Doc.

"Major. I haven't been a Miss since I was eighteen. Yes, the first ones. These last ones, no," Lynne acknowledged.

"Just so. We've sent them on to the FBI in hopes they might do computer imaging with what we have available. But I really don't think we should get too hopeful," Callison asserted.

"You could get lucky, Sheriff. There are lots of possibilities still open for your luck to get better," Lynne said trying to sound encouraging. Lynne watched as Callison shifted in his chair. He was having a hard time being there with her. She held no animosity toward him, other than the fact that he had been rude to her and rigid in his behavior. Lynne would not go beyond civil nor forget her first estimate of him. He was a big fish in a small pond and that seemed to affect his manners. She wanted to test the water, but she did not want to poke a stick at a snake.

"If it was all the same to me, I'd prefer to wait for the results from the FBI...but, " the Sheriff said, clearing his throat. "But these two old birds seem to think that doing so would be waiting for more trouble. And in spite of myself, I'm inclined to agree with them."

"I see."

"So," Sheriff Callison said leaning forward in the chair. He rested his elbows on his knees and held coffee cup in both hands, seeming to concentrate on the last shallow in the cup. "So, although Charlie and Doc

told me what you said about the murderer, I want to hear it from you
first hand."

"You do?" Lynne asked, surprised.

"Yes. I do," he said firmly. "I've had the opportunity, if you will, to do
a little checking on you. You come highly recommended, although part of
that recommendation suggests you're a hard ass."

"A hard ass, Sheriff?" Lynne asked. "Isn't that what most people would
say about you, if you could ask them to be honest with you? In some circles it's a compliment."

"Now just a minute!" the Sheriff began.

"Really, I mean,...with all due respect, it can be a complement." Lynne
insisted. She had been called worse and they had been compliments from
those who admired her work in investigations and by more than a few
who were still serving long sentences behind bars. Lynne figured compliments were what you made of them.

"Just a minute, both of you," Charlie interrupted. "This isn't about personal opinions, attitudes, or personalities. This is about two homicides,
and maybe more if the two of you don't try to put your egos aside for a
few minutes."

"The same here," Doc agreed. "Seems to me, the situation has something each of you need."

"Like?" Lynne asked.

"Well, for one, you need to be a part of this town. You're the interloper. Our own newest stranger, who expected, even hoped to be
accepted and welcomed to live here. This may not be what you want, or
the way you want it, but it is the way things have turned out. And you
know you cannot bury your head in the sand anymore than you have.
And you, Sheriff. You've got an election coming up. The longer this thing

goes on, the worse it looks for you. Charlie and I are two-thirds of the town council and things could go bad if you don't get off that hobby-horse you have been ridding.

"Look, this whole thing is bad business for the town. We cannot afford to loose more people. Like it or not, we cannot afford to have the tourist trade scared off either," Doc lectured. He was fired up. As far as he was concerned, the antagonism of the two ego-batting contenders was getting in the way of the recovery of hope and security for his community and he was not putting up with it anymore.

Neither the Sheriff nor Lynne responded immediately. They were both startled and surprised by Doc's admonishments and felt a little chagrined at the truth he spoke.

"All right. Let's try again," Callison scowled.

"Fine," Lynne agreed hesitantly.

"Good," Doc said, and settled back in his chair satisfied. They would work together and that would be that.

They were still talking three hours later when Mr. Bowannie came into the living room. He waited patiently, holding back from the circle of conversation. The Sheriff saw him, and motioned to Lynne to look behind her.

"Yes, Mr. Bowannie?" she asked.

"We're ready to start here, if you want."

"Oh. I forgot. I've been a little distracted."

"Yes, I can see that," he said kindly.

"I think we've done everything we can now, don't you?" Lynne looked around at Charlie, Doc and the Sheriff. It had been a long session. They had reviewed each piece of information they could recall. Charlie and Doc had recited a list of persons living in the area who might match the inclinations, behavior, and personality of the man they thought they were looking for.

The Sheriff had noted the names, and said he would focus his efforts and those of his deputies on interviewing the prospective suspects. He had not sounded hopeful, but had acknowledged that it was at least doing something constructively. It was a short list. Six men had been identified. Two Gellmore brothers, Joel Pecket, the owner of the gambling house Tabor's Folly, Wynne Huhette, Clarence Stringer, and John Lambrene, all of whom had extensive reputations for being physically violent and emotionally unstable at times. Each suspect had long been a member of the community.

"If you'll give me a moment," Lynne said to Mr. Bowannie, "I'll show you what I'd like to have done."

"Certainly."

Turning back to the group, Lynne prodded, "Well, what do you think?"

"Time to get to it," Sheriff Callison said, and rose to leave. "I hope this works, for all our sakes. You feel pretty strongly about the psychological makeup you've labeled this guy with, don't you."

"Yes. It is not a matter of simply feeling. I'm basing my statements on tried and true research, psychological profiles of similar situations, experiences and such. Feel for me is an analysis not a tactile issue." Lynne corrected.

"That doesn't surprise me," the Sheriff responded as he stood up and put his hat back on.

"I'll let the tone go this time," Lynne said as her eyes narrowed above a slight smile. "I think some things might be productive."

"Me, too," Doc agreed, as he pulled on his jacket and winked cautiously at Lynne.

"Right," Charlie said, downing the last drop of his coffee.

"I'll put my officers at your disposal if anything else occurs. As agreed, you're my unpaid consultant now," Sheriff Callison reminded Lynne.

"There's always pay backs, Sheriff," Lynne smiled.

"I'm sure there is. I have no doubts about that," he said, smiling to her as he tipped his hat. He nodded to Doc and Charlie and walked out the apartment's landing.

Lynne thought she had seen a glimmer of a smile in his eye. She recognized they had gotten off to a bad start because of their personal and unrelated agendas. Those issues were laid to rest. Mostly.

22

At the end of the week, Bowannie and his crew had done a marvelous job. Lynne had felt badly rushed, but not Mr. Bowannie. He had appeared singularly unperturbed with the change of plans or the need to adapt to Lynne's schedule. He and his crew had worked steadily and carefully, with an eye to the details and time constraints. Lynne had been impressed and pleased with their workmanship. By six o'clock the work was finished. Walls had been double coated in paint, the trim and wallpapering were finished, carpets were laid in the living room and bedrooms, the spare bathroom had been repaired, and the whole floor had been thoroughly cleaned. And, most importantly, her private library had been paneled and the shelving was up and ready for her books. In a little over forty-eight hours, she would be in her new home. She would be living there, working there, and beginning her new business. She felt excited, a little scared, and very ready to move out of the hotel.

She did not know what to call her new home. Was it an apartment, a loft, a townhouse, or her retreat? It seemed huge. She felt like a BB in a matchbox in the 4,000 square feet of living space. The house she and Shelby considered buying in Leavenworth, Kansas had been considerably smaller. The apartment was large enough to get lost in and Lynne wondered if that was what she wanted.

The hotel had been comfortable, but living there had made her feel like a vagabond and a drifter without roots. She wanted and needed roots. The speed by which her apartment had been transformed pleased and excited her. It gave her a real opportunity to claiming a new level of independence and quietude. She had been overly accessible to anyone who wanted to see her while she was at the hotel. The Sheriff had intruded on her more than once late in the evening over the last four days. He had come to ask questions, restate the obvious, and develop questions to ask the men he had placed on the suspicious list.

During the week, the Sheriff had eliminated three of the original five men as suspects. Those three had each served a stretch in the Army, had solid explanations for the times in question, and their prints had been on file. The available prints were compared with the partial fingerprints found at the murder scenes. There were too few points for comparison. The three remaining suspects, Alan Gellmore, Joel Pecket and Clarence Stringer were still firmly on the list. Each had been placed under surveillance after intensive questioning. None of them had offered to provide their fingerprints or assist in the investigation beyond routine questioning. Alan Gellmore had been particularly adamant about not cooperating in any fashion and had threatened to sue for harassment.

Lynne did not feel particularly bad at the narrowing of the list. She had not been impressed with the list of probable suspects from the beginning. The information provided by the Sheriff showed Lynne that none of the suspects was in actuality a good fit with the murderer's profile. Each suspect belonged to the right age group, was an accomplished hunter, and knew Greg to a greater or lesser degree. But not only was there nothing in their background or known psychological histories that hinted at psychotic behavior, they were the wrong build and two were left-handed.

Lynne was convinced that Greg Hanson made a better suspect than victim. The more she learned about Greg and how he'd spent his life manipulating people, the more she was certain that he had somehow directly precipitated his own murder. Greg had more enemies and detractors than he had ever had friends.

As Lynne left the Gellmore building and walked back to the hotel after sunset for the last time, she wondered if all the information was leading her down the right path. There had been more than one occasion in the history of the FBI Behavioral Science Unit and Army Criminal Investigation Division files in which the murderer did not match the statistical probabilities, profile, or scenarios of the investigative efforts. She wondered if she had been too sure of herself, too and arrogant about the way the pieces were supposed to fit together. She ruminated about details, connections, pieces of information, and resorted them again looking for anything gone astray.

She wondered if it could indeed be a traveler. Someone who had legitimate business that would allow him to blend into the background of everyone's consciousness and not look out of place. Or, was he someone who could not or would not practice his pent-up anger at home. She wondered if it was someone who had found an easy venue of expression for his craziness. If he were a traveler, he had to take a lot of time to be familiar with the area and be opportunistic in his selection of victims. Lynne knew that if the murderer were a traveler it would make the task of finding him very difficult. A traveler would have his tracks covered by convenience and a certain tempo of their own. The time it would take to uncover that tempo could lead to more bodies, more questions, and more anguish for the town. A traveler would be almost impossible to discover and harder still to catch. His disintegration into his psychosis would have to be close to the surface and he would have to begin to make enough errors to catch himself. Disintegration and continuing murders were the only available keys if it were a traveling man. They would have to be lucky to find him and Lynne did not trust luck. It was too fleeting, flimsy and usually had other consequences attached.

Lost in concentration, she barely heard the hurried footsteps that ran up behind her in the dark until a hand reached out and grabbed her shoulder.

"Lynne," the man's voice said loudly at her ear.

Instinctively, she spun quickly and knocked the man's hand from her shoulder. She grabbed his wrist, stepped into him, and twisted hard. Her quick pressure and thrust of hip made his arm crack down and away from her. While he was off center, she used her left hand to quickly grab him by the nap of the neck, spin him backward and force his face toward the ground. She held his right arm up behind his back by twisting his thumb and palm back. Imbalanced by the speed of her response and the leverage she used by countering his weight, he spun and slid on the sandy, rock-strewn pavement. Blind to his features in the dark shadow of the alleyway and the distant glare of the bracketing streetlights, she held him to the pavement with her knee in the middle of his back and firm pressure on his arm.

"Lynne!"

"What?" Lynne asked, still operating on instinct and impulse.

"Lynne, it's me! Ray! Ray Billings!"

"Ray Billings?"

"Ray. You know the teacher of sociology, lover of small animals, and friend to the environment. Ray Billings, damn it," he said as he struggled to get his face off the cold ground.

"Oh, my God. Dr. Billings. I am sorry," she said as she stood up and backed away from the man. Flustered, she went back to his side and tried to help him stand up. As she reached for him, he waved her away and rolled to a sitting position. He blinked at her.

"Just stay where you are. I'll get up on my own," he commanded. He rose, dusting the gravel and slush snow from his clothes.

"I didn't know it was you," she began and felt a twinge in her side. As Lynne touched her ribs and wondered if she should see Doc Kennedy to have him tape them up just incase they were cracked.

"That's obvious. Do you usually greet friends in the same manner?" he asked in strained humor.

"No. But if you sneak up on me, I guess I do."

"Sneak up on you? I have been calling to you for the last fifty feet. You didn't hear me?"

"No. No, I didn't," she blushed, knowing it would take a lot of time to let go of twenty years of habits and trained responses. "I was lost in thought, I guess."

"No doubt...do you always concentrate that hard?" Ray looked at her in growing amusement.

"Not always."

"Good. Otherwise, I would have to report you as a danger to the community. We don't need any more walking wounded or dead around here, now do we?"

"No. No, we do not. Can, I...would you care to join me for supper, Dr. Billings?" Lynne offered.

"No more surprises?"

"No more. I promise," she said as she took his arm.

"I'd be delighted. There was something I wanted to talk to you about, however."

"Then we can talk over supper and it will be my treat."

"Great. But you don't have to buy my dinner," he said, holding her hand where she crooked it in his arm.

"It's the least I can do," she assured him.

"Not really, but it will do for now," he assured her.

"Excuse me?"

"That's what I want to talk to you about. But let's wait until we get some food. Shall we?"

"Of course."

Small talk consumed their walk to the hotel, and Lynne had recovered from her embarrassment of the encounter by the time they reached the lobby. She could tell that Ray had managed to recover his dignity by the easy flow of conversation. She vowed not to mention it again and hoped he would do the same. She felt pulled and tossed by all the events, which had occurred, since she arrived in Leadville. She knew the murders, her own snooping, and the insistent involvement in the cases had put her on edge. That would have to change. Lynne felt she needed to accommodate to a lot of changes in her life.

During dinner, Ray ordered a carafe of red wine. They drank and settled easily into friendly conversation. During the course of the conversation, Lynne tried to relax in his company. He seemed as bright, articulate, amusing and mannerly as her first impression. He was interested in what she had to say and courteous in his regard to her interests. It was a pleasant time. When the meal had finally arrived, Lynne was feeling very kindly toward Ray.

"I'd like you to do me a favor," Ray said as he leaned across the table toward Lynne.

"Like what?"

"Like, teach my Sociology class next Tuesday evening. I have to go out of town to a conference in Denver."

"You've got to be kidding?"

"No. Remember, I told you I intended to use you."

"I don't know."

"Look," Ray said smoothly, "you'll love it. Are not all retirees and cops hams by nature? Think of it as giving the students a break from me."

"I just don't…"

"I have to present a paper at the conference. If you don't help me, the students get a free day."

"Would that be so bad?" Lynne asked as she tried to think of a way to wiggle out of the situation.

"Yes. They're students. I need a break from them, but they don't need a break from what they need to learn."

"What would I have to do?"

"We're currently reading and discussing Man and His Symbols by Karl Jung. I use it in juxtaposition of an exploration of ancient and modern dream cultures. Are you familiar with Jung?"

"I've read a number of his books."

"Well, there you have it."

"Still," Lynne squirmed.

"All you have to do is refresh yourself with the book and you'd be ready."

"That's heavy stuff for junior college folks."

"They need it. Otherwise, the only thing they'll ever come away with is a two-year technical degree and narrow little lives. My classes are designed to create a certain cognitive dissonance. To make them question. To make them look for answers beyond themselves," he said as he leaned back in his chair and downed his glass of wine.

"Why not have one of your colleagues do it for you?"

"They are mostly technical instructors and I've imposed on the rest often enough. To be frank with you, I have talked to Doc and Charlie about you. You're a fascinating woman, and although it may be an awkward way to start, I'd like us to be friends."

"I see," Lynne said uncertainly.

"Or, for the time being, we could just say you owe me this one. After all, wouldn't you rather teach an evening class for a few hours than be arrested for assault and battery?" he chided.

"Oh. Now I really do see!" Lynne said laughing. She liked his banter and his temperament made sense to her. He had been friends with Doc and Charlie since he moved to Leadville seven years ago. They liked him, and she liked and trusted Charlie and Doc.

"You'll do it?"

"Yes. I'll do it," Lynne said hesitantly, hoping she would not regret her decision.

"Great. The class is on Tuesday evening, six to nine in room 245 of Bradey Hall. Here are some of my notes," he said, reaching into his jacket pocket and pulling out a small stack of three-by-five cards.

"You knew I'd accept." Lynne asked, and looked at him in surprise.

"I pride myself on knowing people. Most particularly women. And I was hoping," he said as he refreshed both glasses of wine before she could protest.

"Right," Lynne said slowly. She was not sure she liked either his self-assured tone or implication. She stored the information but thought she might have to chalk it up to his professorial ego. The friend issue he had raised was becoming a more remote possibility. She wondered if Doc and Charlie were good a judges of character.

"I was hoping to have the opportunity to get to know you better ever since Charlie and Doc introduced us."

"Oh?"

"Of course. You are the most interesting woman in town. Your career and your courage to head out into the unknown and start a new business…all that and your obvious intelligence makes you worth wanting to get to know."

"I've discovered over the last few weeks that it takes more sweat than courage to start a business," Lynne deflected.

"I like to think that if you would allow me to have the time and opportunity to get to know you, that you would find me interesting as well. I am a great chef, minor wine connoisseur, a devil at table games, and an occasionally sparkling conversationalist. I possess other attributes, but those are for later," Ray assured her.

"Are those the detached scientific observations of a trained sociologist speaking?" Lynne asked mordantly.

"Quotes from friends, actually. Frankly, we are of an age, social class and inclination. You impress me as a strong, capable woman. And, if you don't mind me saying so, you are quite attractive. So, rather than being coy, I will lay my cards on the table," Ray continued.

"I appreciate your...ah...honesty."

"I will,...you know. Get to know you, that is. Let's say I've made a study of you and like you."

"I will let you know,...later," Lynne said attempting to modify the tone of irritation in her voice.

"Oh, and about class, don't forget to be there early."

"Why?"

"Well, you'll need time to find the room, set up, and relax a little. Also, if you are late, the students are just as likely to have left. They are under the impression that if you are a professor; they have to wait ten minutes for you. If you are just a guest speaker, they figure a five-minute wait. It's ritualistic behavior but we can't seem to break them of it," Ray laughed, and waved at the waitress.

"I have to be going," Lynne said as she realized he might be ordering more wine. "I have a lot to do. I'm moving into the apartment," she watched as the smile fell off his face.

"Well, I was hoping we might spend more time together this evening," he softened, and slid the note cards across the table to her.

"I'm afraid I'll have to have all the energy I can muster to work. But I appreciate the thought," she lied.

"Well, let's do this again soon after I get back from Denver," Ray said as he touched her hand and let his fingers linger on hers as she drew the cards toward her.

"We'll have to see. My time is pretty tight for the next few weeks," Lynne said as excuse, and frowned slightly as his fingers maintained their touch on her hand.

"Of course," he said, and withdrew his hand.

"I'll pay that bill," she reminded him.

"No such thing. I'll pay," his tone reproachful.

"That wasn't the deal," Lynne insisted.

"Maybe not, but teaching my class is a favor to me. Allow me to be a gentleman," he smiled at her, and pulled a wad of bills from the breast pocket of his jacket.

"Thank you," Lynne conceded.

"Here's to Tuesday night and more time to our becoming friends," he said, raising his glass in toast toward Lynne.

"Tuesday night," she agreed, but studiously avoided his reference to a future dinner date.

23

Lynne slept fitfully. Dreams bore down on her in loud, vivid and terrifying clarity. She awoke twice, out of breath, panting from exertion, and sweating from some strain that slipped away from her as soon as her eyes opened. The second time she awoke, she got up and fixed herself a cup of cocoa. It was three in the morning. She sat at the table feeling aggravated and annoyed at an interrupted night's sleep. She could not remember anything of the dreams and wondered what her subconscious was trying to tell her. She shrugged, irritated. She had been tense and anxious for weeks. Weeks filled with murders, building repairs, and uneasy encounters with the locals. Then the moving company demands had fallen on her. She was awake. The rest she needed to help her feel ready for the long moving day vanished like the mist of her nightmares.

She finished her cocoa and walked hopefully back to bed. She lay in the dark staring at the ceiling and the pressed patterns of the tin visible by the streetlights. She prayed halfheartedly for sleep to come.

To her surprise, the next thing Lynne heard was the alarm clock waking her at six. She felt groggy and was unsure whether she had been asleep or staring at the ceiling. It did not matter now. The moving van could be arriving in less than two hours. She had to get ready. The smell of coffee wafted up from hotel restaurant.

"A shower," she muttered and rose to meet the day.

When she left the hotel and turned toward her building, Lynne could see trucks sitting in front of the doors to her store. She recognized Mr. Bowannie's truck and knew the work crew would be waiting patiently for her to arrive and let them in. Everything had been arranged. Lynne would get the use of four of Mr. Bowannie's apprentices to help with the moving, while he and the other journeymen continued with the labors on the first and second floors of the building.

Mr. Bowannie had told Lynne last Wednesday that he and his crew had about two weeks of work remaining on the building. Lynne had been relieved. Time had been marching on. It was already the third week of May. She had hoped to have the store ready in mid-June to catch the first flow of tourists. Everything had to go right over the next few weeks if she were to stay on schedule.

As Lynne approached the building, Mr. Bowannie got out of his truck and nodded in her direction. The other workers, seeing Mr. Bowannie get out of his truck, started removing their tools from truck beds.

"Good morning," Lynne said to the waiting crew. "And a good morning to you, Mr. Bowannie."

"It is a fine day, Ms. Fhaolain," Mr. Bowannie said with what appeared to be great formality. The other men and women waited for Lynne to find her keys.

"Yes. Yes, it is a fine day," she returned to Mr. Bowannie. She could feel him at her back and his presence seemed to radiate onto her. It was a warm, grandfatherly feeling. Over the weeks they had worked together, he had been sympathetic, although she had not shared any personal issues with him. Time posed a struggle to her. She felt as though she were between being and becoming. There were things she had left, things she lost, and things that had not yet materialized. No longer an Army officer, no longer someone's lover, an old life vanishing to memory, and yet to become a bookstore owner. She was adrift.

Finally getting the doors open the work crew flowed behind her and into the building. The lights were turned on and they moved directly to their task areas. Certain tools, lunch pails, and clothing had been shed into various corners before starting work. They glanced around their respective uncompleted tasks and took a few moments to recall their intentions and projects they had left with the evening before.

Lynne checked the thermostat and adjusted the temperature upward for the comfort of the crew. She glanced at the milling workers readying themselves and their tools, and then turned and headed for the freight elevator. She had developed a complete confidence in the crew and Mr. Bowannie's ability to coordinate the speed and priorities of the day in the emerging store.

Her task for the day was to decide how to effect a smooth and comfortable arrangement of her furniture and belongings when they arrived. She had brought a complete itemized list of her household items with her but felt uncertain as to the floor plan dimensions. She wanted a little time to draw and fit them into a sketch.

Stepping off the elevator, Lynne walked down the darkened corridor to the doorway. Daylight filtered through the sparse windows, allowing her the opportunity to place her feet surely before her. As she walked into the living room-cum-kitchen, she switched on the wall light. She busied herself with the preparations of the coffee she had not been able to get enough of at the hotel. As the coffee began to percolate, she walked around the kitchen counter and flipped on the lights to the living room. Sitting down on a cleanly covered chair, she tried to organize her thoughts and papers for the household arrangements.

She became mesmerized by the list of furnishings and the blankness of the sketchpad before her. She turned toward the living room interior and let her mind drift with the images of the dancing rays of the sun as they captured and sparkled on tiny flecks of airborne dust. Her new life was beginning to take shape. She would become a part of the community and forever removed from everything she had ever known.

A whispered panic of regret rose from her chest and sliced slowly across her heart. Tears welled up in her eyes.

"Shelby," Lynne whispered the name. The grief, loss and need for mourning she would stuffed down, ignore, and run from rushed up and washed over her. She had avoided every hint, reflection, idea, and memory by work and frenzied activity. And now an idle thought betrayed her. There could be no going back to the way things had been. And she did not know what going forward would mean.

Lynne gasped for air and relief from the darkness of her thoughts. Clutching her arms across her shaking chest, she lost the battle as fear and pain collided. She surrendered to the flood and let it carry her in torrents of anguish.

She did not know how long she sat there holding and rocking herself. Exhaustion overtook her and she laid her head in her arms on the thick arm of the chair, breathing in ragged shuddering sighs. She yielded. Not knowing who or what to pray to, or for, she wept.

As she began to relax when a hand seemed to touch her head and stroke her hair. She thought it was her imagination. Puzzled Lynne slowly raised her head.

"You try too hard to be too strong," Mr. Bowannie whispered.

"I'm sorry," Lynne said, sitting up and wiping her eyes with her hands. Embarrassment spread across her already reddened cheeks. She saw Mr. Bowannie motion to her not to say another word.

"The moving van is here," Mr. Bowannie said and turned to leave.

After he was gone, Lynne went to the bathroom and splashed cold water on her face. She collected herself and, feeling somewhat confident that the stain of tears had disappeared, she pushed the button and went to greet her belongings to their new home.

"Did you tell her about the basement door?" Jonathan Walker asked Bowannie as he watched the men from the moving van ready Lynne's belongings for off-loading.

"No. No need to cause her more worry right now," he said uncomfortably. He would wait for the right time to tell Lynne that Jonathan had found the basement door jimmied open when he had gone down to rewire a shorted light fixture. The door had been damaged. The frame holding the dead bolt had been clawed from its placement. Only the heavy chain-lock bolted to the steel cross member that was riveted to the brick wall had kept the determined intruder outside the building.

"We'll fix it and let it be for now," Bowannie said quietly to Jonathan. He did not want the others to know what had happened if he could help it. Lynne would have to know, but he would choose a better time for the telling.

There was, he had noted on each of their meetings, much happening in the air around her and the hint of forgotten dreams about her. A shadowed essence of ancient earth and sky hovered between her and the world. She could be a crossover. It would have to be known. If she were a crossover, he could not allow her to continue lost in this world to herself and the People. He knew whom to contact to help in his seeing and discover what truth there might be.

24

Lynne awoke for the first time in her new home. Her initial glance at her surroundings left her feeling lost as the sleep drifted from her eyes. Slowly, as she began to focus, she trembled at the uncertainty and displacement she felt. The room was not familiar. Sudden recognition brought the feeling of relief. This was permanence, new order even if it meant total personal reorganization. She flung her legs out from underneath the covers determined to charge forward into the day.

"My life, and welcome to it," Lynne announced in confirmation and amused hope. Running on tiptoe, she headed quickly through the chilled air of the room and grabbed the robe hanging on the back of the bedroom door. She preferred to sleep in the nude, but the chill in the apartment sent the hairs on her arms on ready alert. She turned the water on for a shower and decided to take a long soak.

Mr. Bowannie's work crew would not be for another two-and-a-half hour. Lynne had plenty of time for coffee, breakfast, and an ordering of priorities for the day. Humming to herself, she dashed to the kitchen and scooped coffee into the pot while the tub filled.

There is so much left to do, Lynne thought to herself. I have gotten so entangled in situations and circumstances; I have not taken much time out for myself. Knowing she had allowed herself to be pulled into things and had been pushed into events over which she had little or no choice did not satisfy her. The control she had tried to exert had most often taken the form of trying to say "No" but she'd been running where her curiosity lead her. And in some instances that meant she ended up leading with her chin.

The morning went smoothly. Freshly showered and wrapped in her favorite robe Lynne managed to get some of her thoughts on paper. Tasks were separated into discrete units of need and organization. She wanted to get her belongings in the right places, wind down on repairs to the building, ready the bookstore, prepare for the lecture to the Sociology class, and finally, reexamine the details of the murders.

Lynne had studiously avoided contact with the Sheriff while she tried to organize her own affairs. She did not imagine that the Sheriff had missed her intrusions. She had not been able to offer him any quick solutions or a specific direction of inquiry that might have aided in discovering the perpetrator.

She had been of no use to the Sheriff when the media descended on the town. The details and savagery of the two murders had created a media blitz about the town. They had descended like vultures, picking over the pieces of the scant information and nagging the lurid details over prime time. It was not until a triple homicide occurred in the greater Denver area that the news personalities scattered toward the scent of fresher blood. Having arrived like a lost tornado, they left the same way. Distracted, they lost interest. Leadville receded in importance to all but residents. Lynne pulled on her jeans and heard the deep tones of the front door bell announce the arrival of the work crew. Hopping and shoving her right leg into her jeans, she headed for the freight elevator.

That evening as she was preparing to leave for the sociology class, Mr. Bowannie stopped Lynne on her way out the door.

"Grandfather wishes to speak with you this evening," he announced stoically. He had to balance his intent to convince her to meet with Grandfather, and his inclination to chuckle at the bewilderment on her face. He could see the confusion flash its way across her eyes. She was young. Like many Wasichu, she was unfamiliar with the veritable meaning of the word "grandfather." He watched her face, as the misunderstanding caused her to quizzically regard him and silently speculate how a man of his years could still have a living grandfather.

"I'm sorry?" Lynne said, believing she had not heard him correctly. "I'm afraid I didn't hear you," she apologized as she continued to fish into her backpack for the keys to her truck. "Grandfather. He wishes you to meet with him this evening. I will take you there," Bowannie said, enjoying the play of emotions dancing through Lynne's eyes. She was smart, courteous and gracious toward his workers, whether they had been family members or the others he had taken into his fold. He admired how she had dealt evenly, without anger at people, with the small errors that sometimes happened. The behavior was unusual for a Wasichu and had been mentioned by his workers with respectful surprise.

"Your grandfather? He wants to talk to me?" Lynne asked. She could not imagine why Mr. Bowannie's ancient grandfather should want to speak to her. She wondered if she were being set up for some great joke. Her grandfather had been a past master of jokes. She did not have any trouble imagining that Bowannie might be similarly inclined.

"Yes. He said it was important that he meet with you this evening," Bowannie said. He had related his feelings and speculations about Lynne to Grandfather over the course of the work on the building. Grandfather had been intrigued and had not immediately rejected the possibility of a crossover. The old man had smoked on it, and told Bowannie that he must meet with the young woman Tuesday evening.

"I see," Lynne responded as the questions lingered in her head

"I will take you," Bowannie repeated.

"I…, Mr. Bowannie, I have a class to teach tonight. I promised. I cannot do this now," she explained, stumbling for an answer that would not sound like an excuse.

"Yes, after class would be fine," he agreed. "But Grandfather says it must be this evening."

"Oh." Lynne felt trapped. Her plate kept getting fuller. A room full of students staring at their substitute instructor and now Mr. Bowannie's grandfather wanted her to make an appearance. Lynne remembered that Bowannie and his crew had answered every need without complaint or sour disposition. She recalled that he had graciously spent more time than she knew he had been charging her to prepare her apartment for her. She resigned herself. She owed him, and did not mind this method of payment.

"I'll wait for you in the school parking lot. I'll be there by nine. All right?" Bowannie extended his hand knowing that this Wasichu understood a contract obligation. That gesture would bind this young woman.

"All right…that would be fine," Lynne agreed shaking his hand. It seemed a small enough favor. It would cost her little of what she had least to offer. Time.

Lynne swept down the sidewalk to her truck, and put the thought of meeting Bowannie's grandfather out of her mind. Ahead of her, she had a classroom of strange faces waiting, for her and an anxiety level that was causing her heart to race.

"They can kill me, but they can't eat me…I hope," she said as she headed for the junior college.

Afterwards, she was delighted to find that not only did they not eat her, they didn't even kill her. The class session, although long and daunting, went smoothly. Lynne enjoyed exploring and sharing their ideas about Jung's interest in the universality of symbolism. She particularly enjoyed the discussion offered by a young man and woman who had obviously read a number of the books written by Joseph Campbell. Their interjection of the myths explored and interrelated by Campbell provided an ideal means by which to note the frequency of similar creation myths beyond the relatively limited Western European boundaries explored by Jung. It had been very heady stuff.

Nearing the end of the evening class, Lynne felt as though she was about to get in over her head and beyond the notes Billings had provided her when suddenly the class disintegrated into a social gaggle rather than a structured classroom environment. Hesitant at first to let it go on, she succumbed to the freewheeling of ideas and enthusiasm of the students. It wasn't very military, but it was fun. Walking to her truck after class, she hoped that the good Dr. Ray Billings would not be too disappointed with her performance or the lack of rigor she brought to the classroom.

A truck engine started in the dark of the lot as Lynne approached her parking space. Without turning on its headlights, the truck slowly moved across the dark, and deserted parking lot toward her. Its rumbling engine drew her attention. Lynne hesitated as she reached her truck. She looked carefully at the approaching vehicle. A twinge of concern flitted across her mind as it slowly drew closer to her. She reached into the lower pocket of the backpack slung across her back and felt for the gun tucked tightly against the Velcro. She relaxed her grip and tried to slow her heart when she recognized Bowannie's broad face on the other side of the windshield.

"I almost forgot," Lynne shouted at Bowannie's window, not knowing if he could hear her through the glass and rumble of his motor.

He nodded and waved in understanding. He motioned her to get in her truck and follow him. Lynne was grateful he could not see her blushing in her embarrassment. She chastised herself for being too quick to think the worst and reach for a gun every time she felt a hint of threat. With Shelby's death, her early retirement, and the cross-country move, life had taken on great uncertainty and threat. But the solution would be difficult. The world had spun out of her control. Each new predicament did feel as though it threatened her thin web of security. Circumstances, small and large, appeared to mitigate the hope she held for a re-balancing in her life. As she started the truck, she decided she would have to think about how to remedy the situation before she shot some innocent or fool.

25

Twenty minutes later as she followed the taillights of Bowannie's truck, Lynne realized she had no idea where she was going or how long it would take to get there. She had to laugh at herself. Here she was, following a beat-up gray Ford pickup down the highway and across the mountains. They just as she was feeling thankful that they had not taken off across any darkened side roads, Bowannie's truck slowed and turned onto a gravel and ice-packed lane. Lynne sighed to herself and muttered something about a fool's errand, but continued to follow Bowannie's truck into the night. Holding the vehicle steady on the rutted road took most of her concentration but a small voice played a constant tune of consternation behind her frowning brow. What had she gotten herself into? How long would it be before she could go home? And when could she snuggle down into the warm covers of her own bed? The pothole craters road jostled her inside the cab of her truck as trees crowded in on her from the dark.

Thirty miles further on she saw a cluster of distant lights glowing beneath the open star-studded sky. There were ten small cabins neatly arranged at the base of a looming mountain slope. Lynne brought her truck to a stop alongside Bowannie's in an open space surrounded by the warmly lit cabins.

Bowannie climbed out of his truck and motioned Lynne to follow. Halfway to the cabin farthest from the edge of the clearing, he turned back to motion for her to come. Lynne had been trying to cautiously pick her path amongst the ice troughs and wheel ruts scattered across the yard. She saw him motion to her and jogged to his side.

"You smoke, don't you?" he asked as he turned to her.

"Well, yes, I do," she answered. Lynne hoped she was not going to hear another lecture about the evils of smoking or worse yet, not be allowed to smoke in the house she was headed toward. The idea of having to stand outside on this chill night, when she wanted a smoke did not do anything for her fading generosity of spirit.

"Good. Do you have a full pack?"

"Yes."

"Give it to Grandfather when you first meet him," Bowannie said, and smiled at her.

"Give it to him?" Lynne questioned.

"Custom. Old people like tobacco. It also shows respect," he advised. "It will all be explained to you in time. Really."

"Really?" she wondered, and hoped the old man liked menthol.

The door to the small cabin opened as they approached. The combined glare of a bare bulb and dancing firelight silhouetted a skirted form in the doorway. The woman nodded in their direction and beckoned with one arm toward the comfort waiting inside. Smells of sage and boiled beef met Lynne's nose with invitation.

Lynne discovered she had to partially duck as she went through the cabin door. It surprised her. She had never been under the impression that she was a tall person, regardless of the effect her bearing often signaled to others. And the idea of feeling as though she had to duck caught her attention. The door was low. Behind her, Bowannie definitely ducked to miss the top of the frame. She thought to say something about the odd door but restrained herself when she heard a voice close to her.

"Sit," a young woman said and motioned Lynne to a padded chair next to the fire.

An old man was sitting across from the chair Lynne had been directed to. She shucked off her coat, removed her hat, and nodded at the old man as she sat down. Sitting quietly, feeling the ancient eyes stare at her, Lynne noticed that the room seemed oddly shaped. Surreptitiously she glanced around.

The cabin had been constructed with unusually short logs that caused more circular lines than Lynne had thought possible with straight-edged wooden materials. The room into which she had entered was the spacious center of activity in the cabin. She detected several other rooms off from the central area and figured those were bedrooms or other private areas. The ceiling was constructed of logs and showed a radiating crosshatch to a central hexagon peak. Looking at the ceiling and the slow slope of the roof toward the fireplace, Lynne wondered how much of the cabin continued on the other side of the fireplace. She marveled at the simplicity and practicality of the design. If she were right, the private portions of the house would also benefit from the radiating heat of a centralized fireplace.

Lynne glanced at the woman who had directed her into the house. Her face Lynne gave the appearance of great age, but the quick movement of her hands across the surface of the cast iron stove belied that impression. The woman was busily scooping up something hot and steamy from the pots arranged on the stove and dipping it into large wooden bowls. She picked up several flat pieces of bread, placed them in a cloth napkin, and handed the things to the younger woman.

"Be comfortable," Bowannie urged Lynne as he took his place next to the old man. He settled into the low-backed chair, he nodded to the old man, and spoke quietly to him. The old man nodded and responded with what Lynne took for a soft affirmation.

The extinguishing of the glaring ceiling bulb that had hovered near the entrance softened the lights in the room. A bright glow radiated from the fireplace and a nearby lamp.

Glancing quizzically at Bowannie as the lights were reduced and food was offered, Lynne wondered what might be expected of her. Lynne saw Bowannie's face urge her to accept the moment, and she happily resigned herself to the experience. She held the bowl and bread in front of her, inhaled the delicious aromas, and remembered she had not had a bite to eat since noon. The tantalizing smells drifted up to her nose and made her mouth water in anticipation.

She had been so absorbed in her curiosity about the cabin and the work of the women she had not had really looked at the old man. She did not want to stare, but he was the reason for her being there. She felt a twinge of anticipation and nervousness battling in her.

Grandfather had a remarkable face. It seemed to hold the accumulation of his life. All the joys, wisdom and sorrows were etched in loving lines and soft creases. Lynne wanted a face like that someday. The lines and creases were set by decades of seeing everything without and within. The eyes rested below a strong forehead and nestled in a mesh of deeply embedded crows-feet. His body did not seem bent at all, as had been her first impression. He sat straight and steadily looked at her with wonderful attentive eyes. His gaze was polite but seemed to read and entreat her at the same time.

As she opened her mouth to speak, Bowannie motioned to her with a low wave of his hand. He pointed to her shirt pocket where she had put the extra pack of cigarettes. Feeling abashed that she had been about to misstep with the proper order of things. Lynne reached in her pocket, withdrew the cigarettes and handed them to the old man. Bowannie nodded at her and looked back at Grandfather.

"A gift, Grandfather." The soft tones of Bowannie's voice conveyed deep respect.

The old man took the pack of cigarettes from her hand, barely brushing his fingers across her own. His eyes never left her face. A deep quiet grunt drummed once in his chest as their fingers touched. Lynne felt the skin of his fingers. It had been a warm, dry, and callused probe.

Turning to Bowannie, the old man spoke briefly. Bowannie nodded and turned to Lynne. There was a light of mischief in his eyes.

"Grandfather wants to know how long you've been lost."

"Pardon me?" Lynne asked uncertainly. Lost, she wondered. Did the old man believe that she had stumbled onto his cabin rather than having been requested, almost ordered, by Bowannie to follow him here?

Seeing the concern and confusion cross her face, the old man nodded and spoke directly to her. He had a quick, pleasant voice. But he spoke no language with which Lynne was familiar. When he finished his brief statement, he looked at Bowannie for acknowledgment.

"He says you've been lost to yourself, and he wants to know how long this thing has been happening."

"I'm afraid I don't understand," Lynne lied to Bowannie and the old man. Shelby had been gone for six months. Surely, she reasoned, the old man could not know or even guess about that. She figured that too much was being lost in the translation of what the old man said and what he really meant.

"No, Major Fhaolain, you do understand. Or at least you understand part of the question," Bowannie insisted.

She felt caught, trapped in self-protection. She did not want to bare either her pain to anyone. It was a private wound. Lynne could not talk about Shelby, least of all these strange men.

The old man spoke quickly to Bowannie who nodded and turned to Lynne with gentle urging.

"It is about loss and the lost, the two are the same. He wants to know first of the loss. It is not disrespectful. He is concerned for you," Bowannie explained patiently.

"I...I recently lost someone," Lynne felt a choking close in on her throat, and hesitated for fear that tears instead of answers would come. "We..." she tried to continue. "We had been together for a long time. But,...not long enough. I really don't want to talk about it."

"You were married?" Bowannie asked.

"No. No, we were not married," Lynne, said, fighting to maintain her composure.

The old man leaned forward and spoke in rapid quiet words to Lynne.

"He says you are wrong. You were married. He can see that. He says you were loved. He is sad for your pain."

"Yes, even without a piece of paper, Shelby and I were,...united." Lynne swallowed her surprise heavily.

"Then, you are special. All such are special to the people," Bowannie interpreted the old man's words.

"What does your grandfather know of this," Lynne asked struggling to understand.

Bowannie turned to speak to the old man. He mumbled something in reply. They continued in the exchange for several moments while Lynne renewed her absorption in the stew.

"He is not my grandfather," Bowannie said, returning his attention to Lynne.

"He's not? But I thought you said...?" Lynne looked up in surprise. Now she truly felt lost.

"No. He is a wise man. He is not as old as he is wise. He guides us with his knowledge and his vision. That is why he is called Grandfather," Bowannie said by way of explanation.

"Oh, it's like a title, a title acknowledging his venerable position?" Lynne asked, wanting to get on firmer footing.

"Yes. He is wise but he has always been wise. This wisdom comes from his path. It is a path he was shown when he was given his first vision. The wisdom grows in his life and through his having seen many truths. He says your heart will mend, but you should be patient and kind to yourself." Bowannie continued with brief exchanges between him and the old man who had leaned over to him to direct the conversation. "It is in your own time that you must heal. Good, strong, right, and loving. Such he sees you had with your woman. Memory is now both your joy and your pain. You must respect the memory, but care for your life."

"Thank Grandfather for me, and tell him I will." Lynne knew the old man meant well and appreciated his interest. She wondered with more than little concern, if these people were part of the widening rumor mill of the town that she had been caught up in.

"How is it that he would be my Grandfather?" Lynne asked.

"Ahumm," the old man said, nodding toward her. He turned to Bowannie to laugh while pointing at Lynne with an ancient hand. He spoke low and quickly to Bowannie. For his part, Bowannie seemed absorbed in what the old man was saying and several times appeared to be checking for clarification in a rapid-fire exchange. When the old man finished talking, he settled back in his chair, satisfied.

"He wishes me to tell you a story. It is his story and ours too. It will make the understanding easier and perhaps guide you soon as it has guided us these many years." Bowannie leaned back in his chair and motioned quietly to the younger woman who had been sitting by the heat of the stove.

She rose from her chair, and as Lynne watched, poured what appeared to be piping hot water into three large ceramic mugs. The young woman brought the steaming mugs to the fire and passed the cups first to Grandfather, then Bowannie, and finally to Lynne.

The aroma of the steeping brew wafted up to Lynne. A strange, sharp smell met her nose. Roasted sunflower seeds and rose hips were the only tastes she could isolate as she cautiously sipped the hot brew. It was wonderfully aromatic with a taste gentle to the tongue. Looking into the wide cup, Lynne could see a small tea infusion gadget resting on the bottom. A small metal chain clipped to the edge ensured the retrieval of the device when the preferred steeping and level of flavor had been achieved.

When the formality and comfortable companionship of the tea had been observed, Bowannie began to tell Grandfather's story. Periodically, he would pause as Grandfather interjected what appeared to Lynne as an elaboration or further explanation. She noticed how they never spoke over each other, never interrupted what the other was saying, and patiently waited to ensure that the speaker had said all he intended before responding.

Lynne was fascinated and intrigued. She was used to the racket of the provost marshal's office, Army bases, and investigative divisions where everyone seemed to challenge the other to get their two cents in on the conversation. This evening, company and conversation struck a cord within her that she had forgotten was there. Lynne felt what tension she retained flow from her as she leaned into the comfort of the low overstuffed chair and waited for the story.

Her hands lowered the bowl to her lap as she curled her legs underneath her. The warmth of the fire, a good meal, the soothing mysterious tea, and the interspersed rhythmic tones of Grandfather and Bowannie rocked her in their cozy confines. She listened and drifted with the story.

26

As Lynne listened to the old Indian, Leadville quieted itself into the slumber of another dark and cold spring night. The streets were empty and the last sheriff's car of the evening headed north on highway 24.

He waited silently in the dark and relished the cold clear light of the stars. It was perfect, but then it had been almost perfect for a long time since he had gained the power. He had made things happen, and he wanted to make more happen. He waited until the eleven o'clock chimes on the courthouse had announced the long march toward the last hour of the day before he made his way across town. He was barely able to contain himself in his excitement. He warned himself angrily to slow down, to watch his step, and not to let his ego outstrip his ability. He thought of that and laughed out loud, then quickly hushed himself. There was no way his skills could ever again be questioned or brought to fault. He had proved repeatedly how defenseless they were against him. There was little need for caution. He felt his power flow and glowing in his body.

He approached the building from the eastern end of the alley and stood motionless within the shadows that touched one another to form the deepest black. He willed his thoughts toward the edge of the balcony, down the hallway, and to where she lay sleeping.

He raised his head toward the third floor and imagined her lying in her bed. She would be warm. Soft, rounded curves would respond under the touch of his hand. She would be his to claim. He saw her face nestled against the pillow and her hair ruffled near her eyes in silent dreaming.

He called softly to her and imagined himself standing at the foot of the bed watching the gentle movement of her breath rise and fall under the blankets. He would move to her side and touch the cheek she offered. Gently he would stroke her hair, the exposed arm resting near her face, and the turn of the leg under the covers. She would respond to his caress, to the power of his being, and be stirred in the depths of her dreams.

He would arouse her slowly from that slumber, his passion increasing with each stroke. He saw her movement against the sheets, her legs turn and spread in somnambulist longing. She would moan, deep in desire, as his hands manipulated her dreams and her body toward his needs. Gently, she would awaken and see him standing before her. She would see his power and the beauty of his desire. He would take her beyond care or hope of redemption.

She had been bad before. Like any woman was stubborn and reluctant to know her own desires. She would be as bad for him as he wanted her to be when he exposed the lust sleeping in her heart. She wanted him of that he was certain. He knew it as surely as he knew her boasting was a ruse she used to hide her true emotions. Some women were afraid of their emotions and needed the right man to bring them to awakening. He knew he was the man for her. She was fragile, lost, and needed to understand her purpose in life.

She had been thoughtless and ignored his power by trying to hide in the self-imposed prison of her life. He would free her tonight. He would forgive her after he punished her just enough to make her want him more, and give her the release she waited for.

He thrilled to her imagined touch. He would make her promise to do, to want to do, and beg to do, anything he asked. He would accept the gifts she would offer. She would be a lovely prize.

He looked around the alley and found what he wanted, a way up to the third floor. The building next to hers had been shaped with rough-hewn native stone and protrusions of sharp edges gave the alley side its distinctive rock-wall features. He stood on the top brace of the receiving dock, grabbed the drainpipe notched between the buildings, and boosted himself up to the miniature roof overhanging the alley. He placed his hard-toed shoes onto the rock face protrusions and scrabbled up, using the drainpipe as balance. In fifteen minutes, he hung between the two buildings and cautiously planted a foot on the patio ledge of her loft.

Silence greeted him. He breathed hard, forcing air into his lungs as he rested from his exertion. He laughed under his breath, and it steamed out of his nostrils and mouth to float away on the quiet breeze above the alley. He was a steam engine; he thought to himself and laughed. He wondered if she would be able to see the steam rise from him as he tunneled his way into her.

He dropped noiselessly to the patio floor and waited to see if his landing brought hasty movements inside. He did not want to spoil her surprise. He rose and dashed toward the patio doors but found them locked. He shook his head at the silly woman who thought ordinary men would try to seek her out from his vantage point. No ordinary man would dare what he dared, and no ordinary door would keep him from her. Oh, but he loved the chase. And, he realized if it increased her titillation, well then, so much the better. It would make the taking sweeter.

He took his knife from his pock, flicked open the blade, and worked it between the frame and latch. He easily knocked the catch from its place. Quietly he slid the door back and scooted through the opening. A small rush of crisp night air followed him into the room and swirled about him as he listened to silence answer his intrusion.

A light over the stove created a discrete halo in the kitchen alcove. He wondered why she had left the light on. Was she afraid of the dark? Did she worry about goblins, monsters, and things that might go bump in the night? Tonight there would be bumping. The sweet, hot bumps of her against him as he drove home to the root of her soul.

He moved cautiously across the hardwood floor of the hallway and removed his jacket. He did not want anything to come between them when he found her. At the first door he snapped on the penlight, he held in his left hand. It was an office. Books lined the shelves, flowed across a desk, and scattered across the floor.

He moved down the hall and found a second door to his right. The penlight danced quickly into the interior, revealing a large oversized tub, shower and dressing area. He wondered if she would like a good scrubbing between sessions. He moved on. He looked inside the next three rooms. All three were bedrooms, one larger than the rest. It was her room and he breathed her smell again. He peered closely at the bed. The large posts and dark tones of the coverlet seemed in keeping with what he knew of her brooding nature. But she was not in bed. The bitch was not home where she belonged!

He screamed. He bellowed at the top of his lungs. She was cheating on him! Midnight, when she should have been home to greet him and the bitch was off screwing someone else. He cursed and screamed her name. She had no respect. Cheating!

Oh, he swore she would do bump-tiddy-bump for him now. He raised the knife and blindly stabbed the bed and pillow where he imagined her body to be. Bump-tiddy-bump for you, bitch, he breathed. Bump-tiddy-bump for you. Just for this, he swore, one night will not be enough.

"I'll have you. Twist you and turn you! Make you juice up and then drain you so very dry!"

He swore he would lather her up for days, and days, and days. She made her choice, wanted it that way, and he wanted to see that she got it.

Heedless of his own screaming, he ran down the hall toward the patio doors. He slammed the door behind him. It bounced, and rested partially open to let the cold night air seep into the room. He ran to the edge of the patio, grabbed the drainage pipe and a sharp protruding edge of the stonewall. Hoisting himself up and over the railing as he screamed her name and his revenge into the night.

As he scrambled down the wall his eyes filled with tears. He reached out with his foot for purchase on the receded side railing of the dock, but slipped and landed hard on the wooden floor. He rolled to his feet, ran down the steps, and crossed the alley as the courthouse clock chimed again.

Two blocks away Charlie Watson finished his bookkeeping tasks for the month and walked out his office door. He wondered how much fussing his wife was going to do for his staying out so late.

He had been hoping that he would find her asleep when he got home when he heard the screaming. It startled him. A man's throaty, rasping scream split the air. Charlie turned fearfully and looked at the street behind him. The screams wavered and suddenly choked out. It made goose bumps stand up on his arms and scared him to his toes. He had never heard anything like it before, and as the chills ran up his spine, he knew he never wanted to hear it again.

He dashed quickly to the car and fumbled frantically with his keys before he could unlock the door and climb inside to safety. The car started under his shaking hands, and he roared the engine as he pulled away from the curb. Charlie knew he should notify the Sheriff, but he could not bring himself to drive in the same direction the scream had come from. Cursing his cowardice, he turned up the street toward home. He looked at the bag-phone in the passenger's set of his car, and winced. He had to do something.

As he reached for the phone, he prayed silently to himself that what he had heard did not mean another murder. As his heart squeezed pain through his chest, he was certain he could not.

27

As Lynne's eyelids struggled to stay open, the glow from Grandfather's fireplace seemed to expand and take on a distant orange and red shifting haze as Bowannie translated the tale for the old man. Lynne tried to stay alert, but Bowannie's voice became a lullaby and rocked her in the story of the old man's vision.

"I was born in the month of I'kopu, The Turning Back Moon, of December in the land of our grandfathers, when the Pojuaque Pueblo was abandoned by its people. Those people scattered to other Pueblos to escape the mischief of witches and evildoers. It was a hard year. My mother carried me without the protection of her husband. My father had died two months before of a great coughing. My mother had returned to her mother's house, but the food and fuel for fires was little.

"Until the time of my arrival in this world, she had been called,..." Bowannie hesitated and there was some quick discussion before a decision was arrived at and he might continue. "Yes,...she had been called Primrose Down. It was her coming of age naming."

There was some muffled laughter between them from a quick-shared joke. Then Grandfather is urging made Bowannie return to his story.

"It was an honorable and great name to have been given to one so young, and a woman. She had much learning from the spirits who guided her in this world. But just before I was born, she received another name that, although it caused her much laughter, vexed her now and again. My people faced a hard winter. The crops had been poor, and there was much hunger in the Pueblo. She wanted me strong in this world, and feared I might grow too hungry to come out. So, one day, without him knowing it, she took her father's club from where he had hidden it. His father and his father before back to his great-grandfather had given the club to him. It was all that was left to him and my mother treasured it.

"She took it and walked out across the frozen land in search of a care-less rabbit. She called to Rabbit to give his life, telling him she would honor him by wrapping his soft pelt against my skin so he and I might always know each other. It was bitter cold and late of that day. My mother walked far from the Pueblo, past the barren winter fields, across a small creek, and toward the foothills in search of food.

"She had traveled a long way and the wind was carrying snow and ice. She was weary from carrying me and weary from carrying the heavy club. With the blowing snow stinging her face, she did not see the wash until she was upon it. She stumbled down the bank and startled a deer that had taken refuge there in a cluster of brush. She told me how surprised she and Deer were at the noise she made, and very surprised to see each other. Her hand raised and she brought the club hard against the young buck's head. He staggered and she struck him twice again. He fell dead. She knelt beside him and thanked him for his generosity and greatness of spirit, which led him to give himself to those in need. It took her three hours to drag Deer back to her mother's house. She said I was large and kicking in her belly with excitement for the feast.

"When she returned, people saw her dragging the young buck and they were amazed with what she had done. She shared what could be with our neighbors and ate well for several weeks on the chunks for stew, the harvest of organs, and the marrow broth.

"Her friends urged her to tell and retell the story of how one so small, a woman large with child, had hunted the deer. It was good to laugh and have a belly full of food such as that again. She heard people laughing and calling to her in a new and unfamiliar name. At first, she was puzzled, and then she realized it was the story of the adventure she had told. Deer So Slow, they called and, hiding their faces, ran away from her laughing. It was a great joke, and she shared it with them. The deer had been so slow to outrun a great round-bellied mother. From that day forward, when her family and neighbors wanted to share a laugh or the comfort of their fire with her, they called Deer So Slow to join them."

Bowannie and Grandfather laughed and looked at Lynne. Lynne did not know the point of the story, but the more she thought about it the funnier it seemed. She could almost see that small pregnant woman stumbling through the brush and falling on the deer. Deer So Slow, she thought, and grinned at Bowannie and Grandfather as she watched the old man's joy from the telling of the story. His mother had been quite a woman.

Bowannie cleared his voice and turned back to Grandfather, waiting. The old man began to speak again and draw soft images in the air.

"He says it was ten years later that the great vision first came to him. At first being a child, he did not understand, although the things that he saw swept him up and away with them for days. He had fallen ill and the sickness made his body fall to the ground, leaving his spirit free to fly where the watchers of this earth bid him to go.

"My mother was frightened," Bowannie said, translating, "and tended to my body for the four days of my journey. She did not know then whether I would return or not. I did not know either, but I wanted to know what the spirits would bid me to see and do. So I went.

"Time and clouds moved about me and still they bade me follow. My heart beat fast in my chest, but I could not refuse the call. Finally, I came to a mountain. A great voice told me to look into the valleys below. There I saw our people and all the people who had passed before and would pass away from this land that had been ours. I saw the hoops of the other people, who were like our brothers, shrinking and drying before the harsh dry wind. It would sweep over us because we had lost our center and no longer knew where we stood in the world. It was terrible to see, and I cried like the child I was on that mountaintop.

"I did not know why I had been given this terrible vision or what I was to do with it. I was a boy. I longed for the strength of my people to return and raised my voice to ask how we might find ourselves again. Iyatku came through the sky and floated above me where I stood. She was dressed as Corn Maiden and her garments were white, with great reeds decorating the skirt and ears of corn lashed to her waist. Clouds with rainbows danced across her blouse. Her face shone like love upon me and bade me listen to her. She said that we were not lost. We knew where to stand. It is the center of the world. It is here and wherever people of good heart would go. There would be a passing of many seasons and the road on which we would walk would be long and hard. If we had courage and strength, many would return to the land and us in a time of great change.

"She opened her arms wide. There within the folds of her blouse she held sleeping people who floated against the stars of the summer night. Bright mornings rose, and one by one with the dawning of each new day they arose and found their way on the path and back to the center. 'These are the People too,' she told me. 'Though they are gone from this place now, they shall return. Each is a gift to the land and to the real people. But a gift you must find. Their ways will be strange to you. All may not often spring from the wombs of your women. You will be too few in number to receive all that must find their way back before the next great coming of age on this land. But they shall be yours and belong to the real people. I shall send them to you! She said. They may loose their way on the outside of the center. Look for them; though their faces are as hidden your uncles are in the masks of ceremony and prayer dances. They are still there, underneath, and unaware.

"'This,' she said, and pointed in six directions at once, arching her fingers and striking each point twice, 'This is from where they shall come. This is how you have to be prepared. Take heed. Next time I call, you will know where to go to make ready, to receive those who are lost to you.'"

Grandfather stopped and nodded at Lynne. A smile passed over his lips as he bent low across his knees and patted the rough wooden floor of his cabin. Lynne tried to divine the signal, but could only smile and nod back at him. She felt a little foolish and was not clear on the direction or intent of the story.

Lynne nodded again at Grandfather and he waved to Bowannie who spoke to him briefly and seemed satisfied.

"There is more to the story and the things he saw," Bowannie said, "but he does not want you to become misguided in the knowing. So he will teach you a little each time." Bowannie turned to Grandfather, who waved his hand in a downward stroke that seemed to indicate completion.

Leaning back in his chair, the old man's eyes became distant as he stared into the fire. Bowannie remained quiet, and Lynne restrained her impulse to ask questions. She sensed the moment required observation and acceptance. She had no idea what she was doing, but she did understand that in

any unfamiliar situation, as in any foreign territory, discretion was the better part of valor. She waited and sipped her cooling tea.

She understood that she had not been directed to leave and had not, as
far as she knew, worn out her welcome. She sipped the tea and let the
crackle of the fire and the distant sound of the wind lull softly in her ears.
Her eyes closed. She promised herself she would open them again in just
a moment.

Her shoulders ached and she moved to find relief for them. Lynne
turned her body and snuggled down under the blanket as she breathed in
deeply the wonderful aroma of wood smoldering in the fireplace.

She did not remember starting a fire. She could not remember that
she even had a fireplace in her room, her mind insisted to her. Half
cocking her left-eye open, she saw the dying embers and watched as a
charred log collapsed under its own imbalanced weight. It was real and
she was fine in a dream of her own making. She was not going to fall for
that old scare again.

Pulling the blanket up under her chin, she sighed to herself and easily
returned to the dreamscape of wind, rain, green corn field, squash blos-
soms and the center of the world stretching beyond the horizon.

Hours later, light drifted through the small paned windows of the cabin
and crossed Lynn's face, forcing her to open her eyes. She squinted, wondering about the dream she had had and what Jung might think of it.
Surprise hit her like a hammer's blow as she looked around the room
where she slept. She was not in her bed. She was not in any bed but curled
into an overstuffed chair in front of a cold fire.

She vaulted from the chair but her legs, which had been tucked under
her throughout the night, did not respond. She fell to the floor, narrowly
saving her face as her elbows slammed down first. Hot shards of pain raced
up her arms and danced across her shoulders. She cursed under her breath,

the moment she could breathe again. She sat up, and as she rubbed her bruised elbows, she looked about in bewilderment.

She was in Grandfather's cabin. Bowannie was nowhere to be seen, and Grandfather was gone.

"Just great," she muttered to herself. "Nothing like being invited out and falling asleep. You sure know how to impress the locals!"

She stood up and hurriedly pulled on her coat and gloves as she looked out of the window of the cabin's door. A fog lightly skirted the trees in the open meadow surrounding the semi-circle of log houses. The early morning sun was beginning to peak through the trees and set a rose tableau set before her eyes.

She knew that if she were lucky, if there were no dogs, she could make her way to her truck without disturbing a hair on any sleeping head.

Quietly, hardly daring to breathe, Lynne lifted the latch of the cabin door. It swung easily on its hinges and did not squawk against the bite of the cold.

She ran across the yard to her truck. Sliding across the chilled interior, she was more than a little relieved when it started without complaint. She pulled carefully around the truck parked next to hers and recognized as belonging to Bowannie. She made her escape.

Back on Highway 24, Lynne headed north toward town. The clock in her truck read five-thirty, and she wondered how she would ever apologize to Bowannie and Grandfather for her lapse of manners.

As she drove through town, she saw the lights of the Double Eagle and decided that breakfast and a drink were the order of the day.

28

The Double Eagle was warm and friendly. Lynne did not mind if she looked like an unmade bed as she sat in a booth drinking all the coffee they would bring her. Breakfast plates lay empty in front of her, and a second cigarette's smoke curled up toward the ceiling as she browsed the town's morning paper. She was feeling better and less cramped of muscle. She glanced at her watch and was surprised to see that it was a little after seven.

Gulping down the swallow in her cup and taking a quick last drag on her cigarette, she threw a five-Double Eagle bill on the table and hurried out the door. Bowannie and his work crews were waiting on her, sitting patiently in front of the store, and wondering how long she would make them wait. She did not look forward to having to greet Bowannie after falling asleep in the chair and sneaking out of the cabin before anyone woke up.

Straightening her shoulders as she headed toward the store, she decided to take her medicine, make her apologies and hope they would be accepted. As she turned the corner, Lynne saw the trucks parked in front of the store and eased hers in beside Bowannie's parked vehicle. Looking over at him, she saw him wave and slightly ease a smile to his lips. She smiled back and climbed out of her truck.

"Good morning," she called to him as she headed toward the store doors.

"Good morning, did you sleep well?" Bowannie asked, walking up behind her and waiting as she unlocked the doors.

"Yes. Except for this new pain in my neck, I slept very well, thank you." She opened the doors and the work crew walked in and began to set their tools and equipment for the day's work.

"Good. Grandfather hopes you will visit again soon. I do too," Bowannie said as he followed Lynne to the foot of the stairs.

"He does? You do?"

"Yes," Bowannie affirmed. He turned away from her and waved to John and George to discuss the work effort for the day.

Smiling to herself, Lynne headed up the stairs and felt a cool breeze skipping down the steps toward her. She returned to the steps and checked the thermostat on the wall. It read sixty-eight degrees. That was right. Where was the cold coming from?

She bounded up the stairs. Each landing felt colder than the last. She could hear the furnace chugging through the walls as it tried to ward off the chill in the building. On the third floor, the cold air hit her full. As she walked into the living room, she saw the soft mesh curtain of the patio door fluttering in the opening.

She wandered over to the doors and tried to remember if she had gone out to the rooftop patio yesterday. Dropping her backpack on the couch, she walked across the room to close the door. As she started to slide it shut, she looked down at the latch and saw a clean cut across the plastic coating of the hasp. The bright metal glinted at her as she realized what she was looking at. The door had been forced jimmied open from the outside. Lynne took her hand off the door and left it ajar. She turned and walked back to the couch where she had set her backpack down. Her eyes never left the interior hallway of her apartment as she removed the semiautomatic from its Velcro nest. Raising the gun before her, she walked slowly to the phone and called the Sheriff's department.

Gradey was walking past the dispatcher's desk when the phone started ringing. He had sent Sue to start a fresh pot of coffee. Huffing to himself, he grabbed the clamoring device, wondering who were reporting cattle on the road this morning.

"Yeah, Sheriff's department!" Gradey said, daring the caller to say something stupid to him.

"This is Lynne Fhaolain, at the Gellmore building. I'm reporting a break-in, could you send someone over right away?" Lynne said quietly as she strained her ears for the sound of movement in the hallway.

"What kinda break-in?" Gradey asked, recognizing the woman's name. Irritation spread through him. Callison did not have any use for the woman and neither did he? She thought she was some piece of hot shit. Gradey grinned at the phone and swore that she was just a high-toned piece of shit who would get what was coming to her some day. It seemed as though she had been intent on upstaging the Sheriff almost from the day she arrived. She was a pain in the butt that someone should straighten out.

"The usual kind," Lynne answered. "You know, someone breaks in and you don't know whether or not they're still inside."

"Right, we'll send a car over," Gradey replied, and winked at Sue as she returned to her dispatcher's desk.

"Make it fast deputy, 'cause if he's here and I find him you'll need to bring a body bag," Lynne asserted, and slammed down the phone.

"Stupid," Lynne breathed wondering how the man had ever passed any legitimate process to become a law enforcement officer.

She remembered Bowannie and his work crew were on the first floor. They knew nothing about what she would found upstairs. She hesitated. Should she go downstairs and warn them or tell them about the break-in? Should she just wait for the deputy to arrive before checking the building out? She did not want anything to happen to the crew if the burglar was still around. And how in the hell had he gotten up to the patio, she wondered.

Lynne heard movement down the hall. Flicking the safety off her weapon, she slowly moved toward the direction of the sound.

"This town is not good for my nerves," she swore silently under her breath. Her office door was open. She stared at it, trying to remember whether she had left it that way or not. She moved silently to side of the door, reached around, flicked on the light in the room, and jumped inside.

Nothing challenged her. In relief, she stood up, scanned the interior of the office, but could not detect any disturbance of her books or papers. All her equipment seemed accounted for.

"Where're the police when you need them?" she muttered as she started back down the hall. The Sheriff's department was less than eight blocks down Harrison Street, and she had not heard the sounds of sirens yet. Doing a building search was not the way she planned to start her day.

Lynne walked noiselessly to her bedroom door, sidled up to the door-jamb, and waited. Satisfied, she stood and crossed into the room as she flipped on the light switch. The ceiling light flooded the room and the light on the nightstand responded in kind. Nothing. She started to walk across the center of the room as a large black form charged her.

"Hey!" she yelled and whirled to meet the form whipping toward her. Heart in her throat, she drew a bead on it as it screamed past her. Her finger squeezed back on the trigger. A big black, puffed-up, tail-flagging, black cat ran terrified past her and out into the hallway. Pulling the barrel up and away from the retreating figure, she barely managed to jerk her finger off the trigger as the cat raced out, screaming its insults back at her. Her heart pounded and threatened to leap out of her mouth.

"Damn. Damn, damn, damn!" she cursed, not knowing whether to laugh or cry. That was it! First a burglar and then some mountaineering tomcat in the apartment. She had had about all she could take and stalked back down the hall to check the other rooms. As she finished checking the rooms and her property in the bedrooms and great room, she heard a voice calling to her on the stairs.

"Ms. Fhaolain," the voice demanded authoritatively. "Major?" it repeated, as heavy footfalls bounded up the steps.

"Up here, Sheriff. I'm up here…Watch out for that cat," she prompted. She did not want anyone in the Sheriff's department shooting holes in her building or killing a defenseless cat.

Sheriff Callison sprang up the stairs. Gradey was close on his heels as they rounded the banister. He seemed a little surprised to find her standing in the middle of her hallway holding a gun.

"Something going on here?" Callison asked, eyeing the gun.

"Yeah, something going on. One of your local bad boys broke into my apartment last night," Lynne said, and looked down at her weapon. Lynne tucked it into her belt behind her back.

"Where'd you bury the body?" Gradey smirked at her.

Lynne started to say something about Gradey's parentage as she walked toward him with intent and purpose in her eyes.

"That will be enough, Gradey," Callison commanded. "Why don't you go make yourself useful and check the place out?"

"Right," Gradey said as he roughly brushed past Lynne.

"Why don't you fix me a cup of coffee, Ms. Fhao...Major, and tell me all about it?" Callison said nodding her toward the kitchen.

Lynne shrugged and turned to lead the way back into the kitchen area.

"You always go around loaded for bear?" he asked as he watched her scoop the coffee grounds into the basket.

Lynne filled the coffeepot with water and set it on the cabinet. She set the coffee on to brew before turning around to meet the Sheriff's gaze. She saw his eyes sweep slowly from her legs to her face. The look was been intended for her benefit.

"Only when necessary, Sheriff. And in this town that seems to be most of the time. Or haven't you noticed?" she challenged.

Biting his lips, he thought about how he would love to teach her the proper deference due to a man in his position, but his thoughts were cut short by Gradey's voice yelling at him from a back room.

"Sheriff! Sheriff!" Gradey repeated. "You better get down here!"

Mystified at the sound and urgency, Lynne and Callison raced each other down the hall. They found Gradey standing in Lynne's bedroom next to the bed, staring and pointing at the disheveled covers.

"What?" asked Callison, going around to the side of the bed where Gradey stood. "My, my," he exhaled.

Lynne had followed Callison to the side of the bed. She had not paid any attention to the bed. The crazy, stray cat had distracted her and she had failed to check the room thoroughly. Her mind recoiled. No cat or cougar would shred with eight-inch steel claws.

"That's pretty vicious," Callison said, whistling under his breath. The slashing, stabbing, and puncturing wounds on the bed traveled across the covers, into the mattress, and onto the pillow.

He turned to Lynne and saw the look on her face. It was all he needed to see. "Looks like you really pissed someone off. Any ideas?"

"What?" Lynne asked, startled out of her daze. "Oh,…ah, no. No, I don't." Her voice trailed to a whisper. This was crazy. It was not an attempted burglary. He would come straight to the bedroom looking for her. Chills spread across her chest and shrank her heart into an alarmed tight knot.

"You didn't make it home last night, did you?" Callison said, continuing his questions.

"No. I was out…with friends. Fell asleep. Stayed there." "Good," Callison observed casually.

"Yeah, but how good was it?" Gradey interjected.

"Ass-hole!" Lynne shot back at him.

"Shut up, Gradey. Go get the crime kit and make yourself useful," Callison ordered, and roughly shoved Gradey toward the bedroom door.

"Ah, Sheriff, I was just trying to give some comic relief," he protested as he stomped out of the room.

"Yeah, I know he's pretty useless," Callison said, acknowledging the look on Lynne's face. He watched as her eyes dashed from the bed, around the room, and back again.

"Why don't you go back into the kitchen and leave this to me? You look like you could use that cup of coffee, or maybe even something a little stronger," he said as he put his arm around her shoulders to try to pull her mind back from where it had been wandering. She was small and firm to the touch. He liked the way she felt.

"Yeah, sure, fine," she muttered, allowing him to keep his arm around her. She wanted, needed some small comfort. It had been an incredible piece of luck that she had not been at home last night. Someone or something had been looking out for her while someone else had been waiting to take her life. Anger raged in her.

Callison was amazed at how good her body felt next to his. Shaking his head, he reminded himself that it was not the right time. Clearing his throat, he patted her on the arm and gently guided her toward the door. It had to be tough on her. Stiff military exterior aside, she was a woman after all and had a right to be shaken down to her boots.

As she walked down the hall, Callison decided there were things he needed to do while he waited for Gradey to return.

Lynne suffered through the next four hours in fits and starts. From the time she returned home to find her apartment invaded and her bed desecrated. She felt invaded and at risk. Callison and his deputies were more trouble than they were worth. The sheets, pillow, pillowcase, and mattress had been confiscated as evidence and carted off. They were going to send them to the Colorado Bureau of Investigation. Lynne had been furious.

Charlie Watson and Doc Kennedy had arrived shortly after the Sheriff called for backup at the crime scene. They had been supportive and solicitous.

Charlie had been indignant and worried like any good Dutch uncle. He had offered the security and safety of his home to Lynne, and urged her to stay with him and his wife while she had the work crew repair the damage to the patio door. But she had refused; asserting that Bowannie and his workers could complete the repairs to the door before sundown. They had promised.

Among the first things she did after Doc and Charlie arrived was to have Bowannie, and two other carpenters begun to repair the patio door. George was sent to the nearest hardware store to purchase security alarms for the whole apartment area. She arranged with Callison to have the security devices hooked up to the electronic alert system used by a number of other merchants in Leadville. Any further breaches would be signaled in the Sheriff's department.

Although pleased by the outpouring of attention, Lynne was equally embarrassed by the fuss people were making over her. It was an unfamiliar and uncomfortable turn of events. She refused all accommodations offered. Lynne knew they were studiously avoiding any thought or mention of the burglary as more than that. She did not want to think that the murderer might have picked his next victim and that she was it.

She had sat with Doc and Charlie in the living room as a grinning deputy Gradey helped carry her mattress and linens down the stairs. Gradey looked at Lynne, rubbed his big paw rakishly over the surface of the mattress and poked an index finger into a knife wound on the surface. Staring at her, he wiggled his finger in the hole and made ogling mouth gestures. It did not take a vivid imagination for her to understand the lewd suggestion. She exploded off the couch, and it was everything Doc and Charlie could do to restrain her from ripping Gradey's throat out. He and the other deputies quickly retreated, but not without a great deal of derisive laughter.

"Son of a bitch!" she screamed after them. "Bastards," she cursed, and flung her empty cup of coffee across the living room.

"You should complain to the Sheriff," Charlie offered weakly.

Lynne turned and glared at him, and he shrank into his chair.

"I'm sorry, it's not your fault," she stuttered ruefully. "But, I swear, I'll break his scrawny red neck if he so much as looks at me again."

"That was unconscionable," Doc apologized helplessly. Gradey had been on the city council's short list for expulsion from the force. And for good reason. Doc decided that at the next council he would suggest that the list get shorter.

"If you won't come and stay with any of us," Charlie began, trying to distract Lynne from the rude antics of the deputy; "...maybe one of us should stay with you?"

"No. No, that's all right," Lynne, said, returning to the kitchen and pouring an extra helping of Irish Crème liqueur into her coffee. "I'll be fine here. Bowannie will make sure of that, won't you?" She said as she inclined her head at Bowannie who was helping George electronically wire the patio door.

"Yes," he said, nodding to her. As he turned back to look at the door-frame again, he caught the look in George's eyes. True enough, he thought, and silently agreed with George and the uncertainty he saw reflected in the other man's face. He grimaced and returned to his work.

"Listen," Lynne said, "what I really need to do is get out of here and go find a new mattress and sheets." She tried to look at Doc and Charlie without seeing the worry on their faces.

"Now, Lynne," Doc began solicitously.

"Really, Doc, I do! You don't think I would ever want that stuff back, do you? Frankly, the knifing is one thing, but I wouldn't touch any of it now, not after those deputies get finished doing whatever they might do to it...Would you?"

"No. I guess I wouldn't," Doc sighed.

"Shopping sounds fine with me. Do you want my Martha to go along with you?" Charlie offered.

"Thanks, no. But I appreciate the offer. You could, however, be a dear and tell me where the best shopping might be."

For the next two nights Lynne barely slept. Every noise, shift of wind, and ghostly creak of the floors woke her. On Thursday, old Grandfather sent word through Bowannie that her sleepless nights were disturbing him. Lynne laughed and asked Bowannie how her sleeplessness could bother the old man.

Bowannie explained to Lynne that the old man had dreamed of her. He said that was why he had insisted on her coming to his cabin on the night she could have been murdered. He told her that Grandfather sensed danger surrounding her and, having found her, he did not want her lost again. Lynne had to admit that falling asleep in the chair at Grandfather's house had very likely saved her life. She reminded Bowannie of her training and ability to protect herself with or without a gun, but he only shook his head and mentioned to her how death could find even the bravest heart.

Grandfather, Bowannie insisted, still felt the currents of danger surrounding her and had complained about her pacing up and down the long boards of the apartment. He had insisted they both needed their rest.

"What does he suggest?" Lynne asked, giving up.

"That you go away."

"From here? Just like that?"

Bowannie had to laugh at the look on Lynne's face. "Not for good. For a while. A few days. Rest," he prompted.

"Ah, well, that's different. Here I thought you were trying to get me to leave for good."

"No. Grandfather would not have that so."

"O.K. Maybe he's right. I'll think about it."

Bowannie and his crew finished the repairs, construction of bookshelves, and general tidying up of the building. With the books due to arrive over the first three days of the next week, Lynne decided to take some time off and get out of town.

She arranged with Charlie to watch the store, and Bowannie promised to have the alarm system hooked up to the Sheriff's department before he left. Doc wanted to give her a prescription to help her sleep but she refused, chiding him and accusing him of being a pill-pusher. She did not want to think of her leaving as running away, and she did not want to have her wits dulled by drugs.

By Wednesday evening, she had loaded up her truck and headed down the highway. Doc stood by the doors to the store waving her off as she left. As he turned to get in his car, he stopped and shook the handles on the store for good measure and assurance.

She did not want to leave Leadville but she did need a little peace and time to think. She hoped she was right in trusting Doc, Charlie, and particularly Bowannie to keep her belongings safe. Too much had happened to her over the last three months of her life and very little of it seemed positive just at this moment. She felt anger and confusion mixing wildly in her mind and it made her feel like she was falling apart. Ten miles outside of town, she slowed the truck and barely made it to the side of the road as the tears streamed down her face. Her nerves were frazzled. She cried, letting the confusion, anger and hopelessness wash over her. She cried in bitterness and regret as her head rested on her hands clasping the steering wheel.

A sudden sharp rapping on her driver's side window brought her to full startled alertness. She found herself staring wildly at the face of an equally surprised State Trooper.

"You all right, lady?" he called through her closed window.

"No," she whispered, "No I'm not all right."

"What?" he asked.

She rolled down the window. "Yes. I will be fine. I'm just a little tired right now."

"All right. I wanted to check on you. You shouldn't be sitting out here like this. It could be dangerous," he cautioned.

"No kidding," she said, rolling up her window. "No kidding."

She did not stop again until she hit the town of Durango and checked into the first security-conscious hotel she could find that also offered a sauna, steam room and masseuse.

She spent the next two days and nights being pampered, turning into spaghetti in the sauna and putty under the hands of the masseuse. She would wake in the mornings and run through the quieted streets of the town. When she became tired of running, she would steel herself against the pain and run some more. She took in the Saloon and Canteen follies, drank a little too much, and ate with renewed vigor. She slept dreamless sleeps.

29

Grandfather had been right. She came away from the experience feeling better and stronger than she had in weeks. As she walked back into the store Saturday night, she felt as though she could face anything.

She called the Sheriff's department to let them know she was back and left a message for the Sheriff thanking his staff for their diligence with the security of her building. She called Charlie and told him she was home. He said he would let Doc know she was still alive and well even without his drugs. They laughed and she hung to go make her own security check of the building before she settled down for the night.

After finishing the basement and store area, Lynne glanced at her watch. She remembered the days of work she had ahead of her. The first wave of books would be arriving Monday. She did not want anything to spoil the way she was feeling. At ten o'clock, she completed her check of the building and walked back up to her apartment.

"Home again, home again," Lynne mumbled to the walls as she walked down the darkened hallway to her bedroom. As she approached her bedroom door, she shucked off the shoulder holster and let it and the semiautomatic swing in her hand. She walked through the door and over to where the night-stand stood next to the bed.

As she reached for the lamp switch a crashing blow to the right side of her head caused a dazzling of lights in her eyes. The concussion lifted her off her feet and threw her back across the bed. The holster and gun she had held in her hand was flung across the darkened room. She rolled, fell off the bed, jumped up and ran. Her assailant threw himself after her and they crashed against the door. Pain cracked in her shoulder and back as they collided. She struck out at him in hard quick knuckled jabs and felt her hands make contact with a cloth-covered head. She ducked and spun kicking out as a solid punch connected with her jaw and propelled her through the doorway.

Lynne bounced off the banister and grabbed on to it to protect herself from falling over onto the stairs below. Someone charged at her in the dark and tried to topple her. She jabbed with a hard right and scrambled along the railing, kicking viciously. She heard the gratifying grunts of pain as she rained the blows on his body. She heard him fall and swung a foot towards his crumpled body. As her kick landed, a sharp exhalation of air from damaged lungs exploded from the contact. Frantically, she rose, kicking out as she tried to dash to the landing and to the relative safety of the stairs.

Then she heard him. He was singing to her. His voice reached out to her through the dark. "Bumpa-tiddy-bumpbump. Bumpa-tiddy-bump."

"What the…? " she said as she struggled to get past him. She could hear him rise and leap after her.

Before she could reach the landing, a fist struck her hard between her shoulder blades and sent her sprawling and bouncing into the landing of the stairwell. Her face struck the wall and she tasted blood spill acid-sweet on her tongue. He was on her.

"Damn you!" she screamed, spitting blood from her mouth as she clasped her hands together and pummeled the back of his head and neck. He slid to the floor and sobbed.

"No," came his voice, rasping in the dark. "I'm gonna damn you."

Hair stood up on the back of her neck. She whirled and bounded down the stairs. Touching the banister as she propelled herself down, flying two or three steps at a time, she caught herself at the bottom rail, barely managing not to crash into the floor. Up again and running down the hall, she could hear his footsteps thundering after her. She ran down the second flight of stairs and to the storefront. Grabbing at the doors in relief, she searched their surface for the latches and locks.

She could hear the man pounding his way down the stairs behind her. He stopped and then, with a roar of indignation, a bellowed scream tore from his mouth. He fired at her.

A hot searing erupted above Lynne's left hip. She staggered, and every nerve surged in wildfire as the impact slammed her against the doors. She faltered, grabbed at the wound, and abandoned the doors. Hobbling into the interior of the store, she looked for a way out. Anything would do.

Blinded by the pain and the frantic scrabbling in her mind, Lynne plowed shoulder first into a tall unyielding bookcase as she rounded the corner. She heard him taking one exaggerated step after another down the stairs. His footsteps were a swaggering thunder in her ears.

She dashed around the bookcase, and ran toward the back wall away from the glow of the streetlights shining through the wide windows of the store. She did not want to make it easy for him by staying where he might see her. She did not want to loose, not this fight, like this.

Crouching down next to a slanted bookcase, she scrunched herself up as small as she could next to the floor and waited. Her hands moved along the baseboard and touched a long smooth object. She clutched at it just as his silhouette moved into the light flowing through the window. His shadow stretched across the floor toward her. She waited as he walked down the aisle and drew close to her. Then she rose and ran toward him.

His silhouette straightened. She knew she might have only one chance at him and needed the headshot target he was giving her. She twisted her arm back, cocking it and screamed at him. The hammer flew through the air from her hand but barely grazed his head as it flew past him and continued its flight through the store window.

"Gottcha now, tiddy," he crooned softly, and laughed. "Come 'ere little girl, I got some candy for you," he taunted.

"Go to hell!" she yelled, and sprinted to the freight elevator next to the basement door. Slamming her hand around the darkened elevator frame, she punched the button, and tossed the brick that had held the basement door open down the blackened stairs.

"Naughty, naughty," he called after her. He stood in the backlight of the window. He wanted her to see his silhouette. Wanted her to know he was coming for her. Wanted it to sink into her mind for just a moment more.

"Gonna have to spank you for that. Spank you good and hard," he said as he hummed to himself and walked toward her. "…Then we'll get down to the real personal stuff."

His deep, heavy breathing came closer to her hiding place. Nausea rose in her throat. She slipped behind the basement door and stood waiting and hoping. Two silent prayers crossed her lips. One for deliverance and the other for revenge. Lynne held her breath as he approached, and imagined she could smell the sweat on his body. She closed her eyes, reached inside herself, and gathered all her strength. You might not win this; a little voice worried at her inside her head. It might be the last thing she ever did but a hostile fury followed on the heels of fear. She vowed to make every attempt to rip him apart in the process of defending herself. If she lost this battle, they would know him by his pain, she promised.

He stopped before the door, waited, and listened to the sound of the freight elevator sliding up to the third floor. He paused and stretched his neck toward the basement staircase. He did not move. Lynne waited as the breath she held in her lungs fought for release.

"Tiddy-tiddy bump," he hummed into the darkness, and moved and over to the freight elevator. Then, suddenly spinning, he ran back to the basement steps.

"Now where do you think you are?" he called down into the dark. But a sudden pounding cut off his question on the front doors. A crashing blow splintered the wood, sending the doors flying backward on their frame. Someone entered the store.

Lynne stepped further back from the basement door, ducked down to the floor and coiled in the darkened corner. She held her wounded side, as blood oozed over the knuckles of her fingers.

Her pursuer grabbed the basement door, slammed it shut and locked the latch as he watched the front of the store. He took two steps back toward the book aisles and called out into the dark.

"Help me. Over here," in a falsetto voice he muffled in his hand.

Lynne could hear footsteps running toward her assailant in the dark. Instantly, she knew that whoever it was, they were heading straight into harm's way.

"No!" Lynne cried as she sprang from her hiding place and landed a high swift kick into the left side of her tormentor's face. He grabbed at her and they fell to the floor together. Something fell out of his hand, banged hard on the floor, and slid away from him. As Lynne tried to untangle herself, hard blows pounded her to the ribs, thigh, and shoulders. She jabbed several hard shots and tried to rise to her knees. A fist slammed into her stomach. It dropped her to her knees, doubled her over, leaving her gasping for air.

She rolled away. Wincing, she looked back and saw the figure fling itself against the man who had attacked her. They collided together, fists and arms flying. The sounds of the struggle punctuated the darkness beyond her. Thudding sounds pounded slick and wet against flesh.

"Ahhggg!" a man's startled scream rent the dark. Trying to rise, Lynne heard more shouting through the door to the shop. She started to call to them, but a foot came flying through the air and caught her under the ribs. It lifted her, crashed into her again with more force, and tossed her down the aisle. She sprawled on the floor. Stunned, she crawled against the pain of protesting ribs. He had clawed forward and touched cold hard and metal. A gun!

"Call the Police!" a woman's voice yelled at the entrance to the store and mixed with the commotion beyond.

Lynne grabbed the gun and turned to look back into the darkness. In the thin light of the window, she saw the shadow of a man as he flung himself toward her. A crazed roaring curse cut through the air. She fired twice before his flying body pulverized her with his full weight slamming down on top of her. Lynne was swept away into darkness.

The wail of sirens began to fill the night.Lights in the building were turned on followed by the blundering rush of curious onlookers through the doors. What they saw caused them to gasp and stagger back out into the reviving cold night air. The deputies arrived and the gawkers who crowded the storefront were convinced that the only person still alive in the carnage was Sheriff Callison.

Pushing his way through the crowd, Doc thought he heard someone say that Ray Billings and Lynne Fhaolain were dead. He faltered, and then shoved past the crowd and into the store. Ray Billings lay motionless in death and Sheriff Callison sitting on the floor near the rear of the store, holding a rag to his wounds. As he started toward the Sheriff, he saw Lynne Fhaolain's hand move near her head. Doc did not know what to do first.

30

Her eyelids fluttered and she summoned the strength to open them. Instruments were attached to her that whirled, beeped and gurgled around her bed. A tube had been shoved down her nose and made her throat ache dryly. When she tried to speak, she could only manage a croak. A buzzer started chirping near her head, and the startled face of a Sheriff's deputy popped through the door. He looked at her, and then turned to yell down the corridor.

Lynne watched the door slam shut and heard the sounds of running feet coming down the hall. She let her head fall back against the pillow to wait.

"You gave us quite a scare," Doc Kennedy said, patting her arm solicitously. As he took her wrist to read her pulse, Charlie Watson opened the door and glided into the room.

"Well," he said nervously, "look what the cat drug in."

Doc turned on his heels and stared Charlie down. "That's a fine how-do-you-do. The poor thing almost got killed, and all you can say to her is 'look what the cat drug in?'"

"It's okay, really," Lynne croaked.

"Okay, is it? You look like shit! You've got two broken ribs, one cracked, all on the left side. A lip the size of New Jersey. Two goose eggs on your hard head. A bullet hole in you, and bruises I can't talk about in mixed company!"

"Nice man," Charlie observed. "And just where did you learn your bed-side manners?"

Doc turned beet-red but before he could respond, Lynne croaked out, "Yeah, Doc just where was that?"

"No, don't you give me any sass. You'll need to stay in the hospital this week. I want to make sure you're going to hold together all right," Doc asserted in his best business-like voice.

"I got books, Monday. Tons of them," Lynne protested, and tried to rise off the bed. Her head swam and she sank back down into the bed.

"You mean last week," Charlie said quietly.

Lynne tried to speak but the tube made her throat constrict. Doc got a glass of water and she sipped through a straw until it relaxed.

"Last week?" she gasped.

"Yes." Doc was patting her arm. "You've been unconscious. Almost six days now," Doc said with concern.

"Unconscious?"

"It was nip-and-tuck, Lynne. But you'll be fine. Won't she, Doc?" Charlie said looking at Doc for support.

"Yes. Very fine. But you're not going anywhere real soon."

"The store?" she croaked through her cracked throat.

"The store is fine. So are the books. Bowannie and his people have taken charge of that end of things."

"Have?"

"Sure. I was talking to Bowannie this morning. He said he would be ready to open Wednesday. I even managed to talk my Martha into going down and helping some. She needs to get out more and do something other than make those 'country cute' throw pillows of hers," Charlie beamed.

Doc shot a sharp look at Charlie.

"You'll be happy to know the man who saved your life is doing just fine, " Doc interjected.

"He saved my life?" She vaguely remembered that someone had tried to kill her. She had shot him.

"Why, our own good Sheriff Callison. That's who. He almost got his lung punctured from a knife wound, but I turned him loose after stitching him up. He is fit as a fiddle. Been getting some good press on this. No doubt he'll be our Sheriff for a long time to come...But I suspect you don't want to hear about that just now."

"How'd he know?" Lynne felt around inside her head for pieces of herself still groggy from the medications.

"You told him," Doc said. "He was walking by. You know making sure everything was all right at your place. Then a hammer sailed through the window and almost cold-cocked him. Anyway, that's when he found a piece of pipe in the alley, broke the door and went rushing in."

"Who was it?" Lynne asked.

"Who was it?" Doc puzzled. "Oh, that...Well, that was Ray Billings, Lynne. Callison thinks he might also be the man responsible for the others. I'm sorry, Lynne," he soothed.

"Ray?" Lynne could not believe her ears. Her mind spun over. "I killed Ray Billings?"

"Yes. Seems you were right about the type of man we should have been looking for...smart, a little crazy, and strong. We just didn't know we needed to look so close to home," Doc said, shaking his head. It had been a hard fact to accept. He had liked Ray. Most people had. He'd been full of life and old 'Ned.

"I would never," Lynne started to say.

"We need to get out of here and let you rest. Right, Charlie?" Doc looked to Charlie for agreement.

"Yes. Besides, there are a few other folks that who might want to stop in and say Hi. That is, once you're ready," Charlie conceded.

"Tomorrow," Doc warned.

"Tomorrow," Lynne agreed.

On Wednesday, Doc Kennedy released Lynne from the hospital. Unsteady on her feet at first, she managed to walk out the door of her room. She did not get very far. She was stopped by Doc and ordered into a wheelchair. Hospital policy won over her argument and she was wheeled down the hall. Once outside, Doc let her hobble to Charlie's waiting car.

Bowannie had visited her at the hospital and brought her the weapon she asked for, but insisted that the danger was gone. He only gave in to her demanding insistence when she told him about the recurring dreams she had been reliving of that night. She told him how she had lost her weapon in the first moment of the fight and how it had almost cost her life. She thought that if she had it with her, the dreams might go away. They had not yet.

Bowannie had hesitantly mentioned that the store had become a hot attraction in the region. The story of the fight, shooting, and killing of the murderer had been on every television, radio station, and newspaper in the state. With great rancor he said that he believed every thrill seeker and tourist without imagination in a thousand-mile radius had descended on the store. News crews had not abandoned the site for days.

The only thing that had kept the media away from her was the Sheriff's insistence on her care and protection while she was in the hospital. He had held court for the media and had praised her bravery in numerous personal appearances. He would become the media's darling.

She watched as Bowannie's head shook from side to side. He told her he had even heard the Sheriff had received an offer from a California movie mogul to make a film about his rescue. Lynne felt her jaw tighten at the thought. Just her luck, she observed. She kills the bad guy and they offer him a movie contract. She figured it must be what they called show biz.

But she was pleased. Bowannie told her the thrill seekers and others had been buying books, any book, like there would be no tomorrow. Everyone seemed to be thrilled at the idea of owning a book from a store where a murder had taken place.

However, Bowannie had drawn the line with the tourists. Most of them had wanted him to let them take his picture or sign the books as proprietor of the little shop of murder. He refused and almost started a small riot at one point when he physically bullied one man out of the store. Charlie had come to the rescue and kept Bowannie from the very likelihood of being arrested for assault. Charlie stood in as proprietor pretending to be Lynne's long-lost "uncle." He unabashedly sold the lie, signed books, and rang up the receipts from every cash and credit card bearing customer.

Money and buying tourists had poured into the store and they were still coming. Lynne did not know if she appreciated the free publicity or not. Only time would tell.

"You won't believe the place," Charlie said as he turned the corner onto Harrison. He knew what she was headed into and wanted to prepare her. He simply did not know how she was going to take it.

"What do you mean?" Lynne asked as she leaned forward in the seat and tried to see up the street to the store.

"Well," he began cautiously. "You know what I said about all those media and tourist buzzards?"

"Yeah..." Lynne said carefully.

"Well," he began again.

It had been a short ride to the bookstore and Lynne was anxious to see home again. She smiled broadly when she heard that Doc and Charlie had strung a huge "Grand Opening" sign across the front of the store windows. Bowannie and his crew had been taking care of business for her. And business had apparently been brisk.

"Oh, my god!" Lynne cried out as she looked down the street. She could not see the storefront for the crowd of vehicles and people. Mobile television station vans with huge aerials and satellite disks crowded the street, competing for space with radio station vans and cars cruising for parking spaces. "You've got to be kidding!"

"Sorry, Lynne. It seems the Sheriff called everyone he knew and a hundred others he didn't to announce your home coming....back from the grave so to speak," Charlie said as he kept his eyes steadily on the street in front of him.

"Get me out of here!" Lynne demanded.

"And where else might you go? You may as well face them now, or they'll just come back later. Or hunt you down," Charlie asserted.

Lynne fell back into the seat and jarred her ribs painfully. He was right. It was either now or later. Doing it now would get it all over with.

"Charlie," she said as he pulled in closer to the sidewalk and double-parked the car. "Charlie, we have to talk about the definition of friendship sometime. Real soon. O.K.?"

"O.K." he said sheepishly, ducked out of the car and around to her side.

A cluster of people waited by the door. Lynne tried to work her way inside. She got three feet inside the store and was thinking that she might sprint toward the stairs, when she heard her name yelled across the crowd.

"Lynne Fhaolain, folks. The little lady who helped stop the mad man!" Sheriff Callison announced loudly and grinned at her. He was head and shoulders above the crowd as he stood on a makeshift platform surrounded by admirers.

Lynne cringed. The crowd surged and she found herself being roughed up by the people crushing around her. Callison saw what was happening, jumped off his podium, and charged through the crowd to her. He called for his deputies.

A small area of calm opened up in the sea of people as the uniformed officers surrounded Lynne. The deputies made a wedge and moved her toward the raised platform. She felt as though she was going to her own public execution.

For the next twenty minutes Lynne found herself trying to answer questions, see into the glare of camera lights, and focus after the blinding flashes of flashbulbs. Her back ached and her ribs felt as though they were swelling against the bandages Doc had wrapped her in. Stiffness climbed up across her shoulders and she shifted the holster under her jacket with her elbow to a more comfortable position.

"Can we do some of this later?" she pleaded to the Sheriff. It was his party, and she didn't want any more of it than she had to take. "There's plenty of time, isn't there?"

Callison lost the smile he had been wearing but quickly recovered. Waving his arms and hands widely, he looked out into the crowd in his best 'reelection form' and quieted them.

"That's all for today, ladies and gentlemen. The little lady is tired. After all, she's only just got home from the hospital and we want her with us for a long time to come," Callison said as he motioned for the deputies to begin to clear the people out of the building.

"Come on, come on now. Have a heart. We'll still be here in the morning," he promised, and hugged Lynne to him.

Anger flared like an ache in Lynne and was quickly replaced by real pain as he squashed her against his body. She vowed that if he called her "little lady" one more time, she would knee him on national TV.

The deputies quickly and efficiently began to direct the flow of bodies toward the doors. She could not see Bowannie. Then she turned to look at the back of the store and she saw Bowannie and Grandfather get off the freight elevator. They waved to her. When she saw them, her spirits lightened. She wanted a quiet evening, and sharing it with them seemed the right thing to do.

"Well, little lady," the Sheriff's voice bore down on her and made her wince. He glanced toward the milling throng and waved at those whose eyes he could hold. Lynne thought about her promise and decided to let it go. "We certainly are a hit, aren't we?" He grabbed her again, and hugged her harder as she struggled to get out of his grip.

"Stop it. Just stop, okay?"

"What's eating at you?" He looked at her, perplexed.

"I'm tired. I'm just plain tired. I want to go upstairs and lie down," she said in exasperation. "Is that all right with you?"

"Fine with me. Not at all," he said glumly. "But, I could get really used to this kinda attention!" he said smiling again.

Lynne saw dollar signs and Hollywood dancing in his eyes. He loved it all right. He was on top of the world, and it was a ride he did not want to get off.

"Right," Lynne answered cheerlessly. She stepped off the platform and moved toward the rear of the store where Bowannie and Grandfather waited.

"No, really," Callison called after her. "You'll get used to it. We're going to be famous."

Lynne glanced back to the Sheriff, and saw Callison wink at her. She shook her head in exasperation and watched as he jumped off the platform. As he strolled away, he began sing-singing humming "'bumpa-tiddy-bumpabumpa', 'bumpa-tiddy-bumpabump'"

Lynne had turned away from him and taken a few steps toward Bowannie and Grandfather when the Sheriff's song sent shards of ice up her spine to explode against her mind.

"What?" she asked as her hand went to the semiautomatic.

Behind her, Callison stopped shock still as his eyes widened wildly. A growling moan seeped out of his mouth followed by a scream as he spun around to face her. His hand reached for his gun. It came swiftly out of the holster.

Deputies, tourists and reporters froze in alarm. They watched in disbelief and amazement as the Sheriff moved to kill the woman whose life he saved earlier. They were deer caught in the headlights of rushing calamity.

"Callison! You!" Lynne screamed as she whirled to meet him. She dropped to her right knee and fired three quick shots into his solar plexus. The shots lifted the big man up into the air and crashed him back through the storefront. She watched the shattered window expectantly. He did not rise up again. The only thing she could hear was the thunder in her head.

Panicked screams and shouts quickly muffled the sound of breaking glass. The tableau was broken.

Two of Callison's deputies started to draw down on Lynne. She quickly held up her hand before they could touch their weapons. Her gun was pointing at them, and they watched as she shook her head to silently warn them. They hesitated, not daring to move another muscle.

Carefully, with her left-hand still raised, Lynne lowered the weapon to the floor and pushed it away from her. She did not want to get killed by good intentions. The deputies drew their guns and ran toward her. Lynne braced herself for the rough handling she saw heading her way. They fell against her and on top of her, grabbing her arms and twisting them behind her back. Her face was shoved to the floor as Gradey knelt in the middle of her back. Lynne cried out in pain.

"Wait!" commanded Doc and Bowannie simultaneously.

"What?" Gradey snarled.

"Get off of her and just wait a minute," Doc insisted.

"She killed the Sheriff! That's what happened!" Gradey said as he took his knee off Lynne's back.

"Because he was going to kill her. Are you blind? Did you not see?" Bowannie interjected.

"Well,...I." Gradey fumbled.

"He drew on her. Tried to gun her down. Now what the hell was that about?"

"I,...I don't know?" Gradey asked as he looked to the other deputy for help and found none.

"He's right," called a reporter with a mini camera. "I think I've got it in here." He tapped the side of his camera.

"It was Callison," Lynne said as she lay between the two deputies. "He murdered the others, killed Billings." Darkening shadows spun in front of her eyes. "Search his house.... Trophies, from victims," she struggled to connect her thoughts.

"My god!" Gradey said looking down at Lynne. "You don't suppose?"

"We gotta check," Joe answered limply.

"I think I need a little rest," Lynne whispered as she heard a rush of voices coming at her. The light faded from the room.

Slowly, Lynne's eyes opened and she saw Doc's calm face leaning close to her own. She was in her apartment bedroom.

"Now what day is it?" she asked as she reached a hand up to try to still the pounding in her head.

"The same," Doc said. "Just a little later. We brought you upstairs. Bowannie took his grandfather home after all the excitement. He's back now."

Lynne could see Charlie, Bowannie and Deputy Joe standing at her bedroom door. She waved weakly at them, and they came into the room. The deputy shuffled his feet and looked at Lynne nervously.

"What's 'matter deputy?" she asked, wondering if she were still under arrest.

"I got a call," he said, touching his radio as he spoke. "Gradey said…they found…" He stammered to a halt.

"Gradey told him they found the missing body parts in the Sheriff's refrigerator, in an empty milk carton." Charlie interrupted. "No wonder the son-of-a-bitch said he couldn't find the killer. He did not want to. Not like he didn't have to look at him every morning while shaving."

Lynne struggled to sit up. Doc helped her prop herself against the bed's headboard and arranged the pillows behind her. She felt as though her brain would slosh out of her ears if she tilted her head too far to one side or the other.

"I don't understand," Joe said weakly, shaking his head.

"I think I do. At least, what happened the night he came to kill me," Lynne said. Turning to Doc, she said, "Is there any fresh coffee available?"

"Sure thing," Joe said and left the room to get the coffee. A glass of water and an aspirin bottle was sitting on the nightstand next to her bed. She quickly downed two aspirin to see if they would ease the pounding in her head. Joe returned with the coffee.

"It was the Sheriff who was waiting for me when I came home. He hid somewhere up here as I checked the doors and windows. He had been in charge of connecting my security system into the control center at his office. He knew my schedule. It probably didn't take anything for him to bypass the system and wait for me to stumble into his hands." She took a

quick sip of coffee and felt it slip down her throat. She smiled at Joe gratefully as he slipped some Irish Crème into it.

"When I threw the hammer at him, it was Ray Billings who had been
on the street. He may have been coming by to visit or was just going
home. I don't know, but he was the one who heard the commotion and
broke down the doors to get inside. He ran headlong into the Sheriff and
me. Then I killed him."

"You couldn't have known," Bowannie offered sympathetically.

"No, you couldn't have known. But you didn't kill him either," Doc
confirmed. "In the autopsy. The killing wounds had come from a knife. A
puncture wound had gone deep up into his chest. It sliced into the aorta.
Callison killed him. Lynne, he was a dead man before he fell on you."

"Well, he didn't exactly fall on me. Callison probably threw him. At the
time, Ray had seemed to leap into the air. There had been people yelling
and screaming at the door just before," Lynne said wonderingly.

"Rowdies. A group of folks, tourists, they had just left the Double
Eagle. They were wandering back to their hotel. They had to pass by here
on their way. They saw the broken window, the smashed door, and heard
the ruckus inside," Joe interjected. "You know drunks. Their curiosity
overrode their good sense, so they stopped to see what was going on."

"Then that's what did it. The Sheriff had heard them too and knew
he was cornered. He had to get out of the trap had set before he caught
himself in it. Callison did not know I had found the gun. When I shot
Ray, Ray was already dead. But it helped the bastard make the story he
intended to tell even more plausible." Lynne shuddered. Callison had
been cold as ice with calculating nerves of steel. She felt certain that he
would have come back for her again if circumstances had gone differ-
ently. She felt cold. She had hunted others like him before, but never
so personally.

"But I don't understand why? What made him that way?" Joe asked, his hand raking through his hair in bewilderment.

"We may never know why but we'll look into it. Won't we?" Charlie said, looking back at Lynne.

"Maybe…later, much," she hedged.

"Later is good, young lady," Doc said imperiously. "Right now you need your rest. You've got to get well enough to run this bookstore you've been playing around with."

"Right. We better get out of here," Charlie said, turning to Joe and taking his arm to guide him out of the bedroom.

"I'll be staying for a while," Bowannie said to Lynne. "Tomorrow, my daughter will come by to help. She's made more tea."

"That sounds nice. That sounds very nice," Lynne said, sinking under the covers.

After everyone left, she felt the circle of her own thoughts racing and jumbling around in her head. She wondered if anything would ever settle down in her life and begin to make sense again. Leadville and Colorado were a lot more than she had bargained for. She turned out the light on the nightstand and let the dark wash over her. As she drifted toward sleep, she heard footfalls approaching her room and stop near her door.

"Yes?" she said to Bowannie's shadow.

"When you get well, Grandfather told me he wants you to come and tell him a story. It is your turn."

"Story?" Lynne shifted to look at him.

"How Callison got his name." A chuckle drifted through the darkened room toward Lynne.

"I don't understand."

"Sheriff So Slow,...Grandfather says it will be a good story," Bowannie said as he turned away.

Sleep came swiftly to carry her safely toward a new morning.

31

"What?" Doc said plaintively as he watched Lynne place cartons of canned goods inside the 5th wheel. He looked in puzzlement from Lynne's back to Charlie.

"It's pretty simple, really. I traded the store for this 5th wheel," Lynne avoided Doc's eyes as she tried to maximize the space use. She had arrived at the idea a few weeks after her recovery. It had stolen to her like the soft early morning whispers Shelby had used to coax her awake.

"Good Lord, woman, what kinda deal is that? What about your dreams, what about settling down? What about all the other stuff you talked about?" Charlie argued in exasperation.

Lynne turned around to look at her friends and shrugged here shoulders in mock resignation. "It is a pretty good deal really. This 30-foot Road Ranger has all the space I need. I spent twenty years in the military, remember? This is more room than I got in all but the last duty station. And I have spent a lifetime of traveling and re-assignment? So, I have changed my mind. The bookstore was Shelby's dream, it was our dream…" Lynne felt her throat constrict. "I was supposed to be the writer. The deal had been that we would take vacations, gather notes, and I would write travel books for the "Prescott Places and People" series. Four or five states and then every-other year up-dating would have been more than enough work and travel for either of us."

"But," Charlie began.

"Don't even think it…I got a good deal. You know how much these babies cost Charlie?"

"No…but….."

"Well, this one is a year old, camped in for a week, and belonged to Bowannie's daughter. I traded straight across for it and thirty percent continued interest in the store. I'd say I made out like a bandit," Lynne walked past the two old men to retrieve another box of canned goods.

"Just like that?" Doc sighed.

"I'm not hurting for money. You remember that?"

"Yes…but, still."

"I'm pretty lucky Doc," Lynne said turning to look at her friends. "I know what I want to do now and creating the store was the right thing to do. Shelby wanted it and it is its own reality now. So, it was the last thing I will ever be able to do for Shelby. The rest of the reality is that it does not mean a thing to me without Shelby. I was trying to find a way to hold on to the past and be someone I am not. I found out I cannot do that, not safely anyway," Lynne said almost chuckling.

Charlie walked over to the side of the 5th wheel and grabbed one of the folding chairs that had been leaning against a dual wheel. He sat down, rubbed his eyes, and squinted at the sun. "So, what do you figure you're cut out to do?" He asked as Doc sat on a step in the doorway of the 5th wheel.

Lynne pushed a button on the side of the wall and the whine of the awning motor kick into life. In a few seconds, a little shade covered the two old friends while Lynne looked at her supplies and wondered if she had everything she needed for the first part of the journey.

"Well, a couple of weeks ago I called the Prescott folks. They liked the stuff I was writing and sending them about this region. They say I have a lively tone for travel so I cut a deal with them to cover six states, just as a start. Then again,…Colorado, Wyoming, Montana, Idaho, Washington, and Oregon might be all I will ever be able to handle, what with the required updates."

"You're going to travel from state to state and write about…….About what?" Doc said feeling confused.

"Travel, adventure, sports, retirement, and the lure of the great outdoors. I just might be responsible for Leadville and other places getting more tourists to flock to them," Lynne said and winked at Charlie. She knew how he felt about tourists.

"You'll be back?" Charlie asked.

"At least every two years or so. If not sooner. Gotta watch out for my investments," Lynne said grinning at her friends. "In the meantime I'll send you autographed copies of the travel guides as they get published, maybe some photographs and other interesting tidbits, if I run across any."

It was a promise she would make sure to keep.

About the Author

Janet E. McClellan is a twenty-five-year-plus veteran in the field of criminal justice. Her experiences range from patrol officer, investigator, prison official, to chief of police. Janet moved to the Oregon coast a couple of years ago and has vowed never to leave the ocean's side. Her previous works, published by Naiad Press include *K.C. Bomber*, *Penn Valley Phoenix*, *River Quay*, and *Windrow Garden*. This is the first of many books with this publisher. *Tru North* will be returning later in the Fall of 2000.

Printed in the United States
1161700006BA/25